De[illegible]bb, born in Alabama, wrote her first story at age nin[illegible] her first romance at thirteen. It wasn't until she spe[illegible]e years working for the military behind the Iron Cu[illegible] and a five-year stint with NASA – that she real[illegible]ier true calling. A collision course between sus[illegible]and romance was set. Since then she has penned nearly [illegible]undred novels. The *Faces of Evil* is her debut thrill[illegible]ies. Visit Debra at www.debrawebb.com

Praise [illegible]Debra Webb:

'Webb k[illegible]ps the suspense teasingly taut, dropping clues and re[illegible]rrings one after another on her way to a chilling concl[illegible]' *Publishers Weekly*

'Fast-pa[illegible]l, action-packed suspense, the way romantic susper[illegible]s supposed to be. Webb crafts a tight plot, a kick-[illegible]eroine, a sexy hero with a past and a mystery as dar[illegible]he black water at night' *Romantic Times*

'Ro[illegible]uspense at its best' *New York Times* bestselling auth[illegible] Spindler

'C[illegible]ain characters and chilling villains elevate Debra[illegible] *Faces of Evil* series into the realm of high-intensity thrillers that readers won't be able to resist' *New York Times* bestselling author C. J. Lyons

'Bestselling author Debra Webb intrigues and tantalizes her readers from the first word' www.singletitles.com

'Master[illegible]
www.a[illegible]

By Debra Webb and available from Headline

The Faces of Evil Series

Obsession

Impulse

Power (available March 2013)

IMPULSE

DEBRA WEBB

headline

Published by Forever Yours in 2012, an imprint of Grand Central Publishing, part of Hachette Book Group, Inc.

First published in Great Britain in 2013 by
HEADLINE PUBLISHING GROUP

1

Cataloguing in Publication Data is available from the British Library

ISBN 978 0 7553 9688 7

Typeset in Palatino by Avon DataSet Ltd, Bidford-on-Avon, Warwickshire

Printed and bound in Great Britain by Clays Ltd, St Ives plc

Headline's policy is to use papers that are natural, renewable and recyclable products and made from wood grown in sustainable forests. The logging and manufacturing processes are expected to conform to the environmental regulations of the country of origin.

HEADLINE PUBLISHING GROUP
An Hachette UK Company
338 Euston Road
London NW1 3BH

www.headline.co.uk
www.hachette.co.uk

Men cannot always give an account of their impulses

Joseph Parker, *The Ark of God*

Chapter One

Monday, July 19th, 10.31 A.M.

'Did you know that one drop of blood travels from the heart to the toes and back in under sixty seconds?'

Lori Wells tightened her fingers into fists, tugged futilely against the tape binding her to the chair, and forced herself to meet the son of a bitch's eyes. 'Did *you* know all that blood rushing through my veins at this very moment is teeming with the urge to watch you die?'

Eric Spears smiled, made a breathy sound that wasn't quite a laugh. 'You are such a brave girl, Detective Wells. I wonder if that's because your father committed suicide when you were so young.' He inclined his head and stared at her as though memorizing each detail of her face like a lover intent on never forgetting the moment. 'Did you have to help your mother clean up the blood afterwards? Or did your neighbors jump in to help out? *Y'all do that down here in the south, don't y'all?'*

Lori turned away from him. *Bastard.* How could he know so much about her? He hadn't known her name five days ago.

A longsuffering sigh hissed past his lips. 'You're quite boring, detective.' He stood. 'What should I do about that?'

Renewed fear trickled inside her. Lori snapped her head up and stared into those piercing blue eyes. *No.* She would not give him the pleasure. She hardened her expression, refused to let him see the fissure of terror widening inside her.

'What's wrong, *Eric*? Can't get it up if I'm not crying like a scared little girl?' *Don't let him gain control.*

Fury tightened his lips. He drew back his hand.

She braced for the blow.

He laughed at her instinctive reflex. Dropped his hand to his side. 'See, you are a scared little girl. Frankly, I find all that feigned bravado quite tedious.'

'Life sucks like that sometimes.'

He made a sound of agreement. 'It does indeed.' For five or six seconds he deliberated as if undecided how he would proceed. 'You know the reason you're here. Why make our time together more unpleasant than necessary? It'll be much easier for both of us if you cooperate, Lori *Doodle*.'

How dare he call her that! Her father had given her that nickname . . . this scumbag had no right. She didn't need him or a GPS to show her where this was headed. 'Go to hell.'

She wasn't making this easy for him. He would kill her anyway.

Spears turned his back and strode across the room.

Lori quickly scanned the space now that the lights were on, searching for any aspect of her surroundings that might provide some hint as to where the hell she was.

The sedative he'd injected when he'd held her at gunpoint and forced her into his SUV had prevented her from assessing the distance or the traffic sounds as he'd driven her here. She still felt a little groggy. Her mouth was dry. She squared her shoulders, focused on clearing her head. She had to pay attention, to be ready for whatever came next. *Let your training and instincts guide you.*

Focus, Lori.

A warehouse, she decided. An old one for sure. Smelled of neglect and vaguely of oil or grease. Brick walls soared some twenty or so feet to a ceiling where steel beams supported the roof. Naked fluorescent tubes glowed from metal fixtures suspended five or six feet overhead. The smell of disuse permeated the air. She tried to get a better look behind her. Couldn't. Wooden crates lined the wall to her right suggesting the warehouse had been used recently in some capacity. She squinted to read the word stamped on some of the crates . . . Grimes. She'd lived here all her life but that name didn't ring a bell.

Birmingham had its share of neglected and abandoned buildings . . . she'd been in a few but not this one. From her position in the middle of the large open room, she could see a door. Maybe an exit. Maybe just an office or bathroom.

One shot at that door was all she needed . . . if it wasn't a dead end.

Images of what this monster had done to his other victims, all women, rolled like an old-fashioned filmstrip through her mind. Defeat chiseled away at her courage.

Spears grabbed the one remaining chair in the place and dragged it over to where she sat bound with duct tape, wrists, ankles, and waist, to a similar heavy metal chair. He scooted his chair close and straddled the seat, his spread knees flanking hers. She squeezed her legs more tightly together; didn't want any part of him touching her. She didn't even want to draw his scent into her lungs.

Like his subtle aftershave, his wardrobe conveyed an understated elegance. The navy suit jacket hadn't come from a rack in any store where men she knew shopped. The white shirt was crisp and pristine like he'd just picked it up from the cleaners. The jeans fit as if they had been designed by his personal tailor. The icing on the cake – the definitive packaging for his classically attractive blond-haired, blue-eyed features.

If you want to know what evil looks like, look in the mirror.

Jess Harris had definitely gotten that right. Eric Spears, aka the *Player*, appeared nothing like the depraved killer Lori knew him to be. Why did he bother abducting women when he could easily charm them into his lair with that killer smile and deep, smooth voice?

The hunt. Somehow it fueled him . . . drove his heinous desires.

Lori wished she knew half what Jess did about him. Maybe then she could do more than be a damned victim.

Even before she'd met Jess, Lori remembered vividly hearing in the news that not a single one of the Player's victims had ever escaped alive.

Her chest ached. She didn't want to die. Her sister needed her. Her mother needed her. She took solace in the knowledge that at least they were safe. As soon as Chief Burnett and Jess discovered Lori was missing, they would take steps to protect her family.

And Chet Harper. Lori thought of the detective, the man, who wanted so much more from her than she had given. Would she have continued to push him away if she had known this day was coming?

Spears chucked her under the chin, forcing her attention back to him. 'Let's get one thing straight, detective. However much you test me, this isn't about you,' he explained in that calm, clever tone that belied his every action.

'All your hard work to reach the esteemed rank of detective earlier than most means nothing to me.' He tugged at a lock of her hair, twirled it between his fingers. 'That you are most attractive means nothing to me.'

Lori waited, her heart thudding with apprehension, for him to spell out exactly what he wanted from her besides her life.

'I brought you here so Jess will pay attention,' he whispered, leaning forward so that he lingered nose-to-nose with her. 'You think I have her attention?'

Fear buffeting ever harder against her defenses, Lori steadied herself. She would not let him use her to get to Jess. No way.

I might be a victim but I will not be his means of reaching Jess.

'She told me all about you.' Lori forced a smile, inclined her head and studied his face the way he had studied hers. 'What happened? Did Mommy fail to protect you when Daddy decided he preferred you to her? Is that why you hate women so much?'

His hand went to her throat; strong fingers closed tightly, cutting off her airway. 'Do not toy with me, detective. There are things you will never know so don't waste your time and energy trying to analyze me. You'll fail just like all the rest.'

There was nothing amiable about his tone now. The fear she fought to restrain dug its claws in deep even as he released her. She gasped for breath. Her thoughts raced in frantic circles. The things Jess had told her kept colliding with her own instincts.

Should she play his game or resist? What he did to her in the end wouldn't change either way, but could she slow him down or trip him up by choosing one avenue over the other?

'Do you think I have her attention?' he repeated.

'Yes.' Lori cleared her throat, wished she had a drink of water. 'I'm certain you have her attention.'

'That's better,' he said softly. 'Now, tell me about this Chief Daniel Burnett.'

She filled her lungs with a jagged breath, refused to let the fear maintain a stronghold. 'What about him?'

'What's his interest in Agent Harris?'

Lori cleared her mind. *Careful what you say.* Don't give him any ammunition. 'She's a top notch profiler and investigator. We needed her help on a case. Because of you she's probably unemployed.' Anger at what he had done to Jess chased away some of the fear. He had ruined Jess's career with the FBI.

'One does what one must. She created quite the commotion up in Richmond when she so kindly screwed up any chances of a conviction against me.' He lifted his shoulders in a shrug that communicated more arrogance than indifference. 'Diverting attention was essential. Now the world is focused on her inept methods rather than the precise work of a master artist.' A smug chuckle rumbled from his throat. 'Ironic, isn't it?'

'You think? Well, I have a newsflash for you, asshole.' Mad as hell now, Lori looked straight into his eyes. His turned wary and she loved that single moment of triumph. 'Jess Harris is way too smart, way too sharp and far too in demand for a generic piece of shit like you to keep her down. If the Bureau cuts her loose, Chief Burnett will offer her a top position here, just you wait and see.'

That was pure conjecture, but Lori suspected there was no way the chief would let Jess get away again for reasons completely unrelated to her investigative skills. Whatever Spears did to her, Lori could not let him learn that she sensed the chief still had personal feelings for Jess. That could make him a target, too.

'That's right, *Eric*,' she continued, capitalizing on his obvious need to analyze the idea of failure. 'You can't stop her and if you think the Bureau will stop trying to nail you just because you pulled a bait and switch, I'm afraid you're going to be incredibly disappointed. They will get you – with or without Jess on their team.'

His gaze narrowed as if he worried she might be right, and then he laughed, the deep, guttural sound echoing all around her. 'You're quite good, detective.' He leaned close again as if he intended to share a secret. 'Here's something hot off the wire just for you. That game is over. They will *never* achieve their goal.' He reached out, traced her cheek with his forefinger. She shuddered. 'This is a new game and I need Jess to play.'

'You *need* her?' she bit out in disgust.

He shrugged. 'Want her then. Let's not quibble over semantics. Will you help me, Lori Doodle?'

'Do I have a choice?' The answer to that was a big, flashing neon sign in her brain. Whatever she did or didn't do he would somehow find a way to use it. Tears burned her eyes. She blinked them back. She would not cry for this scumbag's pleasure.

'You always have a choice, detective.' His lips lifted again in that charismatic expression that masked the house of horrors beneath. 'You have one now. Live daringly or die quickly. You choose.'

She laughed around the fear crowded in her throat. 'Do you really expect me to believe that if I cooperate you'll let me live? Wow, Santa's here already and it's only July. Give me a break.'

'Oh, I will. You have my word,' he promised. 'For a bit anyway.'

That was what she thought.

'Consider your options carefully, Detective Lori Wells.' He put his face in hers again. 'The longer you stay alive, the more opportunity you'll have to perhaps see that urge of yours to fruition. Who knows?' He straightened, drew back to look her in the eyes. 'You might just get that chance to watch me die. After all, no one lives forever.'

He stood, hauled his chair away from hers. 'While you weigh your options, I'm going to find someone to keep you company.' He laughed. 'Actually, I think I'm the one who needs company. You are b-o-r-i-n-g with a capital B.'

Lori's heart rammed into her throat.

She had to do something . . . otherwise he was going hunting . . .

'Wait!'

He stopped.

'I can't . . . don't leave me here by myself. *Please.*'

He turned around slowly. A grin spread across his lips. 'Ah . . . so you're ready to play, are you?'

His singular motive is pleasure. Jess's voice whispered in her ears. *The only way he can feel it is by torturing his victims in the most depraved ways.*

'Yes.' Lori moistened her lips, wrestled back the fear. 'I'm ready to play.'

Chapter Two

Five Points, 10.42 A.M.

Two uniformed Birmingham police officers waited outside the door to Lori Wells' second-floor studio apartment. Three BPD cruisers sat at the curb, sirens silent, lights dark.

Jess Harris stood next to Chief Dan Burnett's SUV as she scanned the neighborhood. Two apartment buildings and seven houses lined the quiet street. The Five Points address guaranteed an eclectic mix of residents and homes. In all probability there were a few retirees who'd lived here since the first houses were built in the 50s, along with the recent influx of young professionals just launching their careers.

Hopefully some of the retirees had been home and

perhaps saw something useful. Neighbors were already being canvassed.

As if to defy that fleeting hope, her blouse melted against her sweat-dampened skin. No kids in the street; no dogs barking. This morning's sweltering heat kept the children and pets inside and, most likely, anyone else who happened to be home when Lori Wells was taken from hers.

If Jess wasn't scared to death, she would be spitting mad. This was her fault. The Player had followed *her* here – and Lori had paid the price. Her fingers itched to put a bullet right between his eyes.

Let me close again, Spears.

'The crime scene unit is four minutes out,' Burnett said as he came around the hood to join her on the street.

He was shaken as badly as Jess or he would already be inside. Wells was his detective. And she was Jess's friend, even if only for a few days.

How the hell had she let this happen? She'd made a mistake . . . a terrible, terrible mistake. She had to find a way to fix this . . . to stop this sociopath.

'Harper's waiting for us.' Burnett gestured to the apartment complex.

Jess nodded, then followed him across the street,

past the squad cars and up the sidewalk that led to what was now a crime scene. Fear had her in a daze . . . she had to pull it together.

Lori needed her to do this right.

The two officers greeted their chief of police as she and Burnett approached the door. Sergeant Chet Harper waited inside, his expression grim. No, not just grim, sick and terrified.

I'm sorry! Jess wanted to scream the words. *I didn't mean for this to happen.*

Calm . . . stay calm.

She couldn't change what had already happened, but *this* she could do right. The Player would not best her again.

After slipping on the shoe covers and gloves Burnett provided, she entered the apartment, leaving her emotions on the welcome mat. Every case deserved her absolute best, but this one hit a deeply personal chord. Putting aside her personal feelings would require considerably more than the usual discipline.

She could do it . . . she had to do it.

Burnett remained outside to take a call.

'The door was ajar when I arrived,' Chet explained, his tone quiet, somber. 'That bar stool was overturned.' With a gloved hand he indicated the small island with its two stools that divided the kitchen area from the living area of the one-room apartment. 'A glass of orange juice on the coffee table was knocked over as well.'

Jess made her way to the old-fashioned trunk Lori used as a coffee table. The drying puddle of OJ had stained the tan carpet. A half-eaten bagel languished on a napkin. Surveying the space again, this time more slowly, she noted discarded lounge pants and a tee-shirt lay on the floor by the bed. Lori had gotten up and dressed for work. Both doors, closet and bathroom, remained closed.

'What about her cell?'

'I haven't found her phone.'

Chet was visibly rattled. Like Burnett, Lori was his colleague. But for Chet there was more. He wanted a personal relationship with Lori. Jess had a feeling there had already been some serious physical bonding. She also understood that, for now, she needed the emotional distance of referring to the detectives by their last names or respective rank. After working so closely the past few days, she and the two BPD detectives had reached a first name basis.

This event changed everything.

She had to depersonalize the victim . . . *Lori*. Her new friend.

'What about her purse? Keys?'

Chet – Harper shook his head.

'Her car?'

'The Mustang's not in her parking slot or anywhere on the street.'

Didn't make sense that Spears would use Detective Wells' personal vehicle. Certainly wasn't his MO. 'Give me a few minutes, sergeant.'

'Yes, ma'am.'

Jess moved across the room to the closet. Neat, organized. If anything had been disturbed it was impossible to discern. Nothing unexpected in the bathroom other than the evidence that Wells bordered on OCD. Jess smiled, her lips a little stiff, a little shaky. No normal person was this neat.

Then again, what was normal?

Jess trailed her fingers down the robe hanging next to the shower. 'Be strong, Lori,' she murmured. 'I will find you.'

Tears burned her eyes and she blinked them away.

Returning to the main room, Jess took one last long look around the apartment before getting out of the way. The evidence techs had arrived and Harper waited near the door. Jess walked over to wait with him. She wished there was something she could say to reassure him, but there wasn't.

The truth was, there was very little chance this would end well. Dread and anger constricted her throat. The Player had made his move. There was no going back. No stopping him from taking the next step.

It should have been me.

'The carrier is working on tracking Lori's cell phone,' Burnett said as he joined them at the door, distracting Jess from the painful thoughts warring inside her.

'I received an update from the officers canvassing the neighbors. So far no one saw Detective Wells leave,' Harper added, his voice reflecting the same devastation his expression carried. He looked from Burnett to Jess, then at the floor as if holding her gaze was too much to ask.

Harper and all the rest knew . . . this was Jess's fault.

Stay on track. Evaluating the scene and making conclusions had to be done from an objective place. *You cannot screw this up.*

'It won't matter if we find an eye witness.' Jess kicked aside the fear and self-pity and considered the anomalies in the apartment's otherwise neat appearance. 'Detective Wells left alone.'

'What're you thinking?' Burnett sounded surprised by her conclusion.

'There was a struggle,' Harper argued, confusion joining the mix of powerful emotions cluttering his face.

'These aren't signs of a struggle, gentlemen.' Jess gestured to the overturned glass. 'Wells was having breakfast when she received a call that startled her.' She pointed to the stool on the floor. 'She knocked that over when she grabbed her purse and keys.' OCD or not, most people dropped their keys on the surface nearest the door they used most often.

'Whoever called, it rattled her. Scared her even. Detective Wells was in a hurry to get out of here. That's why she didn't care if she locked the door or not. That's also why you haven't found her cell. She carried it with her when she left in her Mustang.'

'I called her mother and her sister,' Harper countered, clearly confused. 'Neither answered. They're probably already at work. Her mother is—'

'Do her sister and mother live together?' Another possible layer of the scenario fell into place for Jess.

'Yes, ma'am.'

'Get a unit over there now.' A new worry robbed her lungs of air. 'Right now.' The emotion she had hoped to keep at bay washed over her.

Lori Wells had rushed out of her home with no care as to whether she secured the premises. Something had her scared to death. The most primal emotion known to man, or woman, was the protective instinct. Put a loved one in danger and all reason evaporated.

Burnett made the necessary call.

Jess turned to Harper. 'We need to get there as quickly as possible.'

If she was right, and Jess had a sinking feeling she was, they could very well have three victims instead of one.

Overton Heights, 11.38 A.M.

As Jess had anticipated, Lori Wells' red Mustang was parked in the driveway alongside a gray Impala that belonged to her mother. From the passenger seat of Burnett's SUV, Jess peered past the tinted glass to survey the house and front yard. The house was a 70s style split-level, part brown brick, part beige siding. It sat on the 'up' side of the street, the driveway ascending the steep bank and disappearing into the attached garage. Nothing moved. Nothing appeared out of place or amiss.

But, inside would be an entirely different story. She

wanted to get in there. It took every shred of patience she could muster to sit here and wait for the tactical team to do their stuff.

If they got inside . . . and the Wells family had been murdered . . .

Pain pinched her face as Jess suffered a new trickle of panic. The need to call her own sister, just to hear her voice, expanded against her ribs. Lily and her family were safe at home, under police protection. If there was trouble at Lily's, Jess would know. Burnett would get a call.

Fate apparently heard her thoughts and wanted to ratchet up the tension a little tighter. Burnett shifted behind the wheel and reached for his cell. That band of pressure narrowed around her chest. Why the hell did he keep the damned thing on vibrate all the time? A little warning would be nice.

'Does her sister have a car?' Jess asked Harper while Burnett spoke quietly to his caller. At eighteen, odds were Terri Wells, Lori's younger sister, either had a car or used her mother's.

'It's in the shop, ma'am,' Harper said from the backseat. 'Terri drives a blue Chevy Cobalt. Lori – Detective Wells told me it's in the shop.'

Lori was gone . . . her family could be dead –

dammit, Jess needed to be in there! What the hell was taking so long?

Damn Eric Spears and his games!

He was here, in Birmingham. No more speculation. Not just a hireling, the monster himself . . . the *Player*. This morning's delivery of that damned package was all the proof she needed.

He'd taken Lori and sent her badge to Jess – at the chief of police's office – by special delivery.

Dread joined the pain and frustration expanding in her chest.

The son of a bitch had started one of his games *here* . . . just for her.

Take a breath and concentrate, Jess.

Burnett ended the call. 'The carrier confirmed that a tower in this area was the last location Detective Wells' cell pinged.' He slid his phone back into the holster at his waist. 'Looks like you called this one right out of the gate, Jess. Your instincts may have saved valuable time.'

Jess absorbed the information. She was on the right track. Wells rushed away from her apartment to come here. That confirmation didn't make Jess feel one bit better about what they would find inside. The chances of Detective Wells' mother and sister having survived an up close encounter with the Player were vague to nonexistent.

The valuable time she may have saved would prove meaningless in the Player's grand scheme.

He never left evidence or witnesses or bodies at the scene of an abduction. At least not as far as the Bureau's research had determined. If anyone was alive in that house, a whole new precedent would be set. He'd already changed his game by targeting Jess rather than a close family member of the victim with that damned package.

That could mean other steps in his sadistic methods had changed.

Please don't let them be dead.

Jess wanted in that house . . . now. She wanted everyone inside alive. And she wanted to find Detective Wells . . . before he was finished with her.

'What's taking so long?'

Burnett assessed her with a long, worried look.

'I know. I know,' she said before he could point out the obvious.

No matter that Spears would undoubtedly be long gone from the Wells home, standard operating procedure dictated that they use caution entering the scene. BPD's Tactical Unit had used the street that ran along behind Overton to approach the house. When the unit was in place, they could move in.

Jess checked the time. Two more minutes, maybe.

The seconds ticked off like hours.

'Let's gear up.' Burnett opened his door and climbed out.

Anticipation sent her pulse into a rapid fire rhythm as Jess did the same. Her legs were rubbery with fear. She battled it back, had to find and stay in that neutral place. The one that allowed her to function with the highest measure of objectivity . . . no emotions and distractions allowed.

Harper was already out and pulling on his Kevlar vest. Burnett passed one to Jess. Despite holding an administrative position, she had to give him credit; the man maintained a preparedness level that surprised her. He carried a veritable 'what if' arsenal in his high-end Mercedes. From fire power to evidence collection to tools and first aid supplies.

Old habits died hard, she supposed.

She pulled on the vest and slung her bag over her right shoulder. Not that she could actually say anything about anyone's enthusiasm in the readiness department. She lugged around a considerable investigator's arsenal in her bag, including her Glock .40 caliber handgun, which contributed greatly to her lack of good posture.

She and Lori had laughed about the difficulties of being prepared while still looking chic as a female investigator.

Men didn't have that problem.

Jess listened while Burnett confirmed their communication links were operational, then she followed him and Harper up the steep bank between the Wells' home and that of the nearest neighbor, using the thick hedges for cover. Members of the tactical unit were now in position and checking the windows in preparation to make an entrance.

The tactical commander gave the order to go through the door. Anticipation roared through Jess.

Finally.

The damned stilettoes slowed her progress. When she'd dressed this morning she had done so with saying goodbyes and driving away in mind. A new job offer with BPD and *this* were nowhere near her radar.

Why couldn't Spears have followed her until she was out of town, maybe confronted her at a gas station between here and Virginia? Or just have waited for her there?

Because he knew *this* would deliver the most devastating blow.

He thrived on the fear of his victims and he knew this move would prompt that all-too human emotion in both the victim and in Jess.

She could not let him win.

By the time she reached the steps of the split-level home's front porch, weapon drawn, the tactical team had entered the house.

And Jess understood with complete certainty that she had spent far too much time behind a desk and computer screen. She was seriously out of breath and her calves were aching. Damned shoes.

An eternity elapsed one tiny fragment at a time before the next announcement echoed across the com link.

All clear. Two vics . . . alive.

Relief trembling through her, Jess shoved her weapon back into her bag and rushed through the open front door.

Thank God.

Harper immediately went to Detective Wells' mother to remove her bindings. The unit commander freed the sister, Terri.

Jess took a mental step back and again attempted to clean away the emotions. She checked the front door. No sign of forced entry which meant the door had been unlocked for Spears and had remained so after his departure. Otherwise a battering ram would have been used by the tactical team.

The large L-shaped living room that flowed into the dining room appeared in order. Two of the dining chairs had been dragged into the middle of the living room and used, along with duct tape, to secure the mother and daughter.

'He took my sister!' the younger woman shouted as soon as she was free. She swiped at her face with the backs of her hands. 'He took Lori! You have to find her!' Sobbing, she rushed to her mother.

They hugged, understandably hysterical.

Burnett leaned close to Jess. 'I'll take the sister.'

'The kitchen,' Jess suggested. The sooner they got these two separated, the less likely they were to get duplicated details. Witnesses were far more likely to recall events from their memories if that recollection was not muddled by listening as another retold those same events.

'Mrs Wells,' Jess said over Harper, who was crouched down in front of the lady attempting to calm her with gentle assurances, 'if you're up to it,' Jess directed a pull-it-together look at Harper, 'we have some questions for you.'

'Let's move to the sofa,' Harper suggested, 'where you'll be more comfortable?'

The mother looked to be late fifties. She was still dressed in her robe and house slippers. The sister had apparently been already dressed and ready to head to work when their unexpected visitor arrived. Harper mentioned that she had a summer job at a local bookstore. The mother worked part time at a daycare center. Both had the same dark hair as Lori, but not the green eyes. Both were distressed at being pulled apart as Burnett ushered the daughter into the kitchen.

When Harper had settled Mrs Wells on the sofa, Jess turned to him, 'Why don't you get Mrs Wells a glass of water? And, sergeant . . .'

Harper met Jess's gaze.

'Take your time.'

Harper didn't argue, though the protest flashed in his eyes.

Jess sat her bag on the floor and shrugged out of her vest. Most witnesses found police gear intimidating. This was Lori's mother . . . even if she possessed some familiarity with how police work was conducted, her daughter was missing and she was terrified.

Jess perched on the edge of the sofa and reached for the other woman's hand. 'My name is Jess Harris. I'm going to do everything I can to help find your daughter. I know this is an awful time.' She gave the woman's trembling hand a squeeze. 'But we need your help to figure out how to proceed. Okay?'

Mrs Wells nodded, then drew in a shuddering breath.

'Let's start at the beginning,' Jess prompted gently.

'I was fixing breakfast when he knocked at the door.' Mrs Wells tugged at the lapels of her robe, dragging it tighter around her. 'I thought maybe it was Lori dropping by before work.' A trembling smile lifted the corners of her mouth. 'She does that sometimes. Especially if she knows I'm making pancakes.'

Jess gave her a reassuring smile. She understood. Pancakes trumped a bagel any day of the week.

There was a peep hole in the door but Mrs Wells hadn't checked. Jess didn't have to confirm that deduction. The woman would feel guilty enough when the full ramifications of her actions had time to set in. No need to add to her burden.

Spears had wanted in. He would have gotten in one way or another.

'You opened the door,' Jess suggested, 'but it wasn't Lori.'

Mrs Wells nodded, the tears welling again. 'He . . . he

barged in. He had a gun in his hand. He told me to sit down.' She knotted her fingers into the fabric at her throat. 'Terri was still in her room. I prayed she would overhear him and call the police, but she didn't.' Mrs Wells gestured toward the hallway on the other side of the room, 'She came flying in here and he grabbed her . . . oh God.' Her body quaked with remembered terror. 'He stuck that gun to her head.'

Mrs Wells fell apart then and Jess waited patiently for her to collect herself. This was a parent's worst nightmare come true.

'He told me to call Lori and tell her that her sister hadn't come home last night . . . and that one of her friends was missing, too.' Again she struggled to compose herself. 'Lori said she was on her way.' Tears flowed down her cheeks. 'He used that tape then. Bound us up so we couldn't move. He put the tape over Terri's mouth.' Her lips trembled. 'But he had questions for me while he waited for Lori to get here.'

'What kind of questions?' A chill seeped into Jess's bones.

Harper waited a few feet away. Jess gave him a nod and he placed the glass of water on the table next to the shaken woman.

'He . . . he wanted to know any nicknames she had

as a child.' Her chest shook with a big breath. 'Her father called her Lori Doodle. At first I refused to answer him but he poked that gun in Terri's face and threatened to make me sorry if I didn't hurry up and answer.'

Harper offered the poor woman a handkerchief. She swabbed her eyes and cheeks.

'Did he have other questions?' Jess asked, encouraging her to go on.

She moistened her lips. 'He wanted to know why she's afraid of heights.' Mrs Wells shook her head. 'I didn't know what he was talking about.'

Unfortunately, Jess did. '*Is* Lori afraid of heights?'

Mrs Wells shook her head again, more adamantly. 'No.' She laughed, an agonizing, fragile sound. 'Why, that girl climbed every tree in this yard when she was a kid. That man was a liar. He came in here saying that Lori was terrified of heights back when he knew her.' She moved her head side to side. 'I don't believe he ever knew my Lori.'

Jess tried without success to slow the pounding in her chest. 'Did you set him straight, Mrs Wells?'

She nodded firmly. 'I told him that if he ever knew her he would know that Lori isn't afraid of a thing in this world except water. After she nearly drowned when she was ten she even stopped taking a bath. Only showers. Never a bath.'

Jess held still, waited for the rest.

'He laughed and said something like *oh yes, that's right*.' Her face creased with fear and misery. 'Then he taped up my mouth and waited for Lori to get here.'

The endless possibilities of water sources and how each could be used for torture whirled in Jess's head. She blinked away the too vivid images. 'Mrs Wells, can you describe the man who did this?'

Harper pulled out his cell and prepared to take notes. Seemed everyone but Jess had moved on from paper and pencil. She liked to take and study her notes the old-fashioned way. Really she just loved the smell of a freshly sharpened pencil and clean, crisp paper.

That such a trivial thought crossed her mind was irrefutable proof that she was on shaky ground.

Spears had her right where he wanted her . . . terrified.

'He was tall, at least six feet.' Her hand shaking, Mrs Wells gulped a drink of water. 'Blondish brown hair.' She shook her head. 'Mostly blond, I guess.' She frowned. 'I think he had blue eyes.'

Eric Spears' image formed in Jess's mind as the lady spoke. 'Any distinguishing facial features? Scars? Birth marks?' Spears had none of those. As certain as Jess was that it was him, she couldn't assume anything.

Mrs Wells considered her memories for several seconds. 'No. He was . . .'

Jess waited, knowing full well what she would say next but determined not to put any words in her mouth or to prompt her in a particular direction.

'He was well dressed. Like some fancy lawyer or something.' Her eyes fixed on Jess's. 'He was a good looking man. Not the sort you expect to do something so horrible.' Her voice faltered on the last.

Her own hand far from steady, Jess reached into her bag and withdrew her cell phone. She brought up the one image she carried of the man whose birth certificate, passport and social security number flagged him as Eric Spears – the one she knew without doubt was the Player – and showed it to Mrs Wells. 'Is this the man?'

Her breath caught. 'Yes.' She nodded. 'That's him.'

Jess lowered the phone to her lap. 'What happened next?'

Harper grew more and more agitated with each question. He hovered not three feet away. His ability to be objective was as skewed as Jess's.

'He waited at the door until Lori got here. When she opened it, he hid behind it.' Mrs Wells shrugged. 'I guess she was so stunned when she saw us all bound up that way she just sort of stood there, staring.' The poor woman inhaled a shaky breath. 'He walked up behind her and told her to hand over her gun and her cell phone.'

She paused, her face a mask of stark fear, obviously remembering that disturbing moment.

'Lori refused at first, but he warned her that if she didn't do exactly what he told her that he would kill me and Terri and then her. I wanted to beg him to take me instead, but the tape . . .' She shook her head. 'He ignored all the sounds I was making.'

The crime scene unit arrived, two techs loaded down with equipment. Mrs Wells looked from them to Jess.

'It's all right, Mrs Wells. These gentlemen are here to collect any evidence that might help us find Lori.' Jess tried to prop her lips into a passable smile. Didn't work. 'They'll make a little mess, but I assure you it's an important step in finding this awful man who barged into your home this morning.'

She hated to call this cruel killing machine a man. He was a monster. A sick, despicable monster who tortured and murdered women for pleasure.

A new rush of terror tied her gut into knots.

When the techs had set up their gear, Jess gave the other woman's hand an encouraging squeeze. 'You're doing fine. Your help is vitally important to us, so please go on with what happened this morning.'

Mrs Wells nodded. 'Lori gave him her phone and gun and he made her leave with him. I . . . I . . .' She dropped her face in her hands and sobbed. 'There was nothing I . . . could do.'

Jess put her arm around her trembling shoulders. 'Lori knows there was nothing you could do. I promise you her top priority at that moment was yours and Terri's safety. She's a good detective, Mrs Wells. She knows what to do in any situation. I want you to try and remember that.'

'Who is this man?' Mrs Wells turned to Jess. 'What does he want?'

'We can't be sure just yet.' Sharing details of Spears' merciless MO would serve no purpose at this time other than to terrify her even more. Sadly, odds were she had heard about the Player on the news and would eventually put two and two together but she wasn't going to hear it from Jess. At least not now. Now it was all Mrs Wells could do to handle the questions. 'Can you tell me what he was wearing? Specifically.'

Mrs Wells frowned. 'A dark suit jacket. Black or navy.' She touched her throat. 'A white shirt. And maybe jeans.'

'You didn't have a chance to look outside and maybe see what he was driving?' Jess suspected the answer was no but it never hurt to ask. Maybe she had glanced out the window on the way to the door and noted a different car on the street and thought nothing of it. Often witnesses remembered additional details if enough specific questions were asked.

'I thought it was Lori at the door. I never even looked outside.'

'Mrs Wells,' Jess figured this was all the relevant information the lady would be able to recall at this time, 'do you need medical attention?'

'No. No.' She latched onto Jess's hand. 'I just need you to find my daughter.'

'I understand. One last question, ma'am.'

The older woman gazed expectantly at Jess.

'Was the man wearing gloves? Or anything in an attempt to camouflage or distort his face? Anything at all?'

'No mask, no sunglasses. Nothing like that.' She hesitated. 'But he was wearing gloves. The latex kind like the doctors and nurses wear except they seemed thicker.' Realization dawned in her eyes. 'Like my beautician wears when she colors my hair.'

'Thank you, Mrs Wells.' Jess pushed to her feet. 'We

may have additional questions for you later.'

Jess left Harper with the woman and went into the kitchen.

Burnett had gotten the same story from the daughter, Terri.

When Terri had returned to the living room to join her mother, and he and Jess were alone, Burnett asked, 'Why would he let them see his face?'

Good question. With no good answer.

Until two months ago, Spears had been nothing more than a wealthy, reclusive businessman based in Richmond as far as the world around him had known. Then Jess's investigation had drawn a line from him to at least six heinous murders committed by the serial killer dubbed the Player. This previously unknown subject, the Player, had eluded authorities for a minimum of five years . . . and his body count had risen to at least thirty. No matter that her investigation had fallen apart, Jess knew for a certainty – at least in her mind – that Spears was the Player. But she couldn't prove it. There wasn't a single piece of evidence tying him to so much as a parking ticket, much less a murder.

The Bureau had had no choice but to let him go. The ensuing media frenzy regarding the botched investigation had rendered a devastating blow to Jess's career.

Her superior had sentenced her to administrative leave until the dust settled. She had jumped at the first opportunity to get the hell out of Virginia. But she'd made a mistake in coming here, to her hometown of Birmingham.

He had followed her.

Now suddenly he abducts a police detective and leaves two witnesses who can identify him as Eric Spears?

There was something very, very wrong with that picture.

The most probable scenario was that Spears was prepared for this to be his final game, in this country at least. Jess had brought scrutiny to his life and, to some degree, he would never escape the shadow of suspicion she'd cast. That new reality cramped his style. If this was his swan song, the game and whatever he deemed his goal were all that counted. He wouldn't care who saw him. He was out of here anyway. But then, why wear gloves? That part didn't add up.

Harper appeared at the door. 'Ma'am, Mrs Wells needs to speak with you.'

Jess and Burnett exchanged a look before moving into the living room. The techs were making a mess of Mrs Wells' tidy home. She and her daughter remained on the sofa, clinging desperately to each other.

Mrs Wells looked up at Jess. 'You're *Agent* Harris?'

No need to explain that was likely only temporary. The Bureau would never allow her to resume her duties at Quantico even if she wanted to. At the very least, she would be shipped off to some low profile assignment where she couldn't screw up anything important. 'Yes, I'm Agent Harris.'

Mrs Wells started to speak, then put her hand over her trembling lips for a moment as she composed herself. 'Terri reminded me that he – that awful man – told us to give Agent Harris a message.'

Ice filled Jess's veins. 'What was the message, Mrs Wells?'

She blinked rapidly to staunch the tears. 'He said to tell Agent Harris that she knows what he wants.'

Jess nodded, let the words penetrate fully.

Spears was right.

She knew exactly what he wanted.

Chapter Three

Second Avenue Flowers & Gifts, 12.15 P.M.

He opened the door.

A bell jingled overhead.

The smell that hit him reminded him of death. He hated that smell. Resurrected memories of his sad mother and his pathetic father. He should never have allowed them to live in misery so very long. They had been much happier once he'd planted them in the backyard.

He sighed. Their worthless bodies had served as splendid fertilizer. There wasn't a single bloom in this shop more magnificent than those in a certain flowerbed in his backyard in sunny southern Cali.

Life was full of unexpected little gifts.

The two ladies behind the counter looked up, stared a second, then smiled.

His lips widened and he knew without the aid of a mirror that his eyes twinkled. Women loved his smile.

'Good morning, ladies.' He sauntered up to the counter. Their eyes clocked his every step. 'Your shop is,' he looked around, infused approval into his expression, then leveled his attention on the two, 'quite lovely.'

The older of the two giggled. 'Thank you. May we help you with something this morning?'

Her cheeks flushed with pride. He liked watching a woman's pale skin deepen with color. Even a woman as unattractive as this one.

She was short. Not that she could help that. Bad genes. Her middle bulged beneath her floral print apron from days of snacking between meals and nights of piling up on the sofa in front of the television and shoving more fat-laden calories into her too wide mouth. That was entirely her own selfish doing.

What a disgusting little pig she was and a sheer waste of air space. Perhaps she would make nice fertilizer, too.

'You certainly may.' He pointed to a large arrangement of fresh flowers. 'I'll take one like that.'

'Oh,' the other woman said, joining the banter, 'this must be a very special occasion.'

He leaned on the counter and gifted her with another handsome smile. 'Absolutely. For a very special lady.'

The younger woman laughed, the sound kind of sultry. She had an intriguing voice. All full of enthusiasm and southern twang. Unlike the short little pig next to her, she was tall and thin. Scarcely any breasts at all. More bad genes.

A woman without breasts was utterly useless. Who would want to play with such a stick?

'I'll make you one fresh,' the pig offered eagerly. 'Pink roses, oriental lilies, peonies, snapdragon and heather. I'll even throw in some green hydrangea. That'll add a special touch.'

'Is the clear glass hurricane vase like that one,' the stick pointed to the arrangement he'd indicated, 'all right for your lady?'

'It's perfect.'

Stick smiled. She did have rather lush lips . . . too nice for such a plain, thin face. A few swipes of the properly sharpened blade and her mouth would be far more suited to her uninspired body. The image of her standing there, her mouth a round hole oozing blood . . . big fat drops falling right past her flat chest and splatting on the counter . . . teased him.

His cock swelled. But there wasn't a single other

trait visually interesting about her . . . certainly nothing to maintain a decent erection. Then again, with such a rich voice, her screams could very well prove titillating.

Not that he needed a distraction at the moment. He had an appointment already. Another little piggy. All plump and eager just like the one rushing to gather flowers for the arrangement.

'Why don't you fill out this card and the envelope,' Stick suggested, pushing a small white envelope and generic card across the counter toward him. Then she offered a pen. 'We can deliver.'

He made sure his fingers brushed hers. She blushed. 'Thank you.' He glanced at the nametag pinned to her tragic chest. 'Ellen. I'd love you to make the delivery for me.'

When the stick joined the pig in preparing his order, he slipped the business card from his pocket and placed it inside the envelope before addressing it. No need to worry about leaving behind fingerprints. No need at all. This was a public place with thousands of full and partial prints just lying around on every surface. Connecting this face with any of them, including the ones he left, would be impossible. That dead end would only make *her* more desperate.

He stared at the name.

Jess Harris.

His cock stirred again.

He had dreamed of touching her for weeks now.

Soon, he promised himself as his erection strained against the fly of his jeans.

Very soon.

Chapter Four

Birmingham Police Department, 2.50 P.M.

Dan Burnett braced against the counter in the men's restroom and stared at the face in the mirror. That man was a stranger to him. The outright fear in his eyes was not the norm. That same emotion twisting in his gut was way out of character.

He was the chief of police. Protecting the citizens of Birmingham was his job.

And he'd failed. He hadn't even protected one of his own.

Now Detective Wells would pay the price. Not one victim was known to have survived this twisted son of a bitch.

He was sick about it, worried . . . and damned scared.

There were steps he should have taken as soon as he recognized that a suspected killer was believed to be in his jurisdiction. Now God only knew how many would suffer for his lack of foresight.

Jess was the expert on the Player, but Dan knew plenty and one thing was guaranteed: he wouldn't stop with just one victim.

In the conference room, the deputy chiefs of every division in the department, Special Agent Todd Manning from the Birmingham Federal Bureau of Investigation, Jess, Harper, and the mayor, for Christ's sake, all waited for him to lead the task force toward resolving this situation.

Waited for him to point the way to finding Detective Wells and capturing a demonically clever repeat killer that no law enforcement agency had been able to irrefutably identify, much less nail.

Twenty years of police work, four as the chief of police, and he had never felt this unsure of himself.

Hell, he hadn't caught his breath after finding Andrea and the other girls who'd been abducted by a far less capable evil. For three weeks the whole city and the surrounding communities had lived in terror while those five young women had been missing. There hadn't been a single lead, not a scrap of evidence.

Truth was, he hadn't found them. Jess had. Every cop working that case had been stumped until she kicked them all in the ass, grabbed them by the noses and led the task force in the right direction.

All five, including his former stepdaughter, had been found alive because of Jess's unrelenting determination and innate skill at looking beyond the routine.

He shook his head, kicked himself again for taking the easy way out. Andrea was still his stepdaughter. Their relationship hadn't changed just because the marriage to her mother had ended. On some level he had convinced himself that the connection to a victim was part of the reason he'd needed Jess's help on that case. Or maybe somewhere deep inside he'd recognized that Jess had always been better at everything than him.

Instead of offering her the position of deputy chief over a new unit, he should have stepped aside and urged the powers that be to offer her his position.

Dan scrubbed a hand over his face and blew out a breath wrought with frustration and mounting uncertainty.

'What the hell are you doing?' Wells needed him and he was hiding in the men's room feeling sorry for himself. Anger, mostly at himself, howled with the need to make this right. To rescue Wells and stop the Player when no else had been able to.

Squaring his shoulders, he straightened his tie. Time to stop wallowing in guilt and to do his job.

The Bureau had backed off to some degree until, they insisted, there was evidence this was, in fact, the Player – the deviant Jess felt certain was Eric Spears. As a courtesy an agent was on duty, along with a BPD uniform, with Jess's sister. Manning was here for the strategy briefing or, more likely, to keep tabs on Jess's involvement. That was the extent of the Bureau's commitment for now.

Dan suspected the underlying motive behind their position was Jess. She was the Bureau's scapegoat in the whole Player/Spears debacle that was still playing out in the media. And, frankly, with both Jess and Manning at the table, the Bureau had fulfilled Dan's request for support.

This was his mess and he had to clean it up.

A rap on the door interrupted his gut-check session.

His frustration at the intrusion quickly shifted to full-on dread at the idea that there might be a new development. He did not want to hear that Detective Wells' body had been found.

Anxiety added a couple more knots to his gut.

'Burnett? You still in there?'

Jess.

Maybe not bad news. Just an unavoidable pep talk. Even after nearly two decades apart, she knew him too well.

Dan stretched his neck, drew in a deep breath and turned to the door at the same instant it opened.

Jess frowned. 'Everyone's waiting. What're you doing?'

How could they have spent those two decades separated by geography and their distinctly different views on their volatile history and her radar still work this well?

Until he'd asked her to come to Birmingham and advise on a case, they had seen each other only once in that entire time. The thought of that one encounter bombarded him with searing flashes of memories . . . *the frantic ripping off of clothes . . . the desperate sounds of mutual need . . . the feel of her warm, slick body moving beneath his . . . alive with his touch.*

He cleared his head. 'It's the men's room. Take a wild guess.'

She rolled her eyes. 'Yes, but what are you doing *now*?'

'Waiting for *you* to move so we don't keep everyone

else waiting any longer.' She was the one blocking the door.

After a searching look, she finally backed up, then waited for him to exit before allowing the door to close.

Maybe that old intimate connection still worked for him, too, considering he could feel her watching him, assessing his every blink, as they strode along the corridor to the conference room.

She had something on her mind.

Stopping short of the door, he turned to her. 'What?'

Jess crossed her arms over her chest. 'As a wise friend once said to me, it's okay to be afraid.'

It disgusted him that he was that transparent.

'Look,' she added on a weary sigh, 'I'm terrified for her myself. But we have to pull it together.'

Any irritation he might have felt at her accusation fizzled in light of the fact that he was the friend who'd given her that sage advice just a few days ago. And she was right.

Now she'd used the word *friend*. Apparently she had decided it was okay for them to be friends. He wasn't sure when she'd had time to arrive at that conclusion but he was damned glad she had. From the moment she rolled back into town just five days ago, they'd been embroiled in a life-and-death race with escalating stakes. Looked as if that wasn't going to change any time soon. He needed her support . . . he needed *her*.

'Thank you, Chief Harris,' he acknowledged. 'Point taken.'

'*Chief* Harris? That's a little premature, don't you think?' she countered. 'You only made that offer this morning.'

'You accepted,' he reminded her.

'Sort of.' She waved her hands back and forth. 'And that's deputy chief, by the way. But we can talk about that later. This situation is complicated enough without making that announcement right now. We need everyone's attention on the investigation, not on why or how I was selected for a newly created position in the department.' She started for the conference room again but hesitated. 'Besides, depending on how this turns out, you may want to retract your offer.'

Before he could argue Jess joined the others around the conference table while he stared after her, stunned and frustrated that she still believed this situation was her fault.

The Player had apparently taken on the part of nemesis to Jess and he wanted to punish her. She had no control over his actions. As brave as she wanted to appear, Dan could see that she was, as she had admitted, terrified for Wells . . . terrified for her family and anyone else who stood between her and Spears.

The problem, in Dan's opinion, was that none of that worry was spared for herself.

Making sure he stayed squarely between her and this maniac was the one thing he didn't fear. If Spears or whoever he was wanted Jess, he would have to get through Dan to reach her. He half hoped the scumbag would be stupid enough to try.

With renewed purpose, Dan entered the conference room. The attention of those seated tracked his movements as he approached the head of the table.

'Mayor Pratt, Sheriff Griggs, Agent Manning,' he said, 'I appreciate your being here to support our department. Let me bring you up to speed.'

As Jefferson County sheriff, Roy Griggs had more experience than anyone in the room. Dan was genuinely grateful to have him on this team.

One of their own was out there . . .

'Two witnesses have identified Eric Spears as the man who took Detective Lori Wells from her mother's home at approximately seven-thirty this morning,' he started as all around the table grim faces absorbed the bad news. 'We issued an APB and, if we're lucky, someone will have seen him.'

Silence held the floor as all absorbed the gravity of the situation.

Dan cleared his throat. 'No one in the neighborhood where Detective Wells' mother resides saw or heard anything. We've had no further contact from Spears. The courier who delivered the package this morning that included her detective's shield described the person who ordered and paid for the delivery as a Caucasian male, between sixty and sixty-five. His appearance was disheveled, ragged. You can find dozens matching that same description lined up at the homeless shelters and soup kitchens. We're not expecting viable results from that lead.'

Still no comments or questions.

'Despite showing himself at the Wells home and leaving behind two uninjured witnesses, Spears paid someone, who could also potentially identify him, to set up the delivery. It would be impossible to hazard a guess at this stage as to why he would act in such a conflicting manner.'

'You're assuming the unsub is Spears,' Manning commented with an indifference that infuriated Dan. 'For the record you have no substantiated evidence here to that end and, as you know, Spears was cleared during the Bureau's investigation in Richmond.'

His condescending remarks broke the silence.

And Jess sprang out of her chair.

'Two witnesses made the identification, Agent Manning. I'd call that pretty substantial. For the record, it was my conclusion, in the Player investigation to which you're referring, that Spears is the Player, whether we were able to prove that or not. He has contacted me five times in the last four days.' Her cheeks flushed with swiftly rising anger. 'Detective Wells' badge was sent to me in the same manner as the Player sends gifts to the families of his victims.'

'Agent Manning.' Dan stepped in before first blood was drawn. 'At this time, we do have sufficient reason to believe Spears is our man. With the positive identification from a recent photo by two witnesses, we are inclined to proceed under that assumption.'

'This recent photo,' Manning countered, 'was not an official photo and hardly admissible as evidence. A photo, I might add, that *Agent* Harris has on her cell phone.' He turned to Jess to stoke the fire he'd lit. 'I find that convenient and somewhat unsettling. Why carry the photo of a person of interest from a previous case in your cell, Harris? This guy must have really gotten to you.'

Dan clenched his jaw. *Agent* Harris. Though Manning didn't know Jess personally, obviously he'd heard enough to want to twist the dagger the Bureau had shoved in her back. Or maybe he had orders to treat her as a hostile in this investigation. Officially, she was still a special agent employed by the Bureau. In fact, she outranked the smart ass running his mouth.

Jess remained standing, braced for battle. 'I do have a photo I took during my interview with Spears. I came to Birmingham to advise on a case immediately following my work on the Player investigation and there was no time to clean out my photo library. Do *you* have a problem with that, Agent Manning? It's not like I yanked his photo from the Bureau's database and wear it in a locket around my neck.'

Manning held up his hands. 'I'm not the enemy, Harris. I'm here purely as a courtesy to BPD. My orders as to how to proceed come straight from—'

'I know where your orders come from,' Jess retaliated. 'And I also know what the Bureau thinks about my handling of Spears and the case in Richmond. But whatever you and all of them think,' she sliced her hands through the air, 'this is Spears. I know him better than anyone else and I know this is him.'

'Like you knew it was him before?'

That was enough. 'What happened in Richmond is irrelevant as far as we're concerned,' Dan clarified for the record. 'This is our case and, as I've already stated, we intend to proceed under the assumption that Spears is our perpetrator based on witness identification.'

'It's your mistake to make, chief,' Manning relented. 'The Bureau feels your time and resources would be best utilized focused on a broader search. You requested we weigh in and we have.'

'Duly noted,' Dan rejoined. 'Let's move on.'

The agent settled back into his seat. Dan had known Todd Manning for about three years. Generally, he was amiable and cooperative. There were always battle lines drawn when joint task forces formed. This time, those sensitive areas were magnified. Because it was one of BPD's own. Because of Jess.

Dan picked up where he'd left off. 'We have teams methodically checking public storage facilities, abandoned warehouses and buildings, as well as homes that have been abandoned by owners and not currently monitored by realtors.'

'That's like searching for a needle in a haystack,' Griggs submitted, his tone as doubtful as the expression he wore.

A rumble of agreement went around the table.

Dan couldn't argue with that. 'Based on Agent Harris' previous dealings with Spears, he likes plenty of privacy when he does his dirty work. He's new to the area and our hope is that prior planning was not up to his usual cautious standards which may serve to our benefit.'

'He had maybe three days after his release in Virginia,' Jess spoke up, 'before abducting Detective Wells. There is nothing in his background that indicates he has spent any time in the south, much less this area. I'm thinking he scrambled to put this game together, which is definitely to our benefit. He may have made mistakes he wouldn't ordinarily make.'

'Once again,' Manning cut in, 'you're assuming this is Spears and that you actually know his MO, if he even has one. I feel compelled to underscore our position that narrowing your search parameters this way is a mistake.'

How many times were they going to go over this? When Dan would have said exactly that, Jess dug in her heels.

'Are you going to discount the fact that almost every aspect of Wells' disappearance matches the MO used by the Player, witnesses aside, when he abducted his victims?' she demanded. 'The same ones he tortured and ultimately murdered?'

'Almost being the key word,' Manning fired back. 'Could be a copycat using the Player's MO. Since your investigation in Richmond could not tie Spears to the Player, I can't see what you hope to gain by pursuing only that avenue.'

What the hell bug crawled up this guy's ass? Dan gritted his teeth to prevent telling him to shut up or get out. Besides, the mayor was here and he had no choice but to be on his best behavior. On some level he got that there was merit to the Bureau's position, but the connection to the Player – to Spears – was what they had. Waiting around for some other scenario to surface would be an even bigger mistake than going with the wrong one.

'I, for one,' Griggs spoke up, 'have confidence Agent Harris knows what she's talking about. Five young women who survived as much as three weeks being held hostage would agree with me.' He turned to Jess. 'Agent Harris, I've just sent a message to my second in command and asked him to organize as many teams as possible to hit those same type locations in the county. I'm sure BPD has its hands full with covering Birmingham and the various surrounding communities. We'll call in our auxiliary deputies. Whatever we have to do, we'll do it.'

Jess nodded, the emotions tearing at her composure shadowing her face. 'Thank you, sheriff.'

'We're about to go public,' Deputy Chief Harold Black from the Crimes Against Persons Division spoke up, 'with a 25K reward for anyone with information leading us to Detective Wells' location and/or the person responsible for her abduction. We expect that reward to increase substantially over the next twenty-four hours. This initial reward is coming from the North Alabama Police Officers Association. They are, as we speak, rallying their members to help with the search.'

'That kind of help is what we need.' Dan was damned glad to have all the boots on the ground he could get.

The men and women of the NAPOA, all retired police officers, with the proper training, could contribute greatly to the search. Gina Coleman, his top contact with the local media, was directing the news releases – including a blitz featuring a rendered drawing created from Spears' photo since the Bureau warned that using the actual photo opened all involved in the investigation to a law suit. That was a point Dan couldn't ignore.

Gina wanted a sound bite from Dan later today if he could make the time.

'We have flyers going up all over the city,' Deputy Chief Hogan of Patrol Division added.

With the ball rolling and Manning settled down, Dan prepared to take his seat.

'Chief Burnett, I apologize for interrupting.' Tara Morgan, his receptionist, hovered at the door.

Dread swelled with the threat of a second tidal wave of trouble. Dan excused himself. Once in the corridor, Tara stepped to the side of the conference room door, signifying she preferred not to be overheard by the others.

Couldn't be good news.

'There are two gentlemen from the Federal Bureau of Investigation here, sir. I explained that you were in a briefing.' She twisted her fingers together. Nervous or flustered. 'But they want to see you. Privately. Now.'

Dan glanced at those seated around the table. Why would Manning fail to mention that others were coming?

'Show them to my office,' he said to Tara. 'I'll be right there.'

Dan ignored the tension tugging at the muscles along the length of his spine and returned to the briefing. 'Sergeant Harper, I'd like you to carry on here.'

Harper was shaken but he knew more about Wells' personal life than anyone else. He was as familiar with the Player case and Eric Spears as Dan. And he would keep the others from closing out Jess. Despite the tension throttling through him, he almost laughed at the idea of Jess allowing anyone to close her out. She would tell Dan exactly that if he dared to say any such thing out loud. Still, someone had to referee.

'Agent Manning, if you would, I'd like you to accompany me to my office.'

Dan didn't wait for the agent and he didn't make eye contact with Jess. Whatever this was about, he figured it involved her. Until he had a handle on what was about to go down, it was best she stayed right where she was.

When they were out of hearing range of the conference room door, Dan glanced at the other man. 'You didn't think it necessary to mention your colleagues were coming a little late to the party?'

Manning stalled, a frown making grooves in his face. 'I wasn't aware anyone else from the Bureau would be coming.'

If the guy was lying, he pulled it off without a flinch. 'Let's see what this is about.'

Manning followed Dan to his office.

The two gentlemen seated in front of his desk rose and turned to greet him.

'Chief Burnett,' the older of the two said as he stepped forward, 'I'm Supervisory Special Agent Ralph Gant, unit chief, Behavioral Analysis Unit 2.'

Jess's boss from Quantico. He looked exactly like the arrogant prick Dan had pictured based on the way he'd treated Jess. Dan disliked him on sight.

He accepted the hand Gant offered. He'd anticipated the local Bureau's involvement at a higher level when they dropped the blinders and admitted Jess was correct. What he hadn't anticipated was Gant's appearance and the lack of a heads-up before that happened.

'This is Agent Clint Wentworth, Office of Professional Responsibility,' Gant added, introducing the other man.

Dan got the picture now. This *was* about Jess, not his case . . . and it was definitely trouble.

Wentworth offered his hand as well; Dan gave it a shake. Manning introduced himself. Apparently he had never met these two either.

'I wasn't briefed,' Manning said, 'that anyone from Quantico was coming.'

'The decision was made just this morning,' Gant explained, giving Manning the minimum amount of information possible.

At least Dan wasn't the only one in the dark here.

'Have a seat, gentlemen.' He moved around behind his desk and waited until the three were settled.

Manning dragged up a chair to join his colleagues.

Dan sat and offered his undivided attention, as difficult as that was to do. He had an investigation to get off the ground. 'I have a briefing going on in my conference room,' he said when no one seemed inclined to get to the point. 'One of my detectives is missing and time is of the essence.' Impatience screwed tighter around his forehead. Why the hell were they here?

'We have reservations as to whether your unsub is Eric Spears,' Gant said. 'Certainly, it's far too early to call this the Player's work. After the disaster in Richmond, there are legal ramifications that need to be considered. Keeping Spears' name out of this until there is some sort of evidence would be prudent. That said, the reason we felt compelled to make this impromptu visit is our escalating concern with Agent Harris' ability to be an asset to your investigation under the circumstances. However, this is *your* investigation.'

Dan's guard went up. 'We consider Jess an incredible asset. In fact, we've offered her a deputy chief position. We're all hoping she'll stay.'

Another of those awkward moments passed.

'I would strongly urge you to reconsider that offer for now,' Gant recommended.

Dan's patience had run out. Now he was just pissed off. He stood. 'As I said, I have a missing detective and a strategy briefing. Unless you have some relevant input to this investigation, I'd say we're done here.'

The three stood in one choreographed move, like dancers in a chorus line.

'Manning, why don't you wait for us in the lobby?' Gant instructed.

Dan's tension moved to the next level.

The silence thickened, pushed the air out of the room as they waited for the door to close behind Manning.

'I'm not sure you have the full story on what happened with the Spears investigation,' Gant said.

'I know all I need to know.'

Disregarding his comment, Gant went on, 'We believe Agent Harris may have suffered a meltdown of sorts. Recent discoveries have led us to believe it would be in her best interest to seek psychiatric evaluation and counseling. I assure you this is standard operating procedure when an agent's actions are called into question. Her cooperation, however, is essential. If she chooses not to comply, we will be forced to pursue separation from service measures based on our conclusion that she is no longer fit for duty.'

Outrage blasted any good sense Dan had managed to hang onto right out the door with the dismissed agent. 'I'd say what she needs is legal counsel.'

'This is your mistake to make, Chief Burnett. But bear in mind that we feel her fixation with the idea that Spears has followed her here and whatever is actually going on will not end well.'

'I've seen his messages to her,' Dan thundered just a decibel or two below shouting. 'Two witnesses to my detective's abduction identified him.'

'She received messages before,' Gant reminded him unnecessarily. 'Followed leads he gave only to her . . . but there was no connection found to the man, Eric Spears, she continues to insist is the Player despite a total lack of evidence. Those anonymous emails she received during our investigation in Richmond were sent from her own home.'

The ramifications of that statement sent Dan's concern for Jess up several degrees. The Bureau was building a case against her and if she had any idea, she hadn't said a word. 'There's no way Jess sent anything to herself.' This was way over the edge.

Gant exhaled a big breath. 'I want to agree with you

more than you can possibly imagine. But we have no choice but to consider what this development means. The sender used a path that was nearly impossible to trace, and when we did find the source it was one we didn't want to see. But our hands are tied. We cannot simply ignore the possibility.'

'You must understand, Chief Burnett,' Wentworth jumped in with his New England accent and visible impatience, 'that Agent Harris' conduct during the final weeks of the Player investigation, even without this stunning evidence, was questionable. OPR must investigate her actions for her own benefit as well as the Bureau's.'

Jesus Christ. They were trying to railroad Jess for more than allegedly screwing up an investigation. Dan took a moment to get his initial reaction in check. 'Whatever you believe, Jess is an essential part of our team and, unless you're planning to take her into custody, that's not going to change.'

'We came to you,' Gant contended, his own impatience showing, 'as a courtesy. For now, the decision is yours to make but we needed to ensure you were fully aware of Agent Harris' situation. The outcome of our investigation could prove detrimental to yours when all is said and done. The unsub in your case, if and when he's caught, could very well use this decision against you.'

Dan struggled to make sure his voice was calm when he spoke. 'Why are you dismissing our *stunning* evidence? We have two witnesses who ID'd Spears. *We* can't ignore that. And I would gladly take Jess's findings into a courtroom any day.'

'We would certainly like to interview those witnesses,' Wentworth responded. 'At this time, however, our evaluation of the situation remains unchanged.'

'We're not suggesting you take Spears off the table as a person of interest,' Gant clarified. 'But an ID made from a cell phone snapshot by two witnesses who were no doubt compromised by emotion is not conclusive evidence that Spears is your man. A good attorney, and Spears has the best, could suggest Harris prompted the witnesses. We must tread carefully here.'

What was the deal? 'Maybe you think that just because I'm a police chief in Alabama that I can't hear beyond what you're telling me. This hammering at the same issues is getting a little old. You must have more than what you're disclosing. You and I both know that anyone could have sent those emails via Jess's home computer.'

Gant and Wentworth exchanged a look.

Oh, yeah. There was a lot more.

'Before we were forced to release Eric Spears, he confided in me that he thought Agent Harris had an interest in him beyond the investigation.' Gant shook his head. 'I ignored the assertion. These things happen sometimes. Suspects take shots at the agents involved with their cases. It wasn't until after we released him that evidence beyond the emails was brought to our attention suggesting he may very well have been telling the truth.'

'You're taking the word of a killer over Jess's?' The timing had dread twisting in Dan's gut. Spears had only been released three days ago. Whatever had happened, it was fresh and Jess hadn't been informed.

'We can't prove he's a killer,' Gant repeated, openly exasperated with Dan's resistance. 'Whatever he is, I'm compelled, for Jess's protection, to investigate his claim. Particularly after last night's development. New, incriminating evidence was discovered in her home.'

'Are you saying you searched her house without her permission?' Jess was going to be livid. Dan was mad on her behalf. What the hell was wrong with these people? Jess had given them nearly twenty years of dedicated and distinguished service. Didn't that count for anything?

'We didn't need her permission. Last night there were two apparent robberies in her neighborhood, her house and a neighbor's. Her neighbor was murdered. The door to Jess's home was standing wide open, the local police entered to ensure there were no other victims.'

'No one called Jess.' Dan would have heard about that.

'After what the local police found, they called us first.'

Dan braced for worse news.

'Pictures of Spears were all over the walls of her home office. Photos of herself cut and taped together with photos of him, as if they were a couple. And there was a message.' Gant heaved another of those burdened sighs. '*Why did you leave me*? The words were written on the wall of her living room, using her neighbor's blood.'

Shock grabbed Dan by the throat. This bastard didn't just want revenge, he was infatuated with Jess. 'He's setting her up. You have to see that.'

'Off the record,' Gant admitted, 'that's our initial conclusion, but we also can't rule out that she's a danger to herself and others. I've worked with Jess for seventeen years, Burnett. This case got to her. The one certainty in all this is that Jess is in trouble and we have to get to the bottom of the source.'

Dan shook his head. 'Whatever you think, she sure as hell didn't dress up like Spears and abduct my detective.' This whole scenario was absurd. Even the break-in at her home sounded fishy to him. He said as much to the other man.

This madman had killed an innocent person to send Jess a message.

'That's the reason I'm here,' Gant admitted. 'I feel compelled to support Jess in this investigation. What I'm sharing with you is not for public dissemination or even for others within BPD. We'd like to conduct our own, parallel investigation into the theory that Spears may be involved in what's happening here. We're not going to ignore that it may very well be that he's the one who has an interest, as he called it, in Jess.' Gant held up his hands stop-sign fashion. 'As much as I would like to assume that's the case and call it a day, we have a responsibility to look at both sides of this.'

They expected Dan to keep this from Jess. How the hell could he do that?

'I can't prevent you from doing what you have to do,' he admitted. 'And I'd be a fool not to accept your assistance in finding Spears – or whoever the hell we're dealing with. But I will not be a party to your witch hunt. My only question is, do you or do you not intend to keep your agent assigned to Jess's family?' Dan had a uniform assigned to the family but the Bureau had a responsibility here, too. And, by God, he intended to see that they did their part.

'No question,' Gant answered without hesitation. 'The safety of all concerned is our top priority.'

'Does that include Jess?'

'It seems you already have that covered, chief,' Wentworth countered smugly. 'Your personal feelings appear to be slanting your objectivity. Since entering your office we've been very accommodating and, frankly, we're not feeling the love.'

Anger, outrage, fury . . . none of those words adequately articulated Dan's internal reaction to the remark. 'FYI, Wentworth, around here you get as good as you give. And you're right, I will keep Jess covered. If you have an issue with that, I'm happy to settle it with you any time, any place.'

For five seconds that turned to ten, Wentworth didn't back down, then he said, 'I have no issue with you handling her personal security.'

That was all Dan needed to know. 'I need to get back to my briefing. Call if you have some development to pass along.'

He had nothing else to say. Evidently the two feds

were a little slow on the uptake since both simply stared at him.

Gant cleared his throat. 'Well. We appreciate your cooperation, chief.'

Dan made a sound that was more grunt than laugh. 'Do not mistake my tolerance for cooperation, gentlemen.'

He didn't wait for a reaction; he walked out.

The situation was crystal clear. Jess was in danger from both sides of the law.

As Dan returned to the conference room silence fell over the group. He ignored the quiet and settled in his seat at the head of the table. 'What have I missed, Sergeant Harper?' His attention zeroed in on his detective.

Harper exchanged a look with Jess who was seated next to him.

'Deputy Chiefs Hogan and Black have divided the city and the surrounding communities into quadrants. The search teams consist of three officers each. One by one the locations will be searched and the results reported to the search commander who will report directly to Chief Hogan.'

Hogan nodded. 'We've already cleared several areas. Property owners are cooperating. So far no issues to slow us down. No demands for warrants. Thanks to the preliminary media blitz, the citizens of Birmingham are already responding to our call for help.'

Dan was grateful for any good news. 'That's what we want to hear.'

Deputy Chief Black gestured to the flat panel television mounted on the wall. 'We've just watched the first press release with our public relations liaison officer and Ms Coleman. I've also received several notifications that some of the same groups and organizations that rallied to help with the search for the missing young ladies have stepped up to offer their support.'

'If,' Jess jumped in, 'we can have folks like those walking the streets with flyers with both Detective Wells and Spears' photos – business to business, house to house – we can keep the pressure on . . . maybe make it more difficult for him to come out into the open and snatch another victim.'

'But if he stays hunkered down,' Harper countered, 'how are we going to find him?'

Harper was running on emotions. Dan couldn't fault him for that; he was halfway there himself. Who was he kidding? He was already there.

Jess didn't look directly at Harper as she spoke. 'The

existing profile on the Player is that he is compelled to begin his ritual once each year, taking six victims over a period of eight to ten weeks. Since he has deviated from the pattern the Bureau has tracked as far back as five years, we can't be sure what his next move will be. But whatever that move is,' she turned to the man at her side, 'we can't make it easy for him.'

'Excuse me.' Harper pushed back his chair and exited the room.

Jess would have followed him but Dan shook his head. Harper was having a difficult time with this investigation. He no more belonged on this task force than Dan had belonged on the last one that convened in this room. But Dan would not refuse him the opportunity to do what he could unless he lost it completely.

For the first time since he resumed his place at the table he allowed his gaze to fully meet Jess's. He knew before she said a word she was about to ask the question he did not want to answer.

'What about the Bureau? Is there a reason Manning is MIA?'

Everyone gathered at the table swung their attention to Dan and waited for his answer.

'The Bureau will be conducting a separate investigation.' He turned his palms up as if it weren't really such a great mystery. 'After the media's scrutiny on their handling of the case with Spears, they appear to be looking for close containment.'

Griggs and the others adopted that who-cares look. Jess, on the other hand, understood that something was up. Dan did not look forward to the conversation that would follow this briefing.

'Meanwhile,' he said, turning his attention back to the more immediate matter, 'I'll meet with Gina Coleman in a couple of hours for that sound bite she wants to air on the evening broadcast. We need to get this done.' He surveyed the faces in the room. 'As with all cases, time is our enemy, but never more so than now. Typically we're dealing with many unknowns, that's also different in this case. We have a firm idea of what we're up against. We know how this will go down if we don't stop him.'

Harper entered the room and took his seat. He didn't make eye contact with Dan or anyone else. That was another conversation he didn't look forward to but it grew clearer all the time that it was going to have to happen.

'Agent Harris briefed us earlier on Spears', aka the Player's, MO. No need to rehash that just now.' Dan indicated the case board on the other side of the room.

'If anyone has specific questions, hang around. Otherwise, let's get the job done.'

Mayor Pratt stood and all eyes shifted to him. 'Just let me say, ladies and gentlemen, that I am very proud and impressed by your rapid movement on this case. For the sake of Detective Wells and our community, I expect quick results.'

With that, the mayor took his leave.

Nice speech but it boiled down to one warning: he wanted this taken care of yesterday. That was something Dan imagined everyone in the room had in common. He stood, shuffled his notes together and hoped Jess would wait until they were alone before launching her interrogation.

'Chief Burnett.'

Tara's voice floated above the hum of conversations and the rustle of papers as the rest of the task force prepared to leave. Again she hovered at the door.

Christ. What now?

Dan motioned for her to join him at the conference table. She moved hesitantly through the disbursing group. That she didn't smile had frustration banding more tightly around his chest.

'Chief, a local florist just delivered a huge bouquet for Agent Harris.' Tara chewed at her lip. 'Security brought it up. They said it's okay but considering the package this morning . . .'

'Thank you, Tara.' Dan snagged Harper who was already moving toward the door. 'Come with me.'

Thankful Jess was deep in conversation with Griggs, Dan cut through those milling in the corridor, Harper keeping step. Tara followed close behind.

She'd been right about one thing, the bouquet was massive. Right up front was a small white envelope tucked at the end of a clear plastic holder with Agent Harris scrawled across the front.

But security had been wrong. It was not *okay*. After this morning, any delivery addressed to Jess was considered suspicious.

'Did you open the envelope?'

Tara shook her head.

Harper withdrew a pair of gloves from his pocket and handed them to Dan. His heart rate climbing, he pulled on the gloves and reached for the envelope. It opened easily, not taped or glued. Inside was a small card . . . a business card.

Belinda Howard. Howard Realty. Had Jess bought a house or condo . . . ?

'What's this?' Jess barged into the huddle. The rest of the task force had stalled at the bank of elevators.

Dan showed Jess the name written on the envelope, then the business card that had been tucked inside.

She frowned. 'Who is . . . ?' She shot a look heavenward, blew out a breath. 'My sister.' She fished in her bag for her cell, then stabbed at the screen. 'She invited her friend the realtor over for dinner last night. Why would she send me flowers?' Jess shook her head. 'I swear, the woman is— hey, sweetie, this is your aunt Jess. I need to speak to your mother.'

Dan tried to relax. This was probably nothing more than Jess's sister going overboard with the sisterly thing. But they needed to be sure.

'Lil, what's the deal with this realtor friend of yours?' Jess nodded. 'Yes, Belinda.'

Griggs sent a questioning look at Dan. Dan pointed to the envelope, then the flowers and finally Jess. Then he shrugged.

'She told you what?' Jess shook her head again. 'Lily, listen to me. I did not buy a house. I did not make an appointment to see a house.' Jess rolled her eyes as she listened some more. 'Where did Belinda say she was meeting me? . . . *What?*' The color drained from Jess's face. 'Do you remember his name?'

Dan felt the tension start to build once more.

'You're sure a man called Belinda?' The big bag Jess

lugged around slid down to the floor. 'Absolutely positive?'

Dan and Griggs exchanged a worried look. This was not sounding good.

'Forget that part, Lil, for Christ's sake. You're sure that's the street?' Jess nodded . . . her expression clouded with worry. 'What kind of car does she drive?' Another pause. 'Okay. Okay. Gotta go.'

She ended the call and turned to Dan, her eyes filled with resignation. 'Belinda Howard called my sister just two hours ago and told her I might be buying a house. She said I was meeting her at one to view a listing but that it was a surprise so Lily wasn't supposed to say anything until I told her. Belinda said a man made the appointment but Lily couldn't remember his name.'

Griggs stepped forward. 'I take it you didn't make this appointment.'

Jess shook her head. 'Not even close. My sister invited this realtor lady to dinner last night. She gave me the whole sales pitch. That was the last time I saw her and I certainly haven't heard from her today.' She gestured to the flowers. 'Why would he . . . how would he know . . . ?'

Apparently Wells wasn't the only one Spears had been watching. Dan touched Jess's arm to draw her attention back to him. 'Did anything happen that might have given Spears the idea there was a connection between you and this realtor?' Spears had been watching Detective Wells *and* Jess.

She thought for a moment. 'I don't . . . wait . . .' Her face lit with realization. 'She hugged me when she was ready to leave. You know, one of those things everyone down here does.' The misery in her eyes twisted Dan's heart. 'He's got her, Dan. He's got Belinda Howard.'

Face pale, she turned to the others. 'Liberty Park Lane in Vestavia Hills. She drives a black BMW sedan. Unless one of you made this appointment for me as a welcome home surprise . . . it has to be him.'

To Dan, she added, 'She's short. Pretty. Forty-five, maybe. A little on the plump side.'

'She isn't his type?' Dan understood.

Jess shook her head. 'Evidently, she doesn't have to be. She's connected to me and that's all that matters to him right now.'

Dan dragged a hand over his face. Spears was changing the game again.

And moving faster and faster.

Chapter Five

Liberty Park Lane, Vestavia Hills, 5.05 P.M.

Jess stared at the message written in blood. Uneven streaks had raced down the pristine tan wall, giving the hideous message a ghoulish appearance.

It's a killer deal, Jess.

'Narcissistic bastard.'

She turned her back to the message and considered the small crimson puddle on the hardwood. Not much larger than a saucer, the kind socialites like Katherine Burnett used when serving tea to her guests.

Jess rolled her eyes. The high-class neighborhood reminded her of Dan's mother. Just went to show what stress could do to the brain. Jess's had obviously turned to mush.

That was a distraction she could do without even as badly as she wished she could escape this nightmare. But there was no escaping.

Closer inspection confirmed the blood on the floor had coagulated. No spatter pattern.

Shoe covers making a swiping sound against the wood floor, Jess walked around the puddle and studied the symmetrical circle it made. No surges, splatters or spurts around the edges to indicate there had been a struggle or any sudden movements at all. Almost a perfect round pool of velvety red.

Jess dragged a pair of gloves from her bag before setting it on the floor near the wall on the other side of the room, away from any visible evidence.

'How much longer?'

Pulled from her concentration by his deep voice, she glanced at Burnett who waited in the doorway separating the great room from the entry hall. The two of them had already walked the entire two-story house. But she wanted a closer look at this part before the techs did their business.

And she needed to lose herself in the crime scene. She couldn't do that with him near. He . . . distracted her and, much to her dismay, he was a distraction she didn't seem quite strong enough to ignore.

She was well aware that the crime scene unit waited outside. 'Tell them I need five minutes.'

'Five, Jess,' Burnett warned, 'and then they're coming in.'

'Yeah, yeah.'

Evidence techs could be a pain, especially when they didn't know the background of the investigator traipsing around their scene, risking the possible contamination of evidence.

Jess squatted down and inspected the floor near the blood a little more closely. Rolling down to her hands and knees, she pushed her glasses up the bridge of her nose and leaned her face close to the floor. There was a smudge or smear blurring the shiny surface.

She needed more light. Back on her feet she moved to the windows on the side of the house facing west and adjusted the blinds. 'Better.'

On the floor in the middle of the room was Belinda Howard's purse, its contents purged as if she'd dropped it there. Likely startled by the man who had shown up in Jess's stead. Howard's cell lay inches away from the rest. She had received a call from a private number shortly after noon. When tracked down, Jess suspected it would lead to another prepaid phone registered to

Jessie Harris. Spears liked adding all sorts of little digs at her with his methods.

She surveyed the large open room again.

No . . . Spears hadn't shown up after Howard's arrival. If he had, judging by where she'd dropped her purse, she would have seen his approach from that big window and known a stranger had arrived instead of Jess. But that hadn't happened. He had already been in the house when she arrived. He'd watched or listened as she'd gone through the steps of preparing for the showing. Ready and anticipating Jess's arrival, Howard had probably crossed the room to peek out the window. Spears had stepped from his hiding place and she'd whirled around . . . dropped her purse.

Jess glanced around the empty room. 'Hmm.' But there was no handy place for him to have hidden.

Shoe covers swishing, she shuffled back to the entry hall. A door under the staircase opened to a coat closet. Jess closed herself in the closet and shut her eyes. She relaxed her body. Breathed deeply. She could hear Burnett speaking in low tones to someone outside the front door.

Yes. This was where Spears had hidden. He'd listened to Howard's high heels clicking as she walked around on the glossy wood floor. She had worn high heels to dinner last night, seemed logical that she'd dress similarly for pitching a high-end house like this one.

Spears was loving tossing the unexpected at Jess in this game.

Persuading the realtor who'd courted her to meet him here had come as easily as breathing. He no doubt introduced himself on the phone as Jess's representative. Even without the promise of a commission, Howard wouldn't have been able to resist the charismatic killer.

Jess returned to the evidence that a violent act had occurred in the room, assumed the position on her hands and knees and leaned down to study the near invisible smudge on the floor a third time. Using her gloved finger she touched the smear, lifted her finger to her nose and sniffed. Slight perfumed smell. Not convinced, using her other hand, she swiped at her own cheek with her forefinger and took a whiff of that one. Oh yeah.

'Make-up.'

She surveyed four or five feet around the area of the smear; if the floor hadn't been polished to a mirror finish she would never have noticed it. The whole house showed like a model home designed to sell the neighborhood. The only thing missing was the sparse but elegant furnishings usually staged strategically for such a showcase property.

Pushing back to her feet, she visualized the scenario. Howard had either been lying on her side or face down. Unconscious most likely. Since the blood was near the smudge, he may have slashed her arm or hand and held it right where he wanted it for the pooling of blood. When he had what he wanted, he probably wrapped the wound and went about his business.

The Player planned every step and he never made mistakes . . . until now.

Or so it seemed. But, with all she knew about him and what she saw here, maybe these weren't mistakes.

Still pondering the concept, she wandered, scanning the span of floor in front of her before she crossed it, toward the kitchen. The scented candle Howard had lit for her anticipated appointment had lost the battle with the metallic odor of clotting blood. Jess blew it out, thankful for the slight reprieve provided by the acrid smoky smell that filled her lungs with the extinguished blaze.

She studied the large stainless steel sink. Too clean and polished for him to have washed up there. Of course if he wore gloves there would have been no need to wash his hands. Just peel his gloves off into a bag.

The laundry room beyond the kitchen was spotless, the sink immaculate. As she turned to go back to the kitchen, she hesitated and opened the door of the frontloading washer. She leaned down, peered inside. Nothing. She checked the other appliances and the cabinets, just in case.

Back in the great room, she considered the message he'd left for her. She crossed to the far end of the room and stared at the bloody taunt. *It's a killer deal, Jess.*

Burnett had been visibly rattled by the message. Jess had been frustrated. The words weren't meant to give her a lead on what he wanted. Just another phrase meant to goad her and to make her afraid of what he would do next.

'Bang up job, you son of a bitch.'

Reaching up, she held two fingers together and measured the width of the strokes. Only slightly wider than two of her fingers. Another frown marred her brow. Jess scrubbed at it with her forearm to smooth it away. Frowns were bad . . . wrinkles were worse. Reminded her that she was getting older by the minute and her career was a mess, along with her dysfunctional personal life.

And a sociopath was playing games with her, using other people's lives.

Jess scrutinized the floor close to the wall displaying the message. If there was a single drop of blood it was far too minuscule for her to spot. The techs would find any traces with their handy gadgets.

Had he used a cloth to wipe his fingers, gloved or not, after each swipe so as not to drip on the floor? She couldn't imagine him using his shirt or trousers. Not his style. Though she had done so the time she painted her living room. She'd ruined two blouses and her favorite jeans.

Jess turned back to the small puddle. Had he walked back and forth to dip his fingers over and over?

Too messy; too time consuming. He'd been on a tight schedule.

More plausible, he had the blood in a container. She studied the message again before turning back to the puddle. Then poured the rest on the floor for the shock value. Howard might have been inside his vehicle by then. With her out of the way, he could far more easily come back inside and arrange the scene to suit his purposes.

As usual he came prepared. There was no indication he'd so much as washed his hands here. He'd carried what he needed, then took the items with him when he left with his victim. Knife, blade of some sort, small container for his art work, cloths or disposable wipes for cleaning up . . . and the sedative he used to disable Howard.

No one lay still and quiet while they bled – not even from a paper cut – or while some maniac used their blood for ink.

Even if he'd restrained her there would have been some movement, some amount of squirming, making the smudge on the shiny floor from her make-up more smeared around.

It was all so precise. Classic work for the Player. Yet, rife with evidence. Evidence that was related to the victim if not to him. The Player never left evidence.

Vibration on the floor made her jump.

She turned and stared at the cell phone shimmying on the hardwood, its screen lit. Maybe Howard's husband or boss or a friend . . . wondering how her afternoon appointment had gone.

Jess crossed to where it lay and crouched down to read the screen.

Home calling.

A pang of regret caught beneath her breast. He would ultimately kill this poor woman as a move in this gruesome game of his.

Just to get to Jess.

Belinda Howard didn't fit the profile of his preferred victim but she had been in the wrong place at the wrong time. Jess's sister had invited her to dinner in hopes of persuading Jess to buy a home in Birmingham. And now Belinda Howard would die because of her work . . . because of Jess.

She had to stop him . . . one way or another.

'Jess.'

Time to get out of the way. There was nothing more the scene could tell her. She didn't need fingerprints or trace evidence to confirm who had done this.

His name was Eric Spears. He *was* the Player. Whether anyone else in the world had accepted that reality, it was true.

After grabbing her bag, she almost slipped as she stamped across the gleaming floor. Damned shoes. Damned shiny floor.

This house was . . . way, way out of Jess's budget. Poor Belinda Howard. She'd probably been psyched at the idea of just how much her commission would be on a sale like this. Rushed over, lit the candle, hoping to finally sell a beautiful home that had languished on the market for no telling how long. Another victim of the failing economy.

Burnett waited for Jess to go ahead of him. Always the gentleman.

She offered a smile to the forensic techs she passed on her way out the front door. All flashed her one of those it's-about-time glances.

Harper paced the sidewalk, his cell resting against his ear. He was the detective in charge of this scene when he had no more business here than Jess. But they both needed to be here, lack of objectivity or not, to see that Spears was stopped and Detective Wells and Belinda Howard came home safely.

That little voice Jess didn't like listening to warned that she was wasting her time even hoping that either one would survive.

On the porch, she stripped off her gloves and hopped on first one foot, then the next to remove the shoe covers. Damned high heels.

Belinda Howard's BMW sat in the driveway, which, in addition to the for sale sign, marked the house as being the location of her appointment since Lily couldn't remember the exact address. En route Jess had made a call to the receptionist at the realty office but she hadn't known all Howard's appointments for the afternoon. Belinda, she'd explained, worked spontaneous showings all the time.

This was one appointment Jess wished the lady had missed.

Two uniformed officers were canvassing the neighbors. Unless they got lucky and someone saw the vehicle Spears drove, the effort was another waste of time. Spears might be taunting them with these changes in his MO but he was far from stupid. He had a strategy with an ultimate goal and getting caught wasn't it. He would never allow anyone to see him, as he had with Detective Wells' family, unless it was part of his plan. He wanted Jess to know it was him.

'I need to take a walk,' she told Burnett before he could inquire about her conclusions. She needed to breathe in enough of the humid summer air to force the last of the lingering stench of blood fully from her lungs.

Any neighbors who happened to be home were likely now peeking between special-order blinds and designer drapes, curious about the number of official vehicles fronting the property. Jess doubted this kind of circus toured the neighborhood very often.

Deputy Chief Black was taking care of notifying the Howard family. Jess didn't envy him the task. She stalled at the end of the drive and took another long look around the quiet cul-de-sac. What did you say to the family in a situation like this?

That Belinda, wife and mother, had been taken by a sadistic sociopath who would torture her until he was done. But not to worry because then he'd dump her body in the open for easy discovery.

It's a killer deal, Jess.

If it was her he wanted, why not just come after her?

The answer was one stamped on far too many memory cells. Because it wasn't the kill, the final step, that drove him. It was the hunt . . . the torture and all the steps in between. His pleasure came from the victim's terror.

As his ultimate victim in this game, he wanted Jess to be afraid.

Burnett strolled up beside her. She blinked back the emotions, kept her face aimed away from him. Going all overprotective was his MO without any additional evidence from her. He already hovered on that annoying edge. Allowing him to see even a glimmer of uncertainty would make bad matters worse.

She had noted the way all those other division chiefs had eyed her this afternoon. The news hadn't been announced but the gossip was already taking on a life of its own. It was a common human reaction. Fallen federal agent blows into town and takes the spot that would have been a promotion to one of their people – the ones already on staff with BPD.

Oh, and she couldn't leave out the old lover label. She and Burnett had been a couple all through high school and college. Since Jess would be the only female deputy chief, she had unquestionably gotten the job by sleeping with the boss. Didn't matter that the last time they had succumbed to that particular weakness was ten years ago.

That she had helped find those girls had earned her Sheriff Griggs' respect if no one else's. Then again, he and the others would in all probability see her as responsible for *this*.

She *was* responsible.

Guilt and fear coiled more tightly, separating her from everyone around her with those invisible yet fierce emotions.

The Player never took a second victim until he was finished with the first.

Twenty-four hours. That cold, harsh reality echoed in her brain. That was the approximate amount of time Lori Wells had left to live.

'Twenty-four hours?'

Jess started at Burnett's question. Didn't realize she'd spoken aloud. Just another reminder of how easily she drifted into one distraction or the other these days. 'Nothing.'

Maybe he would change that aspect of his MO, too.

If they couldn't find him fast – and they wouldn't unless he wanted to be found – Detective Wells' only hope was a shift in his well-documented MO.

'This isn't one of his typical crime scenes, is it?'

Jess braced, focused on ensuring her voice was steady when she spoke. One more excuse was all he would need to yank her off this case for her own protection.

'Not at all.' *Get that quiver out of your voice, Jess.* 'There's generally no indication anything untoward happened. Certainly no evidence of any kind.' With effort she pushed aside the memory of the blood on the floor and the wall and concentrated on what she knew, what she could do for Lori – Lori, dammit.

Not Detective Wells. *Lori Wells.* A friend she wanted to know better, to share experiences with. Jess hadn't bothered with friends in a long time.

Damn Spears.

Burnett waited for her to go on. He watched for the weakness that would prove his theory about her not being able to handle the undeniably personal aspects of this investigation.

Keep it together, Jess.

'He sedates his victims to ensure complete cooperation. We discovered it in his last victims – Ketamine. With the injectable form, if the dose is right it works fast and doesn't last too long. Gives him the time he needs.'

'Is she – Belinda Howard – is she alive?' The hope in his voice never made it to his eyes. 'There's not that much blood in there.'

'He doesn't usually make the kill at the scene of the abduction.' Jess almost laughed. 'The way his MO is changing, I'm not sure I can say either way with any real accuracy. At this point I'd have to conclude that it depends upon if he has a use for her. He,' she dragged in a steadying breath, 'disabled her with the Ketamine, probably, made an incision of some sort to get the blood flowing and left his message.'

Just to get Jess's attention. The vic wasn't even his type. None of this was logical, unless she set aside the profile she'd built over five years of intense study, and acknowledged that every step he'd taken this time had been about her. Getting to her, making her squirm. Generating desperation.

'Where does this put Wells on the food chain?'

Jess swept a wisp of sweat-dampened hair from her

face. 'Without exception,' the words she needed to say got trapped on a lump in her throat, 'he disposes of one victim within twenty-four hours of taking the next.'

Burnett didn't say anything for a moment. Then he moved on from the topic, as if lingering there too long was more than he could manage at the moment. 'Hogan called.' Burnett surveyed the street. 'He went to the floral shop personally. Interviewed the two women who work there.'

Jess held her breath.

'It was him, Jess. Spears walked in and made the purchase with cash. Gave a generous tip for the delivery. There's no security video but both women identified Eric Spears as the guy.' Burnett shook his head. 'He waltzed right into a downtown shop and bought those flowers.'

Jess closed her eyes. What the hell was he doing? Was he after her or just in the mood to torture her from afar? Was he so damned sure of himself after the fiasco in Richmond that he was no longer afraid of getting caught no matter how careless his methods?

She opened her eyes, blinked to clear those graphic images from past cases attributed to the Player. There were things she had to do. 'I need to call my sister before she hears about this some other way.'

The media hadn't found their way here yet but that would happen soon enough. Mostly she just needed some space. A minute or two to pull herself together without Burnett hovering.

'Then we have to talk.'

She'd expected that sooner. Like maybe on the way over here. The Bureau was up to something that wasn't going to be fun for her.

No surprise there.

Jess made her way to where they'd parked and climbed into Burnett's Mercedes, then closed out the world. The temperature inside the vehicle was stifling. She didn't care if she melted. Her hand shook as she rummaged through her bag for her cell. Lily answered on the first ring. It took a minute to convince her sister that Jess wasn't buying a house. Several more minutes were required to calm Lily down and coax her to listen after she learned her friend had been abducted. Suffocating became less desirable, forcing Jess to open her door since she didn't have the keys to power down a window.

'Lil, just stop and listen.' Five or so seconds later, her sister complied. 'I know you probably won't understand what I'm about to tell you, but I need you to listen carefully.'

Another round of ranting about the dangers of Jess's job and Lily finally gave up and lapsed into silence.

'This killer is doing everything different this time.' A gray sedan rolled up the street, moving slowly. Another of those aggravating frowns furrowed Jess's brow. 'You and your kids aren't safe at your house. I need you to agree to go away for a while.'

Lily did what she always did. She insisted they were fine. A police officer and an FBI agent were there with them twenty-four/seven. Why was Jess doing this? Why didn't she come stay with them? Why did this awful man take Belinda?

Why? Why? Why?

Still distracted by the sedan, Jess tried to listen to her sister and watch the car pull into the drive at the crime scene. Strange. Maybe another detective or one of the deputy chiefs she'd met earlier.

Her sister hammered on about how leaving their home was out of the question. She insisted Jess was being reckless as always. That the case mattered more to her than her own safety.

In the driveway, next to Howard's BMW, the sedan's doors opened and three men emerged. Burnett didn't move toward them, an indication that he wasn't exactly happy at the arrival. And that he knew their identities.

He waited for them to reach his position on the sidewalk with no welcoming body language.

Had to be Bureau . . . the suits gave them away most every time. Not to mention the way they walked in perfect step. One turned slightly in her direction. *Manning*. Yep, just as she thought. He sort of stood back as if the other two were senior.

'Turn around, dammit,' she muttered.

Lily yelled her name and Jess hauled her attention back to the conversation. 'No, I wasn't talking to you. What did you say?'

This was Lily's daughter's last summer at home before college. Lily wanted that time spent in the house where her daughter grew up.

Jess squinted to get a better look at the suits. One seemed familiar. His posture . . . the way he walked. She snatched off her glasses and swabbed at the sweat on her face with the back of her hand. The familiar suit turned far enough for her to see his profile.

Gant.

What the hell?

Her frustration shifted to Burnett. He might not have expected them to show up here but he knew Gant was in town and hadn't told her.

Then we have to talk.

Her sister's voice droned in her ear, yanking Jess from the troubling scenario building in her head.

'Lily, you listen to me,' Jess snapped. She didn't have time for her sister's naïve civilian attitude. 'Pack your bags because you and the kids are leaving that house today! No arguments. I'll see you in a few hours.'

Jess hung up while her sister still railed at her. She tossed her glasses onto the dash and dug for her sunglasses. It wasn't that she was surprised at Gant showing up. It was the idea that he hadn't called her. Technically he was still her superior.

She jammed the shaded eyewear into place and grabbed her bag. Why would he contact Burnett without talking to her first?

Mad as hell and a whole litany of other negative things she didn't have time to mentally list, Jess climbed out of the SUV, slammed the door and strode toward Burnett, Gant and his two-man posse.

The dark eyewear Burnett wore didn't disguise his dread as Jess neared. His lips formed a grim line and his broad shoulders sagged just a little. He knew what was coming and he wasn't looking forward to her reaction.

As she stepped up onto the sidewalk, Manning moved toward the house, but Gant and the other man

– Agent Clint Wentworth – didn't bother. What was Wentworth doing here? Why wasn't Taylor or Bedford with Gant? Those two knew Spears almost as well as Jess.

Wait . . . wait . . . wait. Wentworth wasn't with BAU. He was OPR.

Jess squared her shoulders against a groundswell of apprehension. 'I wasn't aware we were having a reunion.'

Supervisory Special Agent Ralph Gant gave Jess a nod. 'Harris.'

'What's going on?' Might as well get to the meat of the matter. 'Wentworth, you felt compelled to bring your investigation all the way to my hometown? How thorough of you.' The inkling of apprehension vanished and indignation took its place. Somehow she had thought her years of hard work meant a little more than this.

Gant looked from Jess to Burnett and back. 'Chief Burnett is aware of our agenda here and he is cooperating for the good of all concerned.'

Oh, this just kept getting better and better. 'You're running a separate, parallel investigation. Chief Burnett briefed us on the Bureau's position.' He just left out the part about OPR coming along for the ride.

'We are,' Gant confirmed.

'Well, then,' Jess gave a nod, 'you'll be interested to know that we have two more witnesses who positively ID'd Eric Spears in this case. Inside,' she hitched her head toward the house, 'you'll find another message of a similar nature to the others he has sent to me since my arrival in Birmingham.'

Gant appeared to evaluate the information. Wentworth, on the other hand, wasted no time tossing out his own opinion. 'Since we have no sense of the message inside, we really can't address your assessment. As for the others, every text message sent by this unsub leads back to a prepaid phone registered to you, Agent Harris, and operating in this area. It's hardly evidence that we're dealing with the Player or Eric Spears.'

'Tell us something we don't know, *Agent Wentworth*. We determined the source of his text messages days ago.' She resisted the urge to suggest he needed to catch up. 'We also know that means nothing except that he's trying to get my attention.' A blind man could see that motive.

'Jess,' Burnett said, drawing her frustration from Wentworth to him, 'we'll go over all this back at the office.'

So he did know about this other . . . whatever it was!

'Chief Burnett,' Gant advised, usurping the tirade Jess was about to launch, 'certain aspects of the information I passed along was a professional courtesy and for your information only in your capacity as chief of police.' He glanced at Jess. 'Agent Harris is still in the service of the Federal Bureau of Investigation. I am her direct supervisor. I will brief her on what she needs to know when she needs to know it.'

'And when exactly will this briefing take place?' Jess demanded. She'd kind of like to know what was going on, too. Beyond the obvious, of course. The Office of Professional Responsibility was investigating her. No surprise there. Any time a case went so far south and garnered so much media attention, there was an investigation to determine any possible failure on the agent's part.

'When we confirm or rule out certain aspects of our suspicions,' Gant answered, 'we will brief you then. Until that time, you will remain on administrative leave. Chief Burnett insists upon your involvement in his investigation against my recommendation.'

Jess held up both hands. 'Spears contacted me. This new game he's decided to play somehow involves me.' She planted her hands on her hips, shoving her bag behind her. 'With all due respect, sir, the notion of taking me off the investigation is not only imprudent, it's illogical.' She kept the part about it being totally stupid to herself.

'At this time, we can't conclude that these actions have been set in motion, much less carried out, by Eric Spears. There are legal ramifications to pursuing that end without corroborating evidence. It's our position that BPD should broaden the focus of their investigation.'

'Did you talk to Spears? Confirm his whereabouts?' Jess demanded, despite recognizing that he had a valid point. There were elements in both abductions that certainly suggested this could be the work of another unsub. But she knew it was Spears.

Like you knew it was him before?

She banished the echo from her head.

'His personal assistant claims he's out of the country on business. Bangkok,' Gant said with visible reluctance, 'but there's no passport verification that he left the country. We are attempting to confirm his movements.'

Jess scoffed despite the trickle of uncertainty that endeavored to undermine her resolve. 'Then you can't substantiate where he is at this time. That's convenient.'

'As true as that is, you cannot confirm he's here. All I'm suggesting is that we approach this theory with a little more objectivity,' Gant urged, 'I'm on your side here, Jess. No one wants a repeat of what happened in Richmond. Do us all a favor, take a breath and step away from this investigation before things escalate.'

Good grief! How could her walking away make things better?

Burnett tore off his sunglasses and stared straight at her. 'Jess, do you intend to accept the position I offered you this morning? *Officially* accept it?'

They had talked about that. But with the Spears situation . . . she wasn't sure he really wanted to go out on that professional limb. Following through on that job offer could blow up in his face. Even if he were having second thoughts, Burnett was far too honorable to take back the offer. Jess didn't want him to become another casualty of her crashing career.

'As I said,' Gant countered, 'for now, Harris is still my agent.'

'Give me an answer, Jess,' Burnett pushed, ignoring Gant. 'The offer stands if you're interested.'

Burnett was dead serious. She knew better than to ignore the warning he was flashing with those intense blue eyes. There was something big she didn't know. Whatever it was, he was worried.

Jess rammed her hand into her bag, grabbed her cell phone and tapped a few keys. She hit Send and smiled up at Gant. 'I'm not your agent anymore. I resign.' She turned to Burnett. 'I officially accept your offer, chief. When do I start?'

'Now.' He thrust out his hand. She accepted his firm shake. 'Welcome aboard, Deputy Chief Harris.'

Gant stared at the screen of his cell. 'You can't resign with a text message.'

'I just did.' Jess hauled her bag higher onto her shoulder. 'If you're ready,' she said to Burnett. 'I'm done here.'

'Your resignation will not terminate my investigation into your recent conduct,' Wentworth warned.

Jess didn't bother with a response. She marched back to the SUV and climbed in. This time she didn't shut her door until Burnett got behind the wheel and started the engine.

When he'd pulled away from the curb, she adjusted the AC vents and asked, as politely as her frustration level would allow, 'Can you tell me now why I just quit my job, besides the fact that Gant is an idiot and Wentworth obviously thinks I'm a lunatic?'

The job was down the toilet anyway. The technicalities of whether she would resign or they would make her miserable were all that had remained. But she had expected the actual separation to go down a little differently. A hint of professionalism would have been nice. There were forms, debriefings.

She'd just bypassed all that with a one sentence text – in English with the proper punctuation.

'I planned to tell you after the briefing but then the flowers arrived.'

When Manning hadn't returned right in the middle of the briefing, she had known that this was bigger than the Bureau merely offering support.

Things were about to get ugly.

Truth was, things had already gotten ugly. Spears was at it again and the Bureau was still doing damage control after his last murder spree.

She was as culpable in that one as Gant or any of the rest.

Two news vans rolled into the cul-de-sac. She and Burnett had gotten out of there just in time.

'The Bureau thinks there's some kind of bizarre personal link between you and Spears.'

Talk about a punch to the gut. Jess twisted in her seat to stare at his profile. 'Are you serious?'

'Just before he was released last week, Spears suggested you had an interest of some sort in him beyond the investigation. Gant blew off the idea. But last night, there was a homicide related to a break-in in your neighborhood. One of your neighbors was murdered. Your house was vandalized.'

Her eyebrows lifted with surprise. One of her neighbors was murdered? She wanted to ask which one but he likely wouldn't know. She doubted she would know the name herself. She was never home long enough to get acquainted with her neighbors. And that was irrelevant. What mattered was that another innocent life had been taken. Another wave of anger slammed her.

'Why didn't I get a call?'

Burnett shrugged. 'That's part of the OPR investigation, apparently.'

Yeah, yeah, she knew the drill. They would brief her when the time was right. When she needed to know. 'Wait, what does the OPR investigation have to do with my private residence?'

Long pause. Not a good sign.

'Gant claims the walls of your home office are covered with photos of Spears.'

Her heart knocked against her sternum. 'What?'

'Some were cut and pasted with photos of you,' he glanced at Jess, 'as if you were a couple. Gant suggested you'd had some kind of meltdown. He's worried about you. I got the impression that there's some level of consensus that Spears might have been right about you having an interest in him.'

'Oh, that's just spectacular.' Jess plopped back into her seat. The whole concept was beyond ridiculous. 'It's a set-up.'

But who would set her up like that? She wasn't delusional enough to consider anyone at the Bureau would be involved. She'd dealt with the usual good-old-boys club crap over the years, some peer envy, but no one she had ever worked with would stoop to such a level.

Spears? He was here . . . had been since the night after his release, she thought anyway. Would he have had time to do all that before coming to Birmingham? Considering all he'd accomplished here, Jess didn't see how.

'There's more.'

As livid as she had every right to be, Jess felt more defeated than anything at this point.

Burnett hesitated before going on.

'What?' she demanded.

'A message was left on your living room wall, written in the murder vic's blood.' He glanced at Jess. 'Like the one we just left.'

'What was the message?' She held her breath.

'Why did you leave me?'

She wrestled back the emotions that tried to shake her. This had to be Spears. It had to be. Yet, the timeline and the changes to his MO didn't fit. The idea of someone else being involved was possible, she supposed. But not just a copycat . . . an accomplice. Some serial killers worked in teams, that was true.

Accomplice or not, her gut said it was Spears himself here in Birmingham.

'They're wrong.' She felt it all the way to her bones.

'I don't know about Spears,' Burnett admitted. 'But I know they're wrong about you. You are not responsible for what this son of a bitch is doing.'

Jess appreciated his support.

But, if Lori's body turned up tomorrow, no matter how much he wanted to believe in Jess he might have second thoughts on that one.

Chapter Six

Lori tried to lift her head . . . couldn't. Too heavy . . . like a bowling ball. She licked her lips. Grimaced at the bad taste.

Wake up.

Why couldn't she open her eyes? Her tongue felt thick, her mouth gritty. She could hear a voice . . . far away. Was the voice calling her name?

Her eyelids fluttered open. Images came into focus. Boxes . . . wooden crates.

The warehouse.

Adrenalin exploded in her chest. Fire seared through her veins. Lori's head came up. She shook it, blinked repeatedly to clear her vision.

Spears! Where the hell was Spears?

Her gaze focused . . . zeroed in on a woman, her

head lolled to one side. Lori drew in a deep breath, it caught in her throat.

Blood.

The fog in her brain cleared. The woman was naked, slumped in the chair. Her arms hung down on either side. Blood pooled on the concrete floor around her. Small rips in her breasts seeped more of the precious crimson, like trails of red tears down her waist. Her legs were spread wide and more blood had dribbled down her pale thighs.

Shit.

Lori leaned forward. 'Hey.' She cleared the rustiness from her throat. 'Hey,' she said a little louder.

The woman didn't respond. Didn't move. She wasn't bound. She just sat there. Lori squinted, tried to determine if her chest shifted with the intake of breath. No . . . maybe.

Shit.

Lori launched to her feet. She swayed. Felt confused. She wasn't tied to the chair anymore. Turning her forearms up, then down, she confirmed what her brain hadn't quite absorbed. She was no longer restrained.

Where was Spears?

She looked around the warehouse . . . didn't see him. She rushed forward. Stumbled. Hit the floor.

Caught herself with her hands before her face smacked the concrete. Pain shot through her leg when she tried to scramble up. The rattle of metal drew her attention to her right foot. Manacled to her ankle tight enough to chafe the skin, the chain trailed from her, beyond the chair she'd been secured in, then to a steel column that supported the roof structure.

'Dammit.' She pulled at the chain with her right leg. It gave a little, providing enough slack for her to move around. She staggered forward a step, then another and another. Steadier now, she moved quickly to the woman.

Oh, hell.

Lori reached out and touched her carotid artery. Her skin was cool, almost cold . . . but there was a pulse. Weak, but there. God, there was so much blood.

'Hey.' Lori cradled the woman's face, but she didn't open her eyes.

She was dying. What did she do? Stop the bleeding. Lori glanced around the warehouse. Nothing but the crates.

Desperation ignited in her belly.

The door.

She moved as quickly as the heavy chain would allow toward the door. Three or four feet from her destination the chain snapped tight. Lori moved in all directions as far as the chain would allow. No windows. No other doors. Nothing she could use to help the woman.

Lori rushed back to her. She crouched down and checked the wounds on her wrists, which appeared to be the main source of blood loss. Not so much now. Coagulation had slowed the drain to a steady drip. She'd seen a suicide victim or two who had slashed their wrists and these wounds weren't the worst she'd encountered. It was almost as if the goal was for her to bleed out slowly.

Fury blasted her chest as she surveyed the wounds to the woman's breasts. He'd cut her nipples loose, left them hanging like flaps. Another wider wound under her bellybutton still seeped blood. Together the injuries to her torso made for a sick sort of smiley face.

Fighting nausea, Lori stood and peeled off her blouse. It was summer, the fabric was thin, mostly cotton. Rips echoed in the silence as she tore the blouse into pieces. Carefully, she wrapped the wound on the woman's right arm, then propped the arm in her lap so it no longer hung downward. She did the same with the left. There wasn't a lot she could do for the breasts. The wider wound beneath her belly button gaped open. Uncertain if it would help, she wadded a smaller piece of the blouse and tucked it into the wound.

Using the final length of the blouse, she covered the woman's breasts as best she could. Lori sat back on her heels, her body shaking with the receding adrenalin and the resignation. This woman was probably dying and there was nothing she could do. Tears slid down her cheeks. She should have been more cooperative. If she had kept him entertained he wouldn't have gone hunting for this woman.

She had tried . . . she really had.

Now this woman would die because Lori had screwed up. She was a cop, she was supposed to know how to do this. But this – she stared at the dying woman – she couldn't fix.

She shot to her feet. Turned around, fury raging inside her. 'Where are you, you son of a bitch?'

Lori grabbed the chain with both hands and pulled with all her strength. Harder. And harder still. A scream wrenched from her throat as she collapsed to the floor. Lori tugged at the bracelet around her ankle. No way was it sliding off. 'Goddamn you, Spears!'

Clapping echoed around her.

She jerked to the left. Glared at the monster standing there applauding like he'd just watched his favorite private theatrical production.

Lori lunged to her feet, rushed toward him. The chain stopped her just short of reaching him. Her chest heaved with the need for air. 'She's dying,' Lori said, the words a defeated whisper.

A smile lifted his lips. 'Very perceptive, Detective Wells.'

If she could reach him . . . her fingers curled into her palms with the need to tear him apart.

He dared to move nearer. Anticipation unfurled inside Lori. She didn't move, didn't even breathe. *Come a little closer, mother fucker.*

He inclined his head. 'You're still not scared, are you?'

Jesus Christ, he was insane. Instinct urged her to fight. But that was premature. She needed him confident enough in her surrender to draw him a little closer. Lori forced herself to relax. 'No.' She moistened her lips. 'I'm not afraid.'

He acknowledged her admission with a dip of his head. 'That's why she's dying, detective. You wouldn't play, so I had to find someone else.'

Guilt hardened in her chest. She was supposed to protect . . . to stop men like Spears. Her gaze swung to the woman in the chair.

'That's right, detective. Look at her very closely.'

The sound of his voice told her he was closer but she

didn't look. Let him think she was too caught up in the emotion. Let him come a little nearer. She shook with the effort of restraining the urge to act.

'A woman is never more beautiful than when she surrenders to the inevitable. Her body relaxes. Her respiration slows . . . her thoughts just drift away . . .' He took another small step toward Lori, his attention seemingly fixed on the woman. 'She's so close . . . so very close.'

Lori could see him in her peripheral vision now. One arm crossed over his chest. Elbow of the other propped there, thumb and forefinger supporting his chin as if he were studying a prized work of art.

'If you look closely enough you can almost see the faint flutter of her pulse at the base of her throat. She's lost so much blood, yet her heart continues to beat. She doesn't want to die.'

One more step . . . just one more.

'She wants to get home to her children,' he said quietly. 'To her husband.' He chuckled. 'She begged me not to kill her. To think of her children.' He sighed. 'She had no idea that her every plea . . . every whimper made me want more.'

Lori lunged for him. She hit him hard. He stumbled back. Something slammed into her.

Hard. Fast. Hot. She dropped to the floor . . . her body shook and convulsed. She told herself to get up . . . to move, but she had no control. No connection between her brain and her muscles.

Spears crouched down next to her head. He waved the small Taser he held in front of her eyes. He leaned over her. Smiled. 'You didn't think I'd take any chances with someone as well trained as you, did you?'

She couldn't respond. Still couldn't move. Tears leaked from the corners of her eyes.

He grabbed her by the hair and lifted her head. 'Just look, detective.' He twisted her neck until she faced the woman. 'She's almost gone now. A mere whisper of life remains. *Just beautiful.*' He leaned closer, put his mouth near Lori's temple. 'She'll be gone soon and then there will be another. Maybe another after that. Until Jess understands that she can't ignore me any longer.'

He pulled Lori's face around to his. 'If she doesn't realize what she needs to do soon, I'll just have to make her sorry. Maybe if I show her the beauty of *your* death, she'll see that she can end this game so easily.'

He kissed Lori's forehead.

Inside she screamed.

'All she has to do is come to me.'

Chapter Seven

Lakefront Trail, Bessemer, 6.59 P.M.

Jess took a deep breath and struggled to remain calm.

She and her sister had taken their debate to her bedroom. Lily's husband was entertaining the kids and Burnett in the family room. The BPD officer assigned to this shift was outside having a smoke. The agent, Nora Miller, had offered to put on a pot of coffee.

No one wanted any part of this showdown.

'Jess, honestly,' Lily insisted, 'no one is leaving the house without an escort. Either that nice police officer or the FBI lady goes with us wherever we go. We are never alone, not even in our own home. What else do you want?'

Jess strived for patience. Since they were kids, Lily had always, always thought she knew best. Just because she was two years older didn't mean she was smarter about issues like this. But she wouldn't admit it if her life depended on it.

And it just might this time.

How the hell was Jess going to get that through her thick skull?

'I have spent the last seventeen years as an FBI *lady*,' Jess snapped. At Lily's horrified expression, Jess bit her lips together in frustration before trying again. 'I'm sorry.' Another deep breath. 'I don't think you understand how serious the situation is, Lil.'

Lily plopped down on her bed and crossed her arms over her chest. 'Of course, you would think I don't understand. I'm *only* a wife and mom. A nurse. What could *I* know about life and death?'

Oh God. 'Lil, I—'

'Belinda is a friend. We've attended the same church for ten years. I know how serious the situation is!' Tears brimmed on Lil's lashes. 'I can't believe this has happened. I'm trying to be strong but . . . Jess, this madman is after *you*.'

All the frustration drained out of Jess, leaving her more tired than she'd felt in her entire life. She sat down and hugged her sister close. 'Lil,' she offered softly, 'I can take care of myself. But if I'm worrying about you and your family, then I'm distracted and I can't stop this monster or protect myself or anyone else if I'm distracted.'

Lil nodded as if she understood but she wasn't making eye contact anymore and that was a bad sign.

And everyone thought Jess was stubborn.

'I like your new haircut,' Jess said when her sister remained silent. She swept her fingers through the thick chin-length bob.

In grade school the teachers were always mixing them up. They had the same brown eyes, the same blond hair. Jess was the one who always got into trouble and Lily was the bookworm.

Blake, Lily's husband, would gladly set anyone straight who mistakenly assumed Lily's mild mannered temperament meant she was a push-over.

'Blake hates it.'

Surprised, Jess suggested, 'You know men, they think long hair is sexy.' At least that was what Dan always said.

The thought stunned Jess. Where the hell had that come from? Mortification burned her cheeks. Thank God she hadn't said *that* out loud. She really, really had to get her head on straight. As of a couple of hours ago, *Burnett* was her superior.

Lil shook her head, her lips trembling, tears streaming down her cheeks. 'He's considering taking a new position in Nashville. He's furious I won't agree to go with him. He thinks because the kids are leaving home, I shouldn't have a problem with moving.'

No wonder Lily was fighting so to hold her ground. 'When did this happen?' Except for having only two kids, Lily and Blake could be the Cleavers, their life together was so ideal. Or, at least, Jess had thought so.

Lily glared at her. 'It's been happening for months but you wouldn't know that because you're never here!'

There was that.

'I'm sorry.' Jess hugged her again. Then drew back and produced a smile. 'That won't be an issue in the future, sis, I accepted a deputy chief position with Birmingham PD. I'll be around a lot more.'

Lily's expression brightened. 'That's great. You can move in with me. The kids'll be gone. Maybe Blake, too. We have lots of room!'

Jess lifted her lips into what she hoped resembled a smile but couldn't do a damned thing about the dismay she felt widening her eyes. 'Wow.'

Her sister smiled, swiped her tears. 'It'll be just like when we were kids.' She hugged Jess hard. 'You and me against the world.' When she drew back, her smile widened to a grin. 'We can go to church together, too! There are a couple very nice men your age who're single for one reason or another.'

'Wow,' Jess repeated as she suffered through another exuberant hug. Exactly what she needed. A man who was single . . . for one reason or another. Awesome. Wouldn't they make a pair?

Just like her and Burnett.

Dear God.

Five days. She'd been back in Birmingham a mere five days and Jess felt her life spiraling backwards more than two decades. Already her hard work to take the south out of her vocabulary and diction had vanished. She spoke as if she'd never left. Ten years ago when she'd fallen back into Burnett's arms for a frantic tangle in the sheets, she had sworn she would never, ever be vulnerable to the man again. And here she was, skirting that old flame as if she hadn't gotten burned badly enough the first time.

Evidently she was destined to repeat the same mistakes over and over.

When another ten minutes of discussion failed to convince her sister to leave town, Jess reluctantly gave up for the moment and joined Burnett and the others.

Lily opted to remain in her room until her eyes weren't so red anymore.

Shock and confusion related to the conversation with her sister warred with the worry and frustration associated with the case. None of which was conducive to Jess's focus on the problems at hand.

Burnett and Lil's husband stood near the fireplace, speaking in soft, quiet tones. Their posture warned that the subject matter was far from soft. The kids were sprawled on the sofa, Alice reading a book on her Kindle, Blake Junior surfing on his iPad. The two were as different as night and day. Lil's son had dark hair and eyes like his father and he loved being in the thick of things, athletics, social activities, anything that involved lots of people and a challenge. Her daughter was the spitting image of her – of Jess – and Alice would rather curl up in a corner all alone and read her books.

Mercy, how did she make these people understand that this was not like the movies? This was real, the danger was real. And they didn't seem to have a clue.

As soon as Burnett noticed her lingering in the archway that separated the family room from the kitchen, he shifted toward her. The move was subtle, the slightest turning of his body to face her. Whether it was the way he moved or just the way he looked, tall, strong and steady, Jess had never wanted to lean on those broad shoulders more than she did at that moment.

There she went, falling back into that same old pattern.

God help her.

'She won't budge,' Jess announced.

Saying the words weighed heavily on her shoulders, fueling the urge to lean against him . . . *her new boss*. A single-for-one-reason-or-another man.

Jess blinked. She straightened her weary body, drew her burdened shoulders back. She was stronger than this. Dammit. 'You need to talk some sense into her, Blake.'

Shoulders down, hands in his pockets, and worry cluttering his face, Blake studied Jess a moment. 'You really think we could be targets in this?'

Rather than march over and shake the hell out of him, she held onto her unraveling composure as best she could. 'Belinda Howard was a guest in your home last night. If being here with me made her a target, do you really need to ask that question?'

Blake blinked, looked taken aback.

Okay, maybe he hadn't deserved that. As miserable as he was making her sister just now, Jess wasn't so sure. Nashville? Seriously?

'I think,' Burnett chimed in, 'what Jess is trying to say is that it's far better to be safe than sorry.'

Blake sucked in a harsh breath as if he'd only just awakened from a deep coma. 'All right. I'll make the arrangements with my brother in Pensacola. We'll go there and stay a few days, get some time on the beach.'

Blake Junior looked up. 'That's what I'm talking 'bout!'

Alice made a face at his loud voice and turned back to her reading.

'Good.' Jess felt a wee bit relieved. 'How quickly can you be packed and on the road?'

Blake Junior jumped up. 'Five minutes, Aunt Jess.' He grinned as he hustled out of the room. The kid – man, actually – was as tall as his dad, a little over six feet, and every bit as handsome.

Lord, she felt old.

'We can be on the road by noon tomorrow,' Blake said, visibly braced for battle.

'Tomorrow?' Well, hell. The relief she'd felt faded. 'Why not now?' It was summer. No school for the kids or Blake. What was the problem here?

Blake cleared his throat and met Jess's glare with surprising determination. 'I have an interview in Nashville first thing in the morning, but I'll be back before noon. Lil and the kids can be ready to go and we'll head out immediately.'

The professor had some balls after all, even if he was wrong. What idiot put his job before his family? 'Every minute you delay,' Jess warned, 'increases the risk to your family.' But then, how could she fault Blake when Lil hadn't even been willing to compromise.

'I get my braces off in the morning, Aunt Jess. I can't miss that appointment.'

Jess turned to Alice who was now frowning at her in that wish-you-would-go-away manner only teenagers could pull off. Great. Now Alice was mad at her. 'That's great, sweetie.'

'Deputy Chief Harris,' Special Agent Nora Miller spoke up, 'I know you're concerned for your sister and her family, but I assure you we have things under control. I'll be here all night. In the morning I'll personally escort Lily and her daughter to the appointment.'

The news of the career shift had certainly traveled swiftly. Probably by text. Jess hated text. Although she had enjoyed getting Gant's goat with her resignation text.

'We'll be fine,' Miller added when Jess didn't immediately respond.

Jess stared at the agent. She was thirtyish. Probably four or five years' experience. She seemed capable enough. Tall, athletic build. Brown hair coiled into a conscientious bun. Her made-for-comfort slacks and blouse were neat, conservative. Her shoes were the same: practical, well-polished leather oxfords.

She didn't have a clue either.

Jess couldn't fathom how to respond to her comment without offending the agent and upsetting Lily's family. 'Noon tomorrow,' Jess confirmed, resigned to their decision, 'not a minute later?'

'Not a minute later,' Blake promised.

Jess shot him a skeptical look. 'You'll square that with Lil?'

'Before the kids and I are done, she'll believe it was her idea,' he promised.

This was the best she could do, Jess supposed.

'Thank you for the coffee,' Burnett announced in the ensuing silence.

Jess gave her niece and nephew a hug and warned them to be extra careful. Under different circumstances she would have hauled her brother-in-law out back and demanded some answers. Nashville? What the hell was he thinking? Instead, she gave him an unenthusiastic version of the hug she'd given the kids and, with a pointed glance in the agent's direction, walked out.

Burnett followed Jess out the front door as did the agent who had, thankfully, picked up on Jess's subtle invitation.

Also sensing Jess had something to say to the FBI *lady*, Burnett jerked his head toward his officer standing at the street and said, 'I'll just be a minute.'

When Jess was alone with Agent Miller on the walk in front of her sister's home, she said her piece. 'Agent Miller, I don't know the extent of your experience with killers like this one—'

'Ma'am,' Miller interrupted, 'I spent the first three years of my career in Chicago before coming home to Birmingham.' She smiled – more of a smirk. 'I know my way around the violent types.' She shrugged. 'No offense, but, at this time, we don't know for sure who this unsub is. Whoever he is, I assure you I have things here under control. And I will see that your family gets on the road by noon tomorrow.'

Maybe if she'd left it at her big-bad-city experience, Jess might have smiled right back at her and thanked her . . . but she hadn't . . . and Jess couldn't.

'Seventeen years,' Jess tossed back, 'in too many places to name. I've seen it all, Agent Miller. I've analyzed the psychopaths who leave nothing but a greasy spot that represented what was once a human being. I've studied the true sociopaths who make the characters in a Stephen King novel look like altar boys. This,' Jess dragged in a breath to try and slow the mounting fury, 'is the Player we're dealing with and none of us have any aspect of this situation under control.'

Jess clamped her mouth shut. Too late. She'd already said too much.

Agent Miller nodded. 'All right then. I'll be extra vigilant, ma'am.'

No use denying a brick wall when she hit one. 'Thank you, Agent Miller. I appreciate that. And I'm certain you're aware of the danger to yourself as well as to BPD's finest over there.'

Miller glanced at the officer. 'I am.'

'Excellent.'

What else could she say? Not one damned thing. Jess walked straight to Burnett's SUV and climbed in. Fear, disbelief, worry, confusion, anger . . . all of it bombarded her with renewed vengeance.

Burnett moved away from his officer, nodded to the agent and headed in Jess's direction.

'Dammit,' she muttered. She blinked faster in an attempt to hold back the tears. Didn't work. Hands shaking, she swiped at the blasted waterworks. If Burnett caught her crying . . . Damn Spears. Damn the Bureau . . . and damn her.

Burnett slid behind the wheel and started the engine. He sent a sideways glance her way.

'Don't ask.'

He pulled away from the curb. 'I know better.'

She closed her eyes and searched for a calm place. There was nothing she could do to further protect her sister tonight. All Jess could do was pray that they would be safe until they were on the road. As hard as it would prove, she had to set that problem aside and concentrate all her energies on finding Spears before either of the victims ended up dead.

Victims.

Lori and Belinda.

Jess could not set their names and faces aside and view either one as a statistic in this case. Although most all victims in the cases she had worked over the years were innocent and hadn't deserved the horrors they suffered, this was different for Jess. Personal. That these two women had become victims was her responsibility.

If either one died, it would be because of her actions or lack of action.

The silence set like gelatin while Burnett maneuvered

the evening traffic on the interstate between Bessemer and Birmingham proper.

'We'll pick up your suitcase,' Burnett said, slicing through that thickening quiet. 'I'll have your car brought to the house tomorrow.'

Jess turned to him, the weariness and disturbing thoughts shifting to the back burner. 'I need my car.' She wasn't getting stranded again.

'No you don't.'

Her gaze narrowed. Oh, no. He could forget that idea. 'I am not staying at your house, Burnett. We've had this discussion already.' Like five days ago. His parents were home now so he certainly couldn't suggest their place.

Queen Katherine would have a stroke if Jess showed up there again. She was likely still attempting to restore to rights her museum of a home after Jess's short stay. She should be ashamed of herself for doing a bit of rearranging just to annoy Burnett's mother, but she hadn't been able to help herself. Katherine Burnett had worked overtime to make Jess feel inferior back in the day. She had made no bones about the fact that she did not want her only son to marry a girl from a carousel of foster homes.

Jess had never been good enough. Why the hell that

still bothered her was a mystery that might never be solved.

'You will either stay with me or you'll go with your sister.' He glanced at her, that smug look infuriating her all the more. 'Take your pick.'

He knew she couldn't go with her sister. She needed to be here, on this case. Besides, her presence with Lil would only draw Spears' attention to her and her family more so than the media already had. That wasn't even an option.

Jess faced forward and glared at the vehicle in front of them to prevent Burnett reading her emotions. She was damned close to her wits' end with him and her family. Not to mention Gant and the Bureau in general. 'You cannot tell me where to stay.'

She couldn't buy a house until she sold her house in Virginia. But she could get an apartment. Maybe not tonight but tomorrow. Except she doubted there would be time. A hotel would be fast and easy, no time wasted.

They were wasting time now.

The search would continue all night and she should be out there. He should, too. She glared at Burnett's profile. 'We should be working with the search commander.'

'Forget it. And, for the record, I'm not telling you

anything, Jess.' He met her glower head on for just long enough to emphasize his statement. 'As your superior, I'm giving an order.'

He'd pushed her to officially accept the position and now he thought he was going to control her personal life, too. She would just see about that. He couldn't make her stay at his house any more than Gant could pressure her off this case even if she had to investigate as a civilian. Men were the bane of her existence.

'As my superior,' she informed him, 'what you're suggesting would not only jeopardize both our positions in the department, it could jeopardize this case from a prosecution standpoint. Spears is extremely intelligent. If we're lucky enough to catch him and have enough evidence to charge him, he will twist our every move to make us look incompetent and to somehow taint and discredit every step of our investigation.' Let him outmaneuver that argument!

Eric Spears was more than intelligent, he was cunning. Jess wasn't willing to take the risk. He'd already shown her – he'd shown them all – just what he could do given even half a chance.

Jess closed her eyes. How could Gant, or anyone else, believe the allegations Spears had suggested?

'The risk is necessary.'

Her eyes snapped opened. 'I know you didn't just say that.' Considering the length of time he'd taken to answer, she'd expected better than that. 'And what about perception, Burnett? Fraternization is an unpleasant word in the workplace. It prompts all sorts of even more unpleasant problems. Sexual harassment allegations, EEOC complaints, erosion of the chain of command.' She shook her head adamantly. 'That would be asking for trouble. The whole department is going to be watching us, making judgments. It's out of the question.'

If she was a man they wouldn't be having this conversation. Burnett would respect her ability to take care of herself. End of story. God, she hated that whole male protector thing.

He kept quiet; apparently he'd tuned her out.

'This is not high school, Burnett,' she pressed. 'You're not star quarterback anymore with all your buddies following your every call on the field. You're the chief of police and every single cop in the department, no matter the rank, no matter how much he likes or respects you, is watching and waiting for a mistake to pounce on. It's human nature. We're only a famine away from eating our young.'

The silent treatment continued.

She folded her arms over her chest. 'The Holiday Inn works for me.'

'I won't argue with you, Jess. I've made my decision. You will be my guest for the duration.'

Where was the anger? The frustration? He made the statements way too calmly. She started to demand a better answer, then the answer hit her. He was scared. Scared for her. Well, she was scared, too. Scared for her sister and her family. Scared for anyone Spears might target because of her. Scared and confused and frustrated and . . .

A new thought poked through the tangle of emotions. This was exactly what Spears wanted. He wanted her to feel *this*. Helpless, confused and afraid. As twisted and sadistic as he was, he understood that he did not possess the power to make her fear him, not on the level he needed anyway. The one true fear that throbbed under her skin and deep in her chest was that he would hurt her family.

Or someone he presumed was close to her.

Like Lori and poor unsuspecting Belinda Howard.

And Burnett.

Spears understood that simple truth about her.

Jess turned to Burnett, the impact hitting home. Spears had already made the connection between her and Burnett. He had done that two days ago. Just to taunt them both, he'd sparred via text with Burnett. He'd goaded Burnett with the idea that he wasn't taking care of Jess.

No one needed to protect Jess. Spears had no desire to kill her – at least not yet. Not until he had tortured her sufficiently. And he'd only just begun. The best way to protect her family and anyone Spears hadn't connected to her yet was to stay clear. Knowledge was power, the less she gave him the better.

In Burnett's case staying clear wasn't an option. The only way to protect him was to watch him every minute. Her professional reputation was already tarnished. What was one more thing for folks to talk about?

Burnett's reputation could take the heat. His life was far more important to Jess than his career.

'Whatever you say, chief.'

Dunbrooke Drive, Mountain Brook, 8.55 P.M.

Jess had caved way too easily. Dan wasn't sure why, but he wasn't going to question it. He was just glad as hell she hadn't fought him for once. He would protect her whether she liked it or not. He couldn't trust her not to put herself at risk on this one. The case was too personal to her.

She'd rolled her suitcase to the bedroom farthest from his. Not that he could exactly blame her after that middle-of-the-night kiss he'd laid on her. Was that only three nights ago?

Between the last case they'd worked together and then this one, he'd lost all concept of time. Every minute was consumed with an urgency that took priority over all else. He'd only checked in with his stepdaughter twice. Guilt settled heavily onto his shoulders. The ordeal Andrea had survived left her badly shaken, perhaps more so than he or her mother realized. He wasn't Andrea's father but he loved her and he needed time to be there for her. He also needed to get Jess onboard with her new position. He sensed that she still didn't see that aspect of her future.

But there was no time for either . . . not until Wells and Howard were found and this freak of nature was stopped.

Jess's concerns about the legal and ethical issues related to her being his guest were not a priority for him just now. Whatever the ramifications, he would deal with those when this was done.

He checked the fridge for something quick and easy

to prepare. Stopping by the Publix was one of those menial chores he hadn't bothered with in a couple of weeks. Maybe he could call in a pizza. It wasn't a glamorous meal but he doubted Jess was feeling any more glamorous than he was.

His gaze landed on the bag waiting on the top shelf in the fridge. That would work. Something else to feel guilty about.

He grabbed the bag Gina Coleman, Birmingham's top reporter and a friend, had dropped off last night and sat it on the counter. A feast from Taziki's. Classic Greek salad, basmati rice and grilled chicken breast. His favorite. Gina had reveled in describing each dish with sensual words and teasing body language.

A promise to have dinner with his parents had prevented him from sharing the meal with her. Just as well. He suspected Gina'd had more than dinner on her mind. She was without doubt even more pissed that he'd sent the department PR liaison to meet with her this afternoon to discuss Detective Wells' abduction and the suspected connection to Spears.

She shouldn't hold it against him since he'd been at a crime scene, but that completely understandable excuse still wouldn't prevent her from being miffed.

He pulled two dinner plates from the rack and

arranged the rice and chicken. A quick zap in the microwave and then he'd add the salad. While he waited for the food to warm he checked his cell. A text from Hogan relaying more disappointing news from the search commander. They'd found nothing other than a few squatters in the search of abandoned warehouses and buildings.

Another text, this one from Gina with a solitary question mark as the content.

He didn't have it in him to reply.

How had so much changed in five days?

Two weeks ago if Gina had showed up at his door in a slinky black dress and ultra-high heels he would have blown off the dinner engagement with his parents and had Gina as an appetizer.

Their relationship outside police business was not exactly personal. It was more an extension of who they were on the job. She respected him; he respected her and they were both too busy for the couple's thing beyond engaging in the occasional satisfying round of sex. No commitments. Still, he suspected she had . . . expectations. Expectations that went beyond what he could offer.

The fact that he hadn't felt the need to make any offer last night was out of character. His sexual appetite had never fallen below the ravenous range. Admittedly since taking the post as chief of police, time had been an issue but he'd never failed to rise to the challenge when the right, mutually appealing opportunity presented itself.

The microwave dinged. Dissecting his manhood would have to wait. That suited him since the reason he'd lost interest in Gina or anyone else was currently making him crazy.

He removed the second plate and deposited it next to the other on the counter.

Might as well admit it right now, pal. A good, hard look at the reality of the past few days would narrow the problem down to one defining moment.

Jess's return.

Andrea's abduction had obviously played a large role. As had the other missing teens. He was immensely thankful that all five had been found alive.

Usually a tough day left him hungry for sex. The physical outlet helped him deal with the frustration of his position. But not this time. This time it all boiled down to *her*.

Analyzing the impact Jess's return had wielded on his life, particularly his sex life, was another bad idea.

He added salad and pita bread to the plates.

Grabbing the empty containers and the bag, he walked through the mudroom, paused long enough to disarm the security system, then stepped out the back door. Outside, he tossed the trash into the collection receptacle.

Before going back in, he surveyed the street, looking for any unfamiliar vehicles. Spears had been damned busy. In less than twenty-four hours he had abducted two women, one being a well-trained detective.

The one thing Spears hadn't managed was further contact with Jess beyond the message on the wall at the crime scene. The flowers contained Howard's business card, but no personal note to Jess. No text messages from disposable phones.

As much as Dan wanted to be grateful for that he recognized that it only meant Spears was up to something else.

Add to that the news Gant had delivered. How could Spears have committed murder in Jess's neighborhood back in Virginia last night, left that message, and then rushed here by morning to abduct Wells and then Howard?

Didn't seem possible. Unless the guy had an associate, as Jess had suggested. Basically, they had nothing except four witnesses who had identified

Spears and the certainty that his goal was to torture Jess.

That left them with no place to go until he made his next move.

Circles. That was where they were going. Running around in circles sifting through haystacks in search of the proverbial needle.

The lab was working overtime to analyze the evidence from the floral shop, the Liberty Park Lane house and the Wells' home. So far, they had no matches on prints. There were so many at all three places that, for now, hoping for a hit from one database or the other was the best they could anticipate.

'Bastard.'

Back inside, security system rearmed, Dan returned to the kitchen to find Jess already seated at the island and digging in. She still wore that dress that had bowled him over this morning. Ivory and form-fitting. And the shoes. He was a sucker for a pair of super high heels. Especially when paired with legs like hers.

What in the hell are you doing, Burnett?

Digging that hole deeper and deeper.

She looked up. 'Any news from the search commander?'

'Zilch. Relief teams are continuing through the night.

Griggs reported the same for his crew.' He exhaled a heavy breath. 'They're determined to cover as much ground as possible as quickly as possible.'

Fork halfway to her mouth, Jess paused, seeming lost in thought. 'No matter how hard we've looked at cases attributed to the Player, we found nothing on where he kept his victims. We drew conclusions based on the conditions of the bodies but that's it. Makes sense that he would hold them in a place where he wasn't likely to be disturbed.' She lowered the fork back to her plate. 'He delivered each body to a place separate from the abduction site or the murder scene – not that we ever located a single one of the murder scenes. He keeps it all separate and there are never any mistakes.'

'Seemed to be a number of mistakes today.' That was as far as Burnett was prepared to go with the are-you-sure concept. He trusted Jess's instincts. And, frankly, her conclusions were the only ones on the table.

'Exactly. His MO is different.' She shook her head. 'But then, so is his end game. I don't think it's about the victims . . . it's a challenge directed at me. I keep thinking maybe he's punishing me for getting so close.' She stared at the food as if she'd suddenly lost her appetite. 'I know it's possible I could be wrong . . .'

He waited for her to continue; didn't dare throw in his two cents until he heard her out. This was hurting her badly enough without any help from him.

'If this is some copycat or accomplice as Manning and Gant suggested, then why does he look enough like Spears to have witnesses identifying him that way? Eric Spears has no siblings or close blood relatives. Not any that we were able to find.' She frowned. 'I don't know where that leaves us.'

The misery in her voice tugged at him. 'Eat,' he ordered. 'Get Spears out of your head for a few hours.'

And pray that Lori Wells and Belinda Howard survive the night.

He opened a bottle of Chardonnay, grabbed a couple of glasses and splashed a hearty serving in both. He settled one stemmed glass in front of Jess and to his surprise she didn't decline. They could both use something stronger but the risk of a middle-of-the-night call was too great.

She took another bite of rice, chewed thoughtfully. 'This is really good. Did your mother make it?' She shot him a look. 'I know you didn't.'

'How do you know I haven't taught myself to cook?' He climbed onto the stool next to her and sipped his wine. 'My culinary skills may be quite advanced.'

She laughed. 'Then why does your stove have all the markings of never having been turned on?' She swirled the wine in her glass before savoring a sip. 'Don't try to fool me, Burnett.' Then she tore off a piece of chicken and devoured it, closing her eyes to relish the sensations on her taste buds.

He loosened his tie and released the top button of his shirt. Usually he would have gotten comfortable by now. But Jess was here and he had to be careful about getting *too* comfortable. He was already feeling the effect of her presence in ways that had nothing to do with the job.

'It's Taziki's.' He shoved a forkful into his mouth to prevent having to answer her next question.

'When did you have time to order take out?' As if the answer to her own question dawned on her, Jess stared at her plate, then at his. 'Were you expecting company?' Her gaze lifted to his. 'You should've said something.' She grimaced as if she'd just swallowed a wad of sand instead of gourmet rice. 'Good grief, Burnett, I could've hung out with Harper or something while you . . . you *entertained*.'

'No, I was not expecting company.' Why couldn't she just enjoy the food? He doubted she'd eaten today. He knew for certain she hadn't since early morning.

'Leftovers from last night then?'

'Let it go, Jess. Eat.'

Why he just didn't tell her escaped him at the moment. That was a lie. He didn't want to tell her. This was a conversation he had no desire to have tonight. Or maybe any other night.

She stirred the rice around with her fork. 'You said for me to get Spears out of my head for a while, but I guess you don't want to talk about *this*.'

Now he was losing his appetite. 'No more than you want to talk about why you don't lose the wedding band.'

She was divorced and she still wore the ring. How screwed up was that? Way more screwed up than his need to keep Gina's impromptu visit off the table. Why couldn't women be more like men and just skip to the good part in a given situation?

'I told you it wards off unwanted advances. I have no interest in dating.' She twisted the ring around her finger with the pad of her thumb. 'This way, I don't have to say no.'

Dan kept eating. Didn't want to talk about dating either. To his supreme frustration, the idea of her dating bugged him.

Irrational. That was it. The past five days had been

irrational and crazy and unsettling on a personal level.

'Seriously,' she pressed. 'What happened? You ordered in and she stood you up? Big deal, getting stood up isn't the end of the world.'

'It was Gina Coleman. She showed up with dinner but I already had plans. Both of us were embarrassed. Satisfied?'

Fact was, he couldn't remember the last time he'd gotten stood up. He reached for his wine . . . paused. He shook his head. 'You did that on purpose.'

She shot him an innocent look. 'What?'

'You knew the stood-up remark would work.'

Expression smug, she lifted her glass. 'I've yet to meet a man who will admit to being stood up.'

'So you got me.' He swallowed his pride along with a gulp of wine.

Jess dug back into her meal with renewed enthusiasm. Took a long drink of her wine. 'So . . . an attractive lady shows up with dinner. She probably brought the wine, too. And you turn her down. Man, you're heartless.'

Fine. He was heartless. 'I was already on my way out the door to have dinner with my folks.'

Jess almost spewed wine across the island. 'You blew off the hot reporter for your mother?' At his glare, she waved her hands. 'Okay, okay. I shouldn't have said that. You did the honorable thing.'

Dan filled his glass again. He *had* done the honorable thing.

There was no need for Jess to know his motive. Or that she was right about the wine.

She tore off another piece of succulent chicken and nibbled, then licked her lips. He tried not to watch. Wasn't happening this side of going blind.

'I'll bet hot reporter was pissed.'

Her cell vibrated against the granite and she reached for it.

He appreciated the reprieve.

Jess's breath caught. She turned to him, fear in her eyes, and showed him the screen.

I left you a gift at Detective Wells' apartment.

While they stared at the heart-stopping words another text appeared.

No need to thank me, Agent Harris. It was my pleasure.

Chapter Eight

Five Points, 10.21 P.M.

All the way across town, Jess clutched at the door, ready to bound out of the vehicle. A deep breath wasn't possible. She needed Burnett to drive faster.

To get her there *now*.

The tires whined as he took a hard right onto Lori's street. He skidded to the curb and Jess wrenched the door open.

'Jess! Wait!'

Ignoring him, she rushed up the walk and toward the steps that would take her to the second-story apartment. Sirens wailed in broken harmony with their throbbing lights. Tires squealed as back-up arrived.

A big body rushed around Jess.

Harper.

Jess nearly stumbled. Almost dropped her bag.

Burnett caught her, steadied her. 'You're not going in there until we know it's safe.'

Two uniforms sprinted past. Burnett grabbed the next one. 'Make sure she stays put,' he ordered.

Then Burnett was gone, too.

Lori was his detective. If she was in there . . . Jess's knees betrayed her.

'I've got you, ma'am.'

It could be Lori or Belinda Howard. Adrenalin fired through Jess. What the hell did Spears want from her? Was she supposed to read his mind? Oh, she got the part about him wanting *her*. But where? When? She needed a fucking clue! She was more than ready to face him.

Fury roared in her like a ferocious beast. Her fingers squeezed into fists. Never in her life had she wanted to kill another human being, but she wanted to kill him. She wanted to watch him die a slow, agonizing death.

'I'm fine, officer.' She put a hand to her chest, offered a faint smile. 'Really. Thank you.'

His hands dropped away from her arms. 'Would you like to wait in—'

Jess bolted. Hell no she wasn't waiting.

'You can't go in there, ma'am!'

'Oh, yes I can,' she muttered. What was he going to do? Shoot her?

She was halfway up the steps before he caught up with her. He nabbed her by the elbow. Jess twisted away from his hold and lunged for the deck on the second level. Burnett blocked the door to Lori's apartment.

Jess jerked to a halt. She sucked at the hot, heavy air but it refused to reach her lungs.

'It's not Lori.'

Jess's knees wobbled. 'Belinda Howard?'

Burnett nodded.

'I need to be in there.' Why didn't he get out of her way?

'She's alive, Jess.'

'Alive?' Her breath deserted her again. The Player, Spears, never left a victim alive.

'Just barely,' Burnett warned. 'An ALS unit's en route.'

'Okay.' Jess mentally scrambled to get her bearings. 'Good.' She glared up at him. 'Can you let me pass now, chief?'

Burnett dragged shoe covers and gloves from his pocket and offered them to her. Stepping out of the blasted heels one at a time, she slipped the covers onto her bare feet. Her hands shook hard. She swore at her shoes . . . at her shaking hands and at that monster Spears.

Burnett moved aside. Jess took a breath. *Do this right. Clear your head.*

She walked into the apartment, mindlessly tugging the gloves into place, and instantly slipping into analysis mode. *She had done it hundreds of times.* The overturned stool and spilled orange juice were just as they had been earlier that morning. Signs of the evidence techs' work after Lori's abduction were everywhere. Harper and another officer were doing what they could for Belinda Howard. Jess moved closer. As much as she wanted to see what Spears had done, she didn't want to get in the way.

'Pulse is barely there.' Harper spoke softly. 'But it's there.'

The comforter had been thrown aside. Howard's body was positioned on the bed with her arms stretched out crucifixion style and her legs slightly spread. The wounds on her wrists had been wrapped in something yellow . . . torn cloth.

Why would he wrap her wounds?

Her nipples had been cut away from her breasts, a thin flap keeping them attached. A classic Player technique, always executed while the victim remained breathing and conscious. But the work was sloppy. The blood had dried on the thin fabric, leaving the jagged outlines of the wounds. Jess could understand him wrapping the wound he'd made at the abduction scene to staunch the flow of blood once he had what he needed. But this was more than that.

The incision beneath her bellybutton appeared to be more a gouge than a smooth, precise line, but fairly wide. Something bloody protruded as if he'd stuffed an object in the wound.

There were no other marks visible. No bruising . . . no scrapes. A few similarities to the Player's work were obvious, but the rest was wrong. Howard's skin was unnaturally pale and, of course, clean, even around the wounds. She looked fragile, like a porcelain doll ready to shatter.

How terrified she must have been until the merciful darkness dragged her into unconsciousness.

Between the damage to her breasts and the one to her abdomen, it looked as if he'd attempted a gory smiley face. The Player's contempt for women always showed in his work, although, usually with a little more style. Jess had dug deep into Eric Spears' background in search of the event or events that had set him on that path. He had grown up in southern California.

No siblings or extended family. Parents died when he was in his mid-twenties. He'd turned his aptitude for creating into a wildly successful software business. By the time he was thirty he owned the world of security software. He'd faded into obscurity while his corporation, SpearNet, which was headquartered in Richmond, grew into a giant.

In Jess's assessment, with his professional challenge conquered and with no wife or kids to distract him, he'd found a new hobby to assuage the evil urges pulsing beneath the seemingly normal surface.

But Jess couldn't prove that theory . . . her gaze lingered on Howard. And she couldn't get right with how the evidence was stacking up in this case. Way out of character for Spears' alter ego, the Player.

'Let's cover her up, Sergeant Harper.' Jess pointed to the closet. 'I think I remember seeing clean linens in there.'

'Yes, ma'am.'

Harper got a clean sheet and covered Mrs Howard. Whether she lived or died, there was no need for her to be humiliated any further. The paramedics wouldn't mind. The evidence techs could go to hell.

Jess leaned close to the poor woman and whispered, 'Hang on, Belinda, we've got you now. We'll make sure you get home to your husband and children.'

Pushing back the swell of emotions, Jess walked the room, checked the closet and bathroom. No messages, nothing out of place that hadn't already been disturbed that morning. Why would he bring Howard back here and risk being seen since the residents of the neighborhood were no doubt watching more vigilantly for strangers?

The Advanced Life Support unit arrived, two paramedics burst into the room, weighed down with gear. Harper got out of the way, huddled nearby, a strange combination of shock and relief creasing his face. The victim was alive but it wasn't Lori. Like Jess, he likely felt a nauseating mixture of gratitude and regret. The officer whose duty it was to protect the victim and the scene stepped aside and waited for further instructions.

Burnett lingered near the island, on his cell. Notifying the family or the Bureau. Jess had no idea.

'Sergeant.' It wasn't until the paramedics focused on Belinda Howard that Jess noticed the bottoms of her feet. At the moment that was all she could see.

'Yes, ma'am.'

'Get a swab from the bottom of each foot before they take her away.'

Harper nodded and went in search of the tools for the task. The crime scene unit should be outside by now. If not, Burnett had a collection kit in his SUV. Harper probably did, too.

The Player always carefully cleansed his victims before dumping their bodies. It was another of his vile rituals. That he had forgotten the bottoms of Howard's feet was either an enormous oversight or a clue purposely left for Jess to pursue. As long as it ultimately led her to Lori and to *him* she would follow even the vaguest hunch.

Jess checked the kitchen, opening the cabinet doors one by one, then the fridge and stove. Nothing in the microwave or dishwasher. The apartment was neat and compact, making the effort quick and easy.

Harper joined Jess, the swabs bagged. 'I have a buddy at the lab I can get to process this for us.' He tucked the bag into the interior pocket of his suit jacket.

'As in now?' Jess inquired. The techs would do the same but she wanted the results now.

'Absolutely, ma'am.'

'As soon as we're done here, I'm going to the hospital with Burnett. Go see your buddy.'

'Yes, ma'am.'

'And, sergeant,' Jess surveyed the kitchen area again,

'does Lori do her laundry at a laundromat or at her mother's?'

'Her mother's every Sunday afternoon. They have an early dinner. And yeah, she went there yesterday.'

Oh, yes. The Player had decided Lori would be the one and he'd watched her. That Sunday ritual had made his next move as simple as breathing. She had unknowingly led him right to her mother's home. Afterward, he'd obviously followed Jess to her sister's. He'd lined up his prey that easily.

I will get you, Jess promised.

Several minutes were required for the paramedics to get Howard prepared for transport. An IV was sending much needed fluids into her veins. Communications with the ER's trauma unit ensured they were standing by for the arrival of a critical patient in need of blood and more.

Jess hoped the woman survived. If she did, she would be the first. As thankful as she was that Belinda Howard was alive, this was *wrong*.

The Player never left survivors.

A new kind of fear sent a chill over Jess. Maybe she was wrong and the Bureau was right . . .

Maybe she needed this to be Spears. Was she losing any prospect of objectivity because she needed so badly to be right? To have a second chance to get him?

'Chief Harris.'

Jess snapped from the haze of new worries she'd drifted into and turned back to the bed and to Harper. 'Yes, sergeant.' Her legs felt rubbery as she moved toward him.

'You should have a look at this.'

Jess hadn't realized the evidence techs had already begun their work. The fear that she had this all wrong had bored deep . . . and was swiftly evolving into sheer terror.

What if she *was* wrong? This could be a copycat. The earmarks were hard to miss. Work similar to the Player's, but not quite right . . .

'He left you another message,' Harper said.

Beneath where Howard had lain, words were scrawled in blood. Jess reached out to touch the crimson ribbons . . . dry. The son of a bitch had written the message, waited for it to dry and placed Howard on top of it.

I'm waiting.

Burnett appeared next to her.

Jess didn't look at him.

He said nothing.

'Sergeant Harper, if you'll oversee the collection of evidence and ensure it gets to the lab in a timely fashion,' Jess said, not waiting for Burnett to make the call, 'Chief Burnett and I will go to the hospital and wait for a prognosis on Mrs Howard.'

'Yes, ma'am.'

Burnett gave his detective a nod before they left. He said nothing to Jess but she knew full well he had plenty on his mind. When he was ready, he would reiterate the idea that she was in danger. That she was too close to this case.

And he would be right on both counts. But this madness had to stop. Jess tore off the gloves and the shoe covers and jammed her feet back into her shoes. Who else had to be tortured or murdered or both before this bastard made his final move?

What was he waiting for?

Jess shoved her hair behind her ears, slung her bag over her shoulder. 'Has someone contacted the family?'

'Deputy Chief Black is taking care of that right now.'

Jess should call Lil. Make sure she was okay and give her the news.

Inside, she started to shake. Lil and her family needed to leave tonight. What was wrong with these people? Didn't they get that there was a murderer out there targeting anyone close to her?

'Anything else?' she asked. He had more to say, she could tell by the grim face he wore and the way he avoided eye contact.

'Gant called.'

So that was what all the phone business was about in there. She crossed her arms over her chest. 'And?'

'And he's pissed.'

What was new?

'He has no legal precedent to interfere with your investigation,' Jess argued. 'This is your jurisdiction, for Christ's sake. Your citizens. As long as yours doesn't interfere with his, he can't do a damned thing.' There were some cases where the Bureau could supersede and/or block what local law enforcement did – like in a bank robbery or basically any crime that occurred on federal property. But this was not one of those cases.

She didn't need to tell Burnett that.

What in hell was the problem here? He looked as if he'd had his lunch money stolen by the school bully.

'He threatened to take you into custody and hold you as a person of interest in the Spears investigation he's conducting if you continue to be involved with

BPD's investigation. Apparently, one of the national news channels has slung allegations about our case and Spears and the Bureau's involvement. Spears' attorney was interviewed and he's threatening to file suit.'

Her jaw dropped. 'What did you say to that?'

'It's my job to negotiate these situations, Jess. I can't have BPD at war with the Bureau. And, frankly, I can't prevent him from labeling you a person of interest and doing exactly as he threatened.' He shrugged. 'I told him what he wanted to hear. You're off the case. I'm putting Deputy Chief Black in charge. Crimes Against Persons will take it from here.'

For about five seconds fury blustered so wildly inside her that Jess couldn't have said a word if she'd wanted to until she considered the way Burnett had made the statement. *I told him what he wanted to hear.*

'All right,' she said cautiously, 'so you told him what he wanted to hear. What're you telling me?' She held her breath.

'Screw Gant. He can coordinate with Black. Harper and I will keep you in the loop. Gant can't control what you do as long as he doesn't know about it.'

'So, what do we do now?' It wasn't like she could go to the hospital as planned. The hurricane of emotions inside her was making a logical thought impossible.

Gant wanted her off this case. Logically, she understood that his hands were tied to some degree. Considering the ongoing OPR investigation, Gant couldn't exactly turn a blind eye and ignore her. If OPR pushed hard enough . . . how far would he be forced to take this situation?

And what if he was right and she was wrong?

She couldn't wrap her head around that . . . not yet.

'Black will keep us posted on Howard's condition,' Burnett said. 'You and I are going home to strategize.' He glanced at her without making actual eye contact. 'You have what you need in that bag of yours?'

'Sure.' She gave herself a mental shake. 'No, wait, we need to get my car.'

Her decade-old Audi was still parked downtown. She would need her stuff from the trunk. Why she hadn't gotten it when she got her suitcase hours ago she would never know. Frustration and fear had her running in those damned loops Spears had created just for her. She felt like a guinea pig in its cage riding that wheel to nowhere.

Her working case files were in the truck of her car. She needed the one related to Spears for this off-the-record investigation Burnett claimed she could conduct in spite of the Bureau's warning. As much as she wanted to trust Burnett's motives . . . this felt wrong, too. Was his need to protect her affecting his judgment?

'We'll pick up your car on the way.'

'All right.'

Jess led the way down the stairs from the landing. The rate this was going, by tomorrow Gant and OPR would have her back against the wall. Burnett could only fight him so far . . . then his back would be against that same wall.

Somehow, she had to make Spears, or whoever this was, react. So far she had done all the reacting. It was time to turn the tables. She needed him to make the kind of mistake that would give her something to find him.

Tires squealed. Jess stalled on the sidewalk as a news van rocked to a stop at the curb. Two uniforms rushed to contain the invasion.

Burnett snagged her elbow. 'Just keep walking.'

By the time they reached the intersection of the sidewalk and the street the reporter, not that Gina woman, was shouting questions at Burnett.

'Chief, is it true that a victim has been found alive? Was it Detective Wells or Belinda Howard?'

'No comment,' Burnett slowed long enough to say what no reporter ever wanted to hear.

'Are you making any headway on the case, Chief

Burnett? The Bureau says this is not the work of the Player, is that your opinion as well?'

Jess gritted her teeth, forced one foot in front of the other to keep pace with him and to prevent turning back and giving the reporter an earful.

'What about you, Agent Harris?' the persistent woman shouted as they kept moving toward Burnett's SUV.

Jess stalled.

The warning on Burnett's face was loud and clear and still, for the record, he stated, 'Not tonight, Jess.'

She met that cautionary glare with a threatening one of her own. 'If not tonight, when? When Gant gets his way and I'm in custody? When there's another victim?'

'Agent Harris, would you like to send the folks of Birmingham a message of reassurance that this madman will be stopped?' the reporter shouted.

Jess pulled free of Burnett's grasp and turned back to the reporter. He didn't try to stop her . . . that wouldn't look good on camera.

The hurricane roaring inside Jess abruptly calmed, as if the eye of the storm had suddenly swallowed her.

'What message would you like to send, Agent Harris? Do you have something to say to the man behind the abductions that have Birmingham's citizens cowering in their homes?'

She thrust the microphone in Jess's face. The camera's lens zeroed in on her.

'I have a message for him, yes.' Fury roared in Jess's veins. She stared straight into the camera. 'I know what you want.' That eerie calm settled around her, inside her, once more. 'Man up, you coward. Come and get me.'

Chapter Nine

Dunbrooke Drive, Tuesday, July 20th, 12.54 A.M.

Dan grabbed a couple of Pepsis from the fridge, stretched his neck, and rejoined Jess in the dining room. He'd railed at her all the way home. He'd been so pissed that he'd had to turn around and go back for her car.

What the hell had gotten into her? And why the hell hadn't he stopped her?

On the drive back, alone and following right on her tail, he'd calmed down. He still didn't like that she'd thrown down a gauntlet, but it was done. Maybe she was right. Maybe provoking the perp into a reaction would somehow facilitate their efforts. Whatever the outcome, one thing was crystal clear: he had been correct in his conclusion that he could not let her out of his sight.

Spears or whoever the hell this was had pushed her too far. And now she was feeling the pressure of sheer desperation.

And Gant was livid. Another call from him had come as Dan followed Jess home. Gant used the incident as further proof that Jess wasn't herself. Her fixation on Spears was prompting her rather than the facts in the case.

To some degree the guy was right. Dan could see that. Jess was far more fragile than she realized.

Pepsis in hand, he padded barefoot to the dining room.

Documents and photos were spread across the table. As he watched, she picked up a photo and studied it carefully before moving on to the next one. She paced back and forth, from one end of the room to the other, while she analyzed and compared the information from her prior work on the Player case to this one, searching for commonalities.

The images from those photos and from tonight's scene kept scrolling through his head, only, in his mind, Jess was the victim. He banished the latest round of mental intrusions and set a Pepsi on the table for her, then popped the top on his own. 'Found anything useful?'

She wilted into a chair. 'This is wrong.' She removed her glasses and rubbed her eyes, then shook her head. 'It's just . . . wrong.'

Dan pulled out a chair across the table from her and lowered into it. 'Wrong how?'

'The Player,' Jess began, her voice weary, 'selects his victims, we believe, after careful consideration of one or more candidates who appeal to his urge for pleasure. The abductions are always pulled off without a hitch, suggesting that he learns the vic's routine and determines the best time and place to make his move.'

'But he didn't do that with Wells or Howard. They were chosen strictly because of their connection to you – not just for his sadistic pleasure.'

'Right.' Jess raked her hair behind her ears. 'On top of that, the method of abduction was vastly different. The Player doesn't manipulate a situation, he takes advantage of one. I mean, it's possible he's used a strategy similar to the one he used today, but we have no documented evidence of contact of any sort with a victim or anyone connected to the victim prior to the abduction. Not until now.' She turned her hands up. 'The single commonality so far is the gift he sends announcing he's claimed a victim. Like delivering Lori's badge to me. And the flowers with Howard's card. He uses that technique every time.'

She rubbed at the gold band on her left ring finger with her thumb, turning it round and round. The habit annoyed him. It shouldn't, but it did. The band was a symbol of what she'd shared with another man and he had a problem with that.

He had no right. Hell, he'd been married three times. *Three*. Didn't seem possible. The first doomed union had been a couple years after he and Jess parted ways. Meredith Dority, then personal assistant to the mayor. The whirlwind marriage had been a mistake. Rebound, he figured. He'd still missed Jess. He'd thought a permanent relationship would do the trick. Wrong. The second had come when he hit thirty. It was like *boom,* he wanted to get married. Nina Baron, daughter of Senator Robert Baron, had happily taken that ill-fated walk down the aisle with him. His parents had been ecstatic, especially his mother. One year later, they had divorced, citing irreconcilable differences. That was a time he preferred not to recall.

Then, a couple years ago, he'd married Annette Denton and thought that would be the one. Annette was beautiful, sophisticated. And Dan adored her daughter. Twelve months into the relationship, they'd both been ready to call it done.

He had no right whatsoever to begrudge Jess her one marriage.

Dan snapped out of the trek down memory lane. Just went to show how tired he was. 'Since Howard survived,' he ventured, dragging Jess from her own reverie, 'does that suggest better odds for Wells' survival?'

'Maybe . . . I wouldn't dare guess at this point. Howard's survival and the injuries she suffered are nothing like his usual work.' She shuffled through the photos, selected three and then spread them out in front of him. 'See for yourself.'

Dan studied each one of the Player's victims from his recent spree in Richmond. The bodies were nude, as Howard had been, but his previous assaults had been horrifyingly more savage. He had literally carved up the women's bodies as if they were a canvas for his twisted creative outlet. Damage to the breasts, similar to Howard's, the lips . . . the eyes . . . the fingers and then a path down the rest of their bodies. None of the wounds appeared particularly deep. The goal hadn't been to kill, at least not at first, but to torture with endless points of agony.

Dan shifted in his seat, tugged loose the top two buttons of his shirt so he could breathe. Though the Player appeared to use different torture techniques – probably dependent upon what prompted the most screaming – the end result was the same: the victims were raped and murdered. Once deceased, the bodies were meticulously cleaned and deposited in the most unexpected and open places without a speck of other evidence left behind. His delivery points ranged from a church pew to a public park.

Jess tapped the photo in front of him. 'See how precise his work is? The removal of the nipples almost as exact as a surgeon's in preparation for a lift. He pinpoints major nerve centers, too. See that area of the shoulder where he seemed to concentrate? And here in the upper area of the inner thigh? The eyes?' She leaned back, distancing herself from the photos. 'He knows how to inflict pain. He's mastered the art.'

Dan felt ill. 'You mentioned before that he likes to use their fears against them. That's why he asked about Detective Wells' fears.' He swallowed at the lump that had lodged in his throat.

Jess leaned forward again, pointed to marks on one of the vics. 'Snake bites. Dozens of them. Only one bite was from a poisonous snake. That was cause of death.

But all the others appeared to have been inflicted before death.' She put another photo in front of him. 'This one, the remains of spiders were found in her stomach contents and even a couple deep in her throat. We believe he made her swallow them, probably one by one. Cause of death, myocardial infarction. He literally scared her to death. The rest of the wounds inflicted were just for fun.'

'So . . .' Dan couldn't believe he was about to say this out loud. 'Based on his prior pattern and what we've seen here with Belinda Howard's condition, which bore no marks of a specific fear-inducing torture, the perp we're dealing with isn't Spears or this Player?'

But if it wasn't him, then who the hell was this guy?

Jess propped her elbows on the table and rested her chin in her hands. She didn't answer for a time. She'd been back in Birmingham less than a week and the troubles with Eric Spears had started weeks before that. She was tired, disgusted and scared – even if she wouldn't admit that last part.

He thought of the challenge she'd issued to this maniac that would be run over and over on the news. She was desperate to stop him. And that scared him.

'Even if we learn that Belinda Howard was terrified of a paper cut,' Jess said finally, 'it still doesn't fit the

Player's MO.' She peered at the photos again. 'Based on what we have so far, I'd be a fool to believe this is him.' She lifted her gaze to his. 'But it *is* him. It has to be. The messages he sent to me are the same tone and rhythm. I could get past that by assuming Gant was right and we had a copycat who had latched onto the media frenzy back in Richmond and had targeted me. But we have four eye witnesses who have positively identified Eric Spears.' Exhaling a burst of frustration, she busied herself organizing the photos and reports back into a stack.

'Spears' likeness is plastered all over the city,' he said, hoping to reassure her. The Bureau wasn't happy, but the media blitz and the flyers were out there. 'By sun-up whoever this guy is, he'll have a hell of a time moving around freely.'

Her efforts at pulling the file back to order stalled. 'That's the thing, isn't it?' She shook her head. '*Whoever this guy is*. What if I'm not only wrong about this, what if I've been wrong all along like Gant said?'

Reaching across the table, he took her hand in his, gave it a squeeze. 'Considering this guy looks just like Spears, I say until we have a better alternative, we keep following our instincts. That can't be wrong.'

'That's the part that's driving me crazy. The part I

can't get past even though every other aspect of this case points to someone else.' She threw her hands up in exasperation. 'I can see one witness being way off on the ID, but four? Unless he has a long-lost twin – and we found nothing on any siblings or close family whatsoever, much less a twin – or has a fan who idolizes him to the extent that he went to the trouble to change his entire appearance, this has to be Spears.'

'Let's say it is him, no question,' Dan proposed, 'is there anything in his psychology that could explain this sudden departure from his usual methods?'

She reflected on the question for a few moments. 'The compulsion that drives a sociopath like Spears is immense. Most can't control those kinds of extreme impulses but he has worked long and hard, probably disciplined himself with physical abuse to maintain a rigid level of restraint. He knows what he wants, what he must have, and he goes after it when the time is right. When he's prepared.' She tortured that lush bottom lip of hers. 'He's keenly intelligent and a lot OCD so everything has to be perfect. Methodical. Precise.'

She pushed out of her chair and started pacing again, arms wrapped around her middle like a shield.

'I can only assume that he got distracted for some

reason by the interaction with me and he's fixating on whatever it is about me that intrigues him. That fixation has prompted him to act on pure impulse which is way outside his comfort zone. He's making mistakes and he knows better. Yet he doesn't care because he's lost control to the degree that it makes him feel in control to pretend this is exactly what he intended.'

Dan had given in to plenty of impulses of his own. Ten years ago in the Publix when he and Jess ran into each other for the first time in years . . . neither had been able to control what had happened between them.

She stopped, hauled Dan back from his wayward musings, and faced him.

'It's possible he's turned this into his new reality to block those old feelings of inadequacy and failure that haunted him in the past.' A light came on in her eyes as if the assessment were a relief, then her face fell, scrunched with worry. 'If that's the case, then he's on the edge and the smallest thing could tip him over. The results of a fall like that are immeasurable. Until he's contained, there's no telling what level he'll take this to.'

'So, the longer it takes us to find him, the more dangerous this situation could become.'

She nodded but he doubted his comment registered, she was still analyzing.

'The trouble I have with that scenario is that Spears found control and held onto it with an iron fist for all this time. Otherwise he might not be the wealthy man he is today. Not to mention, if he's the Player, as I believe, he has at least thirty murders on his résumé and not one can be connected to him. He's nothing short of brilliant. Surely a bump in his path as insignificant as my interference couldn't undo all that rigid control.'

She shook her head, clearly exasperated. 'And yet that had to be the trigger.'

Dan had read that about Spears. He'd built an empire out of a small software company – for security systems, no less. A recluse, he worked from his mansion when he wasn't traveling. He spent more time outside the country than in it.

A man like that could have hundreds of victims all over the world.

'Maybe he's given in to the impulse, to his obsession with you,' Dan tossed out, 'and he's lost total control, like you said.'

She lowered back into her chair. 'Maybe. But if we look at the victimology, I'm not convinced even a loss of control or this rush he seems to be in would change his methods so completely. Howard's wounds are not nearly as detailed as his usual work and he's a perfectionist. He would never be so careless.'

Dan could see that it was killing her to be totally confused on a case where she thought she knew the perpetrator so well. 'During the investigation in Richmond, you were thinking maybe he had an accomplice or partner. Could this be his work? Could he be,' Dan shrugged, 'attempting to walk in his teacher's footsteps? Even going so far as to change his appearance? Imitation is the sincerest form of flattery.'

'It's possible. I suspected he had at least one student, protégé, whatever. Even if I couldn't prove it. Considering I received all those emails while he was being held for questioning, there had to be someone else involved. I sure as hell didn't send them to myself – even if they were sent from my home computer.' She made a derisive sound. 'But I would be more inclined to believe this is a relative who bears a striking resemblance to him. The way Lily and I look so much alike. Or . . . or the way my niece looks so much like the both of us.'

'Yet, in five years, the Bureau's investigation found no such relatives.'

'None.'

'That takes us back to Spears himself.' Dan blew out a breath. Talk about going in circles.

'Which presents a whole other problem,' she declared, frustrated. 'No print matches. Who knows if any of those collected at the scenes were his since Mrs Wells said he was wearing gloves. But the women at the floral shop said he wasn't wearing gloves and we haven't found a single print matching his, not on the business card or anywhere else.'

She opened her drink and took a long swallow as she leaned back into her chair. Dan's throat tightened as he watched her tilt her head back, lengthening that smooth, slender neck and then licking her lips after savoring her drink. As tired as he was, as awful as the situation with the case, he couldn't deny himself the luxury of looking at her as a woman. The woman with whom he had once shared everything. The same one he'd walked away from.

The biggest mistake of his life.

'I'm stumped,' she confessed. 'I can't fit what we have in this case into what I know about the man I interviewed in Richmond three weeks ago. I just can't make the leap.'

'Believe it or not,' he said, the idea gaining momentum, 'I think we found our answer. What we have on our hands is a copycat.' Made the most sense in his opinion. That Jess didn't look surprised prompted him to go on. 'And since the name Eric Spears wasn't connected to the serial killer known as the Player until last month, this copycat would have already had to know who Spears was. Had to know and love him enough to have gone to all the trouble to do whatever necessary to look like him.'

She stared at Dan for a long moment without saying a word. Then, as if his pronouncement had abruptly sunk in, her eyes widened. 'Then the real question is, whether or not Spears is involved. If he is, then we don't have just one sadistic killer to worry about. We have two.'

The idea sent dread plowing through Dan's veins.

His cell vibrated. He blinked away the new, troubling concept and stared at the screen. Gant. *Damn.*

Burnett was still on the phone when the doorbell sounded. It would be Harper. He'd sent Jess a text asking if he could stop by. It was too early for him to have results from the sample he'd taken from Belinda Howard's feet, but there could be other news.

After confirming it was Harper, Jess disarmed the security system and opened the door. 'Sergeant, I hope you have some good news. I've reached my limit for bad in a single twenty-four hour period.' Her nerves were shot. The concept that both Spears and his protégé were here . . . working as a team upped the stakes dramatically.

Maybe the ultimatum she issued to the media would goad one or both into making a move against her. Get this over with . . . so she could take him or them down. She recognized the thought as irrational but that didn't stop her from meaning it just the same.

Harper waited while she secured the door. 'We'll have those results by noon, ma'am. The lab is seriously backed up but my friend assured me that we have priority.'

'Good. Anything else?'

Harper nodded, his face grim. 'The yellow fabric used to wrap the wounds on Howard's arms was from a blouse. Someone ripped it into pieces to use as makeshift bandages.'

There was absolutely no way Spears would do that. Had to be the protégé or copycat, whatever the hell this guy was.

'Another piece of that blouse was used to staunch the blood flow from the wound to the abdomen.'

'Do we know what Belinda Howard was wearing when she was abducted?'

He nodded. 'A light green dress. I also reviewed the statements Mrs Wells and Terri made after . . . we arrived.' Pain pinched his face. 'Both Terri and her mother stated that Lori – Detective Wells – was wearing brown slacks and a *yellow* blouse.'

That could mean Lori was still alive and that somehow she had attempted to provide first aid to Belinda Howard. Jess's heart squeezed. She wanted to cling to that sliver of hope. Jess refused to believe Lori was dead. She was strong. She would survive longer than the average victim of a heinous killer.

'She would do that,' Harper said, as if he'd read Jess's mind. 'Try to help, I mean.'

Jess met his gaze, her heart squeezing again at the agony in his eyes. 'Detective Wells had to be alive to administer first aid.' She pressed her lips together before she said too much. It would be wrong to give him any additional assurances.

'That was my thinking.'

Just move on, Jess. 'Any word on Howard's condition?'

'That's part of the reason I came by.'

It struck Jess then that they were still standing in the entry hall. 'Come in, sergeant. I don't know where my head is, much less my manners.'

He touched her arm and she hesitated. He glanced beyond her before speaking. 'How's he taking all this?'

Jess shook her head. 'He's sick about it, just like you

and I. And he's pretty pissed about the TV thing.'

Harper smiled. 'I saw it. You looked pretty tough. If I was this guy, I'd be worried.'

As tired as she was, he made her smile. 'That was the goal, sergeant.'

She led him to the dining room. Burnett was still in the kitchen. The hushed sound of his voice made her want to walk right up to him and demand to know to whom he was speaking and what it had to do with the case.

Then again, it could be that reporter . . . Gina . . . wondering if he was available.

You're an idiot, Jess.

'Have a seat, sergeant.' She gestured to the chairs lining the table. She'd bet a million dollars if she had it that the table had never been used before tonight. This was no home. It was a status symbol. Apparently Burnett's mother had rubbed off on him without Jess here to intervene. 'Would you like coffee? Pepsi? Water?'

An excuse to go into the kitchen was more than welcome.

'No, ma'am, thank you.'

Harper waited by a chair for her to take a seat first. If she could only convince him to loosen up. The ma'am thing got on her nerves. But he was far too courteous and dutiful to ever loosen up when it came to showing proper respect. His parents had taught him well.

She sat.

He sat.

'What's the update on Howard?' Jess braced for more conflicting details.

'She's conscious now and talking a little. Agent Gant and Deputy Chief Black have spoken to her but she was in no condition to give a statement.'

'What about lab results? Toxicology? Anything?'

A small smile breached the somber line of the detective's lips for the second time since his arrival. 'Black has a niece who works in the lab at the hospital. She gave him the results, verbally of course, before the lab got around to releasing their findings.'

It paid to have friends and relatives in the right places. 'What type of sedative was used?'

'Ketamine.'

Special K, the very one the Player used. Not that he was the only one. The sedative, used for human patients as well as equines, was popular with the druggies dragging around a death wish. 'Was she sexually assaulted?'

'No, ma'am, she wasn't.'

One step forward, one back. Not that Jess wasn't

thankful the poor woman hadn't suffered that horror as well. But the Player, Spears, always raped his victims. *Always*. That would seem to corroborate the scenario that regardless of the similarities to his work, this was most likely not Eric Spears. More likely the copycat. With no print matches and no other evidence, identifying a man wearing another's face was not going to be easy.

Burnett appeared in the doorway. Harper brought him up to speed.

Jess waited, her patience growing paper thin, for her turn. 'Was that call about the investigation?'

'It was Gant. He'd like to have a joint briefing with BPD at ten in the morning to review where we are on the case.'

'Does that include me?' Jess knew it was pointless to ask but she did it anyway.

He gave her a fake smile. 'Since my ears are still ringing from the chewing out I got from the mayor as well as Gant about your television appearance, that would be a no.' Before she could protest, he added, 'You have a different briefing at that time.'

'What briefing?' A barrage of new worries entered center ring in her already crowded brain.

'With one of the detectives assigned to your unit.

She'll be bringing you up to speed on how we do things at BPD and showing you around.'

Harper kept quiet. Probably wished he could run for the door.

In other words, Jess was out of all official steps related to the case. Period. She stood. 'Whatever you say. You're the chief.' She turned to Harper. 'You should get some sleep, sergeant.'

Then she walked straight to the guestroom and slammed the door behind her. It was childish, she knew. But she was tired and frustrated and . . . a bunch of other things she didn't want to think about.

With her suitcase plopped on the bed, she dug out her lounge pants and tee and her toothbrush. She tossed her glasses on the night table, peeled off the dress. She'd already kicked off the blasted high heels. When her sleepwear was on, she stamped into the en suite and washed her face and brushed her teeth.

Her hand slowed with the work of scrubbing her teeth as she stared at her reflection. For as long as she could remember she had worked harder than her peers to ensure she achieved her goals.

What else was a girl from no less than four foster homes going to do? She lowered the toothbrush and spat into the sink. She wiped her mouth with the back of her hand. She understood the motives behind her own psychology. Her parents died when she and her sister were kids. They had nothing. At eighteen they were turned out of the last foster home with the same thing they brought in. Nothing. No one understood how that felt until they walked that lonely, frightening path.

Lil had chosen the course perfect for her. She wanted someone to rely on who would give her the home and life for which she yearned. Not Jess. She hadn't trusted anyone else to take care of her. Her parents had deserted her by dying.

Burnett had left her.

But that was okay because by then she had known she could take care of herself. All she had to do was be relentless . . . be the best.

She stared at the band on her finger. Old forty had rolled around and she'd awakened scared that she would be alone for the rest of her life. Middle age did that to a woman. So she'd married a nice man, a fellow agent. Things had been okay at first. But he'd quickly grown disillusioned. Jess loved her work more than him. He'd wanted a social life. Jess didn't have time. He'd wanted children. Jess didn't have time. If she slowed down to do all that she would fall behind . . . and that was unacceptable.

And then she wouldn't be the best anymore.

The idea terrified her.

Dan had asked why she still wore the ring and she'd lied. She wore it because to take it off would show the world that she had failed again. Burnett had left her and twenty years later her husband had, too.

Another truth flashed in her eyes. She saw it . . . couldn't deny it.

She had run away from Birmingham all those years ago because she could never be the best here. She was just a poor kid from foster care, doomed to mediocrity. Katherine Burnett had never let her forget that. Then, twenty-odd years later she ran back after her first true failure at the Bureau.

Part of her still wanted to believe that the failure to bring down Spears wasn't her fault. That she was one-hundred percent correct about him. But maybe she wasn't. Maybe the failure was all hers. The fear of failure had sent her running again.

Just like Spears or his protégé, the lookalike, was scared of failure so he was making mistakes. Acting illogically . . . acting on impulse.

Determination filled her.

Maybe she didn't have this case figured out yet, but she refused to be afraid of that . . . of failure.

Jess rinsed her toothbrush. She stared at the woman in the mirror and gave her a message. 'Not this time.'

She didn't need to be the best anymore and she damned sure wasn't running.

Jessie Lee Harris was here to stay and she would stop this evil.

Dan stood outside the guestroom door. He should have told Jess straight up what the deal was, but he'd needed to do that when they were alone. It wasn't that he didn't trust Harper. Hell, Harper was one of the best detectives he had. Not to mention he would be working in Jess's unit. Decisions related to her position now and later should not influence his opinion of her. And, right now, Harper was emotionally compromised.

Since the shooting when Wells took that bullet intended for Harper, Dan had watched the two grow closer and closer. He didn't have a problem with that building relationship unless it interfered with their work.

So far that hadn't happened.

But Wells was a victim in this case. If Harper wasn't such a damned good cop he wouldn't even be on this case in any capacity. His oversight of the evidence gathered and working as liaison with the search commanders was invaluable.

Still, if push came to shove, Harper might break under the emotional stress. This whole situation between Jess and the Bureau was highly charged and incredibly sensitive. The Bureau, more specifically OPR, wasn't going to give up the witch hunt until satisfied that they were in the clear.

If Dan didn't help her protect herself, Jess was going to be the one burned at the stake. For Christ's sake, look at the way she'd put herself out there by making that statement to the press. She wasn't thinking clearly.

He rapped on the door.

It opened immediately as if she'd been standing on the other side waiting for him. Knowing her, she probably had been.

'Are you going to give me a chance to explain?'

She stared at him a moment, arms crossed over her chest. She'd scrubbed her face clean of make-up, taken off her glasses, and traded that killer dress for a tee and lounge pants.

'I was already in bed. It's late.'

Sure enough, she'd thrown the covers back but that didn't mean a thing.

'You're up now.'

'Fine. It's your house. Suit yourself. Explain.'

'I'm not shutting you out, Jess. But if Gant suspects

for a second what we're up to, he'll make life seriously miserable for you. Detective Wells' life is at stake here and both our careers are as well. We have to walk a fine line between playing nice with the Bureau and doing what we both know is right.'

Arms still crossed, suspicion still clouding her face, she asked, 'You won't keep anything from me?'

'Why the hell would I keep anything from you?' That ticked him off. 'I need you on this. We've known each other most of our lives. How can you not trust me?'

Hadn't they worked this part out already? Shortly after she came here to advise on the case that had his whole department baffled, they'd butted heads about the past. He'd thought they talked it out. Apparently not.

She looked away. 'I want to trust you completely. But the truth is, part of me just can't.' She shook her head. 'I'm genuinely sorry I feel that way, but that's just the way it is.'

As tired and emotionally drained as he felt after Andrea's abduction and this damned Spears case – not to mention the memories and feelings just being around Jess again evoked – he'd doubted anything else could damage him today.

But her words managed to do just that.

'All right then.' He felt at a loss as to what to say next. 'Goodnight.'

He left it at that. Nothing he said would change her mind.

Maybe he'd made a mistake thinking there was still something between them. Twenty years was a long time. A gap that spanned that wide wasn't going to be bridged in a few days.

Maybe not in another two or three decades.

But if misunderstandings and further damage to their tenuous relationship was what it took to keep her safe . . . then so be it.

Chapter Ten

Southpointe Circle, Hoover, 2.00 A.M.

Chet Harper sat in his SUV. He'd been sitting here trying to work up the nerve to get out for five minutes or so.

The streetlights showcased a picture perfect neighborhood. Nice, landscaped lawns. Proud two-story homes. Vehicles tucked into garages for the night. No scattering of cars cluttering the curbs.

In this world all was as it should be.

And it was late. Too late to wake his ex-wife. Too late to see his son. But he needed to see him. To watch him sleep for just one minute and to smell his little boy scent.

Sherry wouldn't understand. She never understood anything about Chet or his work. Why the hell had he ever believed they could make it as a couple? They'd had nothing in common. As a high-powered executive at a research corporation, she'd had no respect for his work. The long hours. The risks.

You could do better, Chet. Your pay sucks.

He stared at the dark house. Nice neighborhood, great school district, well above a mere cop's salary, even with the promotion to detective sergeant.

The house his wife paid for. Not a day had passed without her getting in a dig about his pay and the long hours. Every moment he had resided within those walls he had been reminded that the house was her accomplishment. Not his.

But it had been his home with his son, no matter that the place had been just one more nail in the coffin of his marriage.

Now another man lived there.

The new guy had built a tree house in the backyard. He'd gotten Chet's son a dog when Sherry had refused to allow a dog on the property, much less in the house, when she was married to a measly cop.

Chet opened the driver's door and got out. Somewhere down the street a dog barked. He eased the door closed and moved up the walk. His heart thumped harder with each step.

He shouldn't have come. At the steps leading up to the front door, he hesitated. If he knocked or rang the bell the dog would bark. He didn't want to wake his son. Not for this. His own selfish needs.

Tired, he sat down on the top step.

He'd lost any semblance of a normal life with his son two years ago. Maybe Sherry had been right when she said Chet's life would never be normal as long as he was a cop.

But the life he'd had, he'd cherished.

Waking in the middle of the night and being able to go to his son's room to watch him sleep. Watch him breathe. Waking him in the mornings, his hair all mussed and his eyes still heavy with sleep. Those moments had been precious to Chet. He missed that time with his boy.

The door behind him opened.

Chet shot to his feet and turned, prepared for a clash with the new husband.

'What're you doing out here at this hour?' Sherry, clad in her favorite cotton gown, stood in the open doorway, the springer spaniel at her feet, tail wagging.

For one moment the memories of all the times he'd unbuttoned those tiny pearl buttons and pushed that worn thin white gown down her body held him captive.

How had they lost their way and gone so far down the wrong path?

Didn't matter . . . she had moved on and so had he.

The newer memories of Lori in his arms had his eyes burning again.

Chet held up his hands. 'I'm sorry. I didn't mean to wake you.'

She puffed out a breath. 'You didn't. I have a huge presentation tomorrow and I'm still fine tuning.' She frowned. 'Is something wrong?'

'Tough case.' He shrugged. Might as well tell the truth. 'I just needed to be close to Chester.' He backed down a step. 'It was a bad idea.'

A moment passed.

He was sure she would send him on his way, after telling him what a selfish bastard he was.

'Come on in. I'm pretty sure I won't be getting any sleep tonight anyway.' She stepped back in invitation. 'Might as well share in our misery.'

Startled, Chet cleared his throat to buy time to find his voice. 'What about William?'

'He's in Chicago. He won't be back until tomorrow.' She laughed. 'Today, I mean.'

Grateful she hadn't been in the mood for a scene, Chet crossed the threshold.

'You need coffee? I'm on my second pot.'

Man, she was in a generous mood. He was almost afraid to breathe since one wrong move or word could awaken her I-hate-your-sorry-ass attitude. 'No, thank you. I'd just like to sit with Chester for a few minutes if that's okay. I won't wake him.'

'Sure.' Sherry closed and locked the front door. 'Stay as long as you like.'

So, maybe he was hallucinating. He stared at her a moment just to be sure before turning away.

She stopped him when he started down the hall. 'Chet, are you sure you're okay?'

He managed a nod. 'Just a tough case,' he repeated.

'Understood.'

She headed back to the kitchen and he walked quietly up the stairs. Chester's room was the first on the right. The door was ajar. He didn't like it to be closed all the way. The kid was still afraid of the dark.

Chet eased the door open and entered his son's world of Shrek and Spiderman. A nightlight glowed, providing just enough illumination to chase away the unknown lurking in the darkness. Chet stood at his son's bedside for a long time, watching him breathe, his dark hair sticking up from the tossing and turning he'd obviously done before surrendering to sleep. Chet wouldn't smooth his hair for fear of waking him. Chester was about ready for a trip to the barber shop and his first real haircut, not the little trims his mother gave him. Chet would take him where his father had taken him as a boy.

He wanted everything for his son. Not mountains of toys and gadgets, but happiness and a safe home. He had learned the past two years that those two things were all that really mattered.

But there were so many evil bastards out there like the one who had taken Lori. Was there such a thing as a safe life anymore? Could he possibly hope to protect his son?

He sure as hell hadn't protected Lori.

Like she would have allowed him to protect her. Chet smiled at that, his lips quivering in spite of his best efforts to be strong. Lori would kick him in the ass and tell him she could protect herself. All she needed was a little back-up.

His jaw clenched, he would find a way to give her that back-up.

Hang on, baby.

He moved quietly to the rocking chair in the corner. The same one they had used to rock Chester when he was a baby. Eventually it would have to go. The older the boy got the more independent he became.

The natural course of life.

Chet lowered into the rocker. His body – his soul – was so damned tired.

And he was terrified.

He knew plenty about this Player . . . this Eric Spears. But it hadn't felt so damned real until he had seen the Howard woman sprawled on that bed, abused and defeated and far too close to death.

He'd seen victims in worse shape. The visible damage done to her was not so devastating in the scheme of things. And dead was dead, no matter the condition of the body. But knowing the man who had done those evil things to Belinda Howard had Lori . . . that was nearly more than Chet could bear.

As much as she fought getting involved with him, he knew she wanted to be with him. He'd felt it both times they had been together. She had stronger feelings for him than she wanted to admit.

God knew he had strong feelings for her.

He couldn't lose her. He closed his eyes, tried to hold back the tears. What bad ass cop cried like this? He fought harder, his body trembling with the effort. The hot, salty affront came any way.

Then he prayed. He prayed for his son to be protected

from evil . . . and he pleaded for Lori's life. He prayed she would be strong. And that somehow she understood how very much he loved her.

Then he set the rocker in motion and he prayed for the relief sleep would bring.

Chapter Eleven

Lori heard voices.

Wake up!

The fog was so thick she couldn't find her way through it. She needed to swallow. Couldn't. Her mouth felt so dry.

Open your eyes!

Lori moistened her lips. Wished for a drink of water. It was so hot . . . and stuffy. Made it hard to breathe.

Her lids cracked open the tiniest bit. She tried to open her eyes fully but the lids were too heavy to move. Her tongue felt thick . . . fuzzy.

Harsh words echoed around her.

Who was shouting? A man, she decided. But she couldn't make herself care enough to force her eyes open. Why was he shouting?

Why couldn't she wake up?

Images flooded her brain . . . the naked woman . . . blood. Her mother and sister bound and gagged. Her eyes flew open.

Her heart rammed against her ribcage. Warehouse . . . she stretched her right foot in a slow circle . . . chain.

Spears!

Her muscles bunched to push her body up from her face-down position on the grimy concrete floor.

She froze. Listened again to the voice or voices.

One by one she relaxed her muscles and slowed her breathing. She needed to assess the situation before she made Spears aware she had regained consciousness. She didn't dare move until she had a handle on the situation.

'You're always right, aren't you?'

Spears' voice.

Who was he talking to?

'Whatever I do, it's never good enough. Three years I've devoted to you and it's not enough.'

Was he on the phone?

She would need to turn her head and face the other direction to see him . . . and whoever else was there. Not a risk she was willing to take just yet.

Listen, Lori. Calm down. No sudden moves to draw attention. Was someone else here with Spears besides her and the dying woman? Another victim?

She didn't know how long she had been asleep but the woman was probably dead by now. She'd lost too much blood. An ache pierced Lori's chest. She had been helpless to provide any real assistance to the woman.

Get all the static out of your head! Just listen!

'She's not listening!'

Lori's heart stumbled to a near stop. Had she said that out loud? She moistened her lips again. She didn't think so. *Lie still . . . lie perfectly still.*

'What else do you want me to do? Obviously I don't yet have her full attention. But I will soon, you have my word. Yes, yes! This is my mess!'

She had to see who the hell he was talking to. The conversation sounded as if it was about Jess. He'd asked Lori if she thought he had Jess's attention. Holding her breath, she started to move her head . . . one slow fraction at a time until she was facing the opposite direction.

She tensed. He had his back to her.

'You didn't have a better plan,' he argued. 'You're angry because *I* took the lead.'

Whoever he was talking to, Spears was angry, his voice accusing. With his back turned to her, she dared to lift her head and look around. There was no one else . . . the crates and nothing else except the two chairs. Her gaze lit on the chair with the puddles of blood on either side.

Where was the woman?

Lori's heart started to race.

'Yes,' Spears roared. 'I will make it happen.'

Lori dropped her head back to the floor and froze.

He started to pace.

She didn't dare keep her eyes open more than a crack.

'No. I absolutely can do this.'

His hands were all over the place as he spoke. On his hips. Waving around in the air. Everywhere but holding a cell phone to his ear. But there was no one here. Who the hell was he talking to? Was he using a Bluetooth? She squinted to see if there was anything in or around his ear. Not on this side.

He turned to pace back the other way.

Nothing there either. At least nothing that she could see. Was he arguing with himself?

'I know what I have to do and I *will* do it.' He stopped. Exhaled a big breath. 'You see? You're not good enough and he knows it.' He kicked one of the chairs.

Lori jerked as it skidded across the floor.

He seemed to compose himself for a moment. She couldn't be sure about before, but he was definitely talking to himself now.

He calmly removed his suit jacket, folded it neatly and placed it on one of the crates. He braced his hands on his hips and stared at the chair where the woman had been before he sent Lori off to la-la land.

Then he faced her.

She shut her eyes.

Too late! Too late! a voice in her head screamed.

'Ah, someone's awake.' He walked toward her, each step sending her heart rate climbing higher and higher. 'Don't try to fool me, Lori Doodle. I know you're awake.'

She didn't move. Didn't speak. Didn't open her eyes.

He crouched down, denim rubbed against denim. 'Were you listening to my conversation?'

Don't react. Maybe he would think he had imagined her eyes closing.

He fisted his fingers in her hair and jerked her head up. 'I'm speaking to you, detective,' he screamed in her ear.

She ignored him. Didn't even flinch.

He stood, dragging her up with him. Strong fingers clamped down on her bare upper arms and shook her hard. 'Do not ignore me!' he roared.

Like a rag doll, she hung limply in his hold, let her head loll to one side.

He shook her again, harder. 'Pay attention, bitch!'

She kneed him hard in the groin.

His hands dropped away from her as he doubled over.

She kneed him in the head. Knocked him onto the floor. She kicked him in the gut. In the back. 'Mother fucker,' she growled as she kicked him again.

He grabbed her foot and jerked.

Lori lost her balance and hit the concrete floor flat on her back. The air whooshed out of her lungs.

He scrambled to get on top of her. She got a choke-hold on his throat with both hands. Curled her legs up to keep his body weight off hers.

They rolled. The chain rattled. Twisted up in her legs. He banged her head against the floor. She twisted her face to the right, clamped down on his forearm with her teeth.

He screamed and cursed.

She belted him in the jaw, shoved both hands into his chest. He toppled over. She was on top now. Her hands around his throat, she squeezed and pressed with all her strength . . . all her body weight.

He flung her off. Shot to his feet before she could get up. He kicked her in the ribs.

Her stomach seized . . . she lost her breath again. He sat down on top of her, his legs on either side of her waist, pinning her arms to her side. She squirmed. He bore his weight into her middle. Bile rushed into her throat.

She surrendered. Too tired to fight anymore. He was too heavy . . . too strong.

'Why isn't Jess paying attention?' he demanded.

She licked her lips. Tried to catch her breath. She wasn't answering his stupid questions.

'Answer me!' His scream echoed in the massive room.

She managed a pathetic laugh. 'Fuck you.'

He rammed his fingers into her hair and banged her head against the floor. 'Why . . . isn't . . . she . . . paying . . . attention?'

She stared straight into his eyes and repeated, 'Fuck . . . you.'

The back of his hand connected with her jaw. Her head snapped to the left and more pain roared through her skull.

'Answer the question, detective.'

She licked the blood from her lips and said nothing.

He dragged down the straps of her bra. She tensed.

He squeezed her breasts.

Hard as she tried not to react, she felt her eyes widen with the fear of what he might do next.

He smiled, took a deep breath. 'You're making me hard, detective.' As if to back up his words, he ground his pelvis into her.

White hot rage crashed into her brain, obliterating all else. 'Why don't you just go ahead and kill me, you sick bastard?'

He smiled. 'You know I can't do that, detective.' He squeezed his thighs tighter as he leaned forward. His fingers fisted in her hair, he kept her head pressed against the floor. 'If I do, Jess will never come play with me. You're my bait.'

Lori struggled to turn her face away from his.

'I guess I'll just have to send her another message. I think she'll pay attention this time. She certainly has *my* attention.' He pressed his face closer to Lori's. 'She sent me a message, detective. Jess told me to man up. Can you imagine?' He released her hair, held his arms out in question. 'What else does she want me to do to prove myself?'

The woman. Lori glared at him. 'Where's the other woman?'

He smiled. 'She should be dead.' He sighed. 'However, I may have underestimated the ability of her heart to continue beating after losing so very much blood.' He shrugged. 'Bless her *heart*, she just didn't want to die.'

'You're a sick piece of shit.'

'Sticks and stones may break my bones, but your unkind words can't hurt me, Lori Doodle,' he singsonged in a creepy child-like tone.

He inclined his head to the right and studied her a moment, then cocked it the other way. 'I have another question for you, detective.'

She clenched her teeth. She would die before she helped this son of a bitch.

'When the lungs are deprived of oxygen, do you know how long it takes for a woman of your age and physical condition to lose consciousness and subsequently expire?'

Her body tensed, but she refused to allow him to see any other reaction to the threat.

He waited a moment. When she didn't answer, he sighed. 'I suppose not.'

His hand closed over her mouth and nose.

Fear ignited.

'Let's find out.'

Chapter Twelve

BPD, 10.00 A.M.

Dan surveyed the group seated around the conference table in his office. He and Deputy Chief Black had already briefed the mayor. The leaders of the task force waited now for him to continue with what they didn't have.

No hits on the prints. No traceable evidence to anyone at any scene who wasn't supposed to be there.

'Belinda Howard was in no condition to tell us much last night. However, this morning she gave a somewhat sketchy statement to Agent Gant and Chief Black.'

'Did she identify her abductor?' Harper asked.

Like Dan, he wanted to know that answer first and foremost. Whoever had Detective Wells, Spears or not, the investigation needed to be focused on finding the right perpetrator. He felt confident in the conclusion he and Jess had reached last night. This perpetrator was either Spears or someone connected to him.

Dan shook his head in answer to the question. 'She was sedated for most of the time she was being held.' His frustration hitched up another notch. 'At no time did she see Detective Wells or anyone else.' That news had been deeply disappointing. 'The perpetrator approached her from behind at the house on Liberty Park Lane and injected the sedative. She remained unaware of her surroundings for most of the time she was missing. She has no idea where she was held or for how long. I'm sure you're aware that the Ketamine used to sedate her can cause lapses in memory and hallucinations. Frankly, we can't be certain what memories are real and what are imagined.'

'Isn't Ketamine what Spears uses on his victims?' Deputy Chief Hogan asked.

'I'll defer to Agent Gant to answer that one.' After all, this was Gant's briefing, too.

Gant stood. 'Ketamine is the sedative the Player uses on his victims, as do lots of other criminal types. It's not an uncommon drug when incapacitating the victim is the goal. Let me state once again, for the record, gentlemen, we do not believe this is the Player and we have no evidence that Eric Spears is the Player.' He glanced at Dan. 'As far as the drug, unfortunately, it's available from all sorts of sources, including the Internet and on the street. The liquid Ketamine is somewhat more difficult to find, but it's out there.'

Dan opted not to let the man's unnecessary point about Spears annoy him. 'Howard,' he continued, 'was not sexually assaulted. That is another element that sets this perpetrator apart from the Player.' No use leaving an opening for Gant to get in another dig. 'Additionally, none of the Player's known victims have ever survived an encounter with him.'

'Clearly,' Agent Wentworth piped up, 'Agent Harris is wrong again.'

Dan didn't like judging any person by their physical characteristics. But he'd made an exception this time. Being short, bald, middle-aged with generic black glasses and cheap suits gave Wentworth the undeniable look of a quintessential ass-kisser. Dan hadn't liked him when they met yesterday and he liked him even less today.

'Rarely,' Manning hastened to add, 'does a serial killer deviate so widely from his MO.'

Unlike Wentworth, Manning was well groomed and had the sort of physical traits that would make for fed poster boy of the year. Still, he had his head up Gant's ass, too. Manning's loyalty to the team was no different than his to Jess, Dan supposed.

Jess, on the other hand, wasn't speaking to him. Other than good morning, she hadn't said a word since emerging from his guestroom.

That he intended to resolve. As soon as this briefing was over.

The profile the Bureau had come up with was no better or different than the one Jess had spouted off the top of her head last night.

'Agent Gant will provide the details of the profile he believes will assist in our investigation.' Dan sat down and let the man have the floor.

Gant cleared his throat. 'Thank you, Chief Burnett.' He surveyed the faces around the table. 'We believe we are dealing with a copycat who, motivated by recent media attention, has latched onto the Player's MO to the degree possible. He appears to have zeroed in on Jess Harris. The media attention that spilled over from the Player case to BPD's recent investigation into the missing young women that included Harris' involvement may have brought him here. We are still looking into the theory that this unsub is or was related on some level to the Player and has launched his own attempt at the game. His alleged resemblance to Spears cannot be accurately assessed at time. Considering the only element the two victims have in common is a connection to Harris, we feel confident that our profile is as close as can be reached with such limited information. I have provided a more detailed summary for each of you.'

Deputy Chief Hogan gave a quick overview of the ground they had covered in the search and the disappointing results.

When Hogan looked to Dan, he took it from there. 'We will continue our search efforts. We believe, as Agent Gant said, that we are perhaps dealing with a copycat, but we're not ruling out the possibility of Spears' involvement. He will remain a person of interest if for no other reason than his striking resemblance to our perp. We're hoping the media support will continue to make it difficult for the perp to reach out for another victim. The information flow is our strongest asset. Report anything you feel is even remotely unusual or out of place.' Dan pushed back his chair and stood. 'Thank you for your time. Let's get back out there and find Detective Wells.'

As the others filed out, Deputy Chief Black lingered. 'If possible, chief,' Black said, 'I'd like to have a few more minutes of your time.'

'Of course.' Dan closed the door and gestured to the conference table. A new development was more than welcome, though he doubted that was the reason for this private meeting.

'I'm aware that Deputy Chief Harris' credentials are stellar.'

Dan held up a hand to stop the man. 'Harold, I know the situation with the Bureau has been an absolute mess. But I can assure you that Jess is considering all avenues. She is aware that the perp we're looking for may not be Spears or whoever the hell this Player is. She continues to support our investigation, which I don't have to tell you is a true asset. But maintaining a low profile from this point forward is for her own safety.'

The concerns of those in his department were not lost on Dan. With the events of the past twenty-four hours there hadn't been time or opportunity to address those concerns.

Black gave a single nod. 'I'm sure she is doing her very best from a very awkward position. But that's not what I wanted to discuss.'

The frown that furrowed Dan's brow added momentum to the dull headache building behind his eyes. 'What's on your mind then?'

'There are some rumblings in the ranks about your choice of Harris for heading this new unit.'

Damn. Dan had known that particular issue would come up sooner or later. He'd hoped for later. 'This unit was created specifically with her credentials in mind. This was not a promotion opportunity that anyone in the department has missed out on. This unit might not have seen fruition at all had the occasion to bring her aboard not presented itself.'

'I completely understand. But you surely comprehend how that might feel to some who've worked long and hard to reach a certain rank within the department.'

'Are we talking about someone in particular?'

'For example,' he hedged, 'you've asked me to reassign both Sergeant Chet Harper and Lieutenant Valerie Prescott to the new unit. Prescott has twenty years of police work under her belt. I dare say her credentials rival Harris', excluding the degree in psychology.'

'And a dozen years of profiling for the Bureau,' Dan reminded the deputy chief.

Black nodded. 'True. But I sense the potential for resentment and I felt you needed to be aware. With things as they are, you have been somewhat distracted.'

There was no denying that charge. 'Is it your opinion

that Lieutenant Prescott might prefer to remain in your division under the circumstances?'

Dan should have seen this coming.

'May I speak candidly?'

As hard as he tried not to, Dan went on the defensive. 'That is why we're having this closed door conversation.'

'Prescott will do well working with Harris once her initial resentment fades. But the rumblings department-wide will only be exacerbated by any appearance of a personal relationship between yourself and Deputy Chief Harris. I've known you since you were knee-high to a grasshopper, Dan, and I know your decision had nothing to do with anything beyond her credentials but we have to face the facts here. Our detectives aren't privy to the same insights on the matter so they're going to make judgments.'

Dan compressed the ire that stirred. 'So the rumor is that I gave Jess the job because of our history?'

'I'm sorry to say,' he sighed, 'but that is the case for the most part.'

'We were kids, Harold, and that was a long time ago.' Dan would not entertain this nonsense.

'But the talk is that she's staying with you and though I fully understand the motivation for that decision, others obviously do not.'

The ire erupted into full blown fury. 'Deputy Chief Harris is, for all intents and purposes, in my protective custody. If anyone has a problem with that they need to see me personally.'

'As I said,' Black reiterated, 'I get that. But at your level, Dan, appearances carry a great deal of weight. You need to consider your actions closely. I tell you this because we've worked together for many, many years and I have tremendous respect for you.'

Dan knew he was right, but that didn't make him like it. Jess had made the same point. 'I'll deal with that when we've got Wells back and this case is closed.'

'As we all should. In the meantime, I'll do all I can to defuse the rumors. We don't want this to get out of hand and jeopardize your reputations or this case as it goes forward.'

'I appreciate that, Harold.'

They stood simultaneously, both knowing that finding Wells wasn't going to happen with them discussing department gossip.

After Deputy Chief Black had gone, Dan settled behind his desk to plow through the pile of messages that had built the past week.

He needed to check on Andrea.

He needed to find Wells.

At some point, he needed to figure out how to handle the situation with Jess.

11.21 A.M.

'Thank you, Lieutenant Prescott, for taking the time to show me around.' Jess manufactured what she hoped was an appreciative smile. 'I look forward to working with you.'

Prescott was two years older than Jess. An attractive woman with fiery red hair and calm blue eyes. Her personal and professional lives presented with that same contrast. Suzy homemaker meets Dirty Harry. Prescott was married with three children, two in college and one in high school. In her late twenties, she had worked as a beat cop full time, gone to college part time and managed to raise her kids. She'd scaled the ranks in record time. She was one of the best detectives in the department.

She was smart, hardworking and mad as hell that Jess had gotten this position, which would have been a promotion for her and about a half a dozen other detectives in BPD.

That she had happily reported all of this to Jess meant one of two things. She either wanted to be honest and above board in their working relationship or she wanted to make Jess sweat.

Whatever her motive, she had managed to do the latter with hardly any effort.

Jess wasn't naïve enough to believe that this high level opportunity came without a price. She wasn't surprised about that at all. What did surprise her was that the senior detective assigned to her had the brass balls to tell her to her face. For the most part, Jess appreciated and respected her candor.

Prescott extended her hand. 'I look forward to working with you, too, chief.'

Jess accepted the gesture and wished the sentiment that went along with it was sincere.

'I'll contact you when we're ready to have our first staff meeting.'

Prescott gave her a nod and headed for the elevators at the other end of the corridor.

Jess puffed out a breath. 'Fun, fun.'

'Chief Harris.'

Jess turned at the sound of Harper's voice. She had never been so glad to see a friendly face. She'd gotten the *look* from most everyone to whom Prescott had introduced her. The look colleagues reserved for gatecrashers. The one that guaranteed she wouldn't be accepted as one of them in this decade.

Jess grabbed Harper by the arm and ushered him into the main conference room and closed the door. 'Sergeant, please tell me you have some good news.' Something! Anything they could use to find Lori.

'The lab found several things.' He shrugged. 'The usual dirt and dust stuff and,' anticipation sparked in his eyes, 'grease and automotive oil. Well, he didn't exactly say grease and oil, but that's what all the science talk boiled down to.'

Jess hated to burst his bubble but a person could get those same trace elements on their feet just walking down the street. She started to say as much but then she stopped. The abduction scenario played out in her head.

'If he carried her out of the house,' Jess said, replaying the scene more slowly, 'which would have been necessary with her sedated, he would have put her in his vehicle, driven to wherever he's holding his hostages, then carried her or dragged her in.'

'And if he dragged her,' Harper countered, 'the trace evidence would have been contained to one area, not spread fairly evenly over the entire bottom of each foot.'

'Whether she walked around inside the holding

place or not, one time standing squarely on both feet would have done the job.'

'That's my thinking.'

'Grease and oil would be present on the floor of an old mechanic's shop,' she suggested, mentally running the possibilities.

'A used parts supply store,' Harper offered.

'Or a storage warehouse where old cars and parts are kept.' This could definitely narrow down the search. 'We should look into collectors or guys who hoard vehicles and or parts.'

'I've already passed the information along to the chief and the search commanders. We're getting some help from Support Division on tracking down properties that have been used for those purposes in the past as well as those being used presently.'

'Put the ones no longer in use at the top of your priority list.' This unsub would want some level of assurance that he would not be disturbed. Jess would not refer to him as Spears again. Not unless there was evidence. Maintaining her objectivity was essential. She'd lost it for a time. That couldn't happen again. This was a new day and she wanted to start it off right. 'He needs privacy for his work.'

'Yes, ma'am, already done.'

Why couldn't she have gotten another Wells or Harper instead of a Prescott? Jess felt another punch to her gut. She would never have the opportunity to work with Lori again if they didn't find her soon.

Don't go there, Jess. 'Were any additional evidentiary details released in the meeting this morning?'

'Nothing you don't already know.'

Jess glanced at the clock on the wall. Almost noon. She'd spoken to Lily early this morning. Her sister had promised to be on the road to Pensacola by noon. With the briefing over, where the heck was Burnett? Since the briefing only included the top members of the task force, they had used his office.

'Is Burnett still in his office?'

'He was in conversation with Deputy Chief Black when I left the briefing.'

She wished he would hurry. They needed to be out there taking part in the search. What she really needed was a message from this unsub. She'd sent him one of her own. That clip of her telling him to man up had aired a million times. She'd looked a fright. And he hadn't responded. Not a peep. Dammit.

Jess blew out a disgusted breath.

Doubt tried to shoulder its way into her head, nudging at her new-found determination.

As much as she hated to let go of the idea that she was right about Spears, years of training to formulate an unsub's profile, based on his MO and history and backed by extensive research into the faces of evil, warned her that this unsub couldn't be him. Humans were creatures of habit. It wasn't natural to change those habits so abruptly without some major event. And she just didn't see how the debacle in Richmond, particularly since he'd been cleared, had risen to that occasion.

Still, her instincts screamed at her that he was somehow involved.

'I have to get back to the search,' Harper said, tugging her from the troubling thoughts. 'I'll call you immediately when we find her.'

Jess gave him a hopeful smile. 'Please do, sergeant.' *Find her, please.*

Dropping her bag to the floor, Jess blew out another big breath to dispel some of the tension. Didn't work.

She walked over to the case board and studied the timeline and data Deputy Chief Black and Sergeant Harper had posted since Jess had been removed from that duty.

Spears peered back at her from the photo on the board. 'What're you trying to accomplish?' she muttered.

Why didn't he send her a damned message? In addition to her televised challenge, she had sent several texts to the last number Spears used to contact her.

No response.

Fury lashed through her. 'Tell me something, you bastard! Point me in the right direction!'

The door opened and Burnett rushed in.

Judging by the look on his face, the briefing had gone about like Jess's morning. She had no sympathy. Her bad morning was his fault.

As he moved nearer she saw the worry in his eyes and she knew that whatever had happened wasn't about Gant or the briefing.

'What?' she demanded.

'Your sister and her daughter—'

'What happened?' Fear annexed all other thought.

Strong hands settled on her shoulders. 'Jess, they're safe.'

Oh God. Oh God. Oh God. She couldn't breathe . . . couldn't speak. Jess had brought this evil to her family . . . to the people she cared about most.

'They were at the orthodontist's office. Agent Miller was with them.'

'Dammit, Burnett, tell me what happened!'

'He took Agent Miller.'

Chills climbed up Jess's spine. She shook her head. 'From the orthodontist's office? In the middle of a business day?'

He nodded. 'We need to get over there.'

Jess grabbed her bag. Spears or the copycat, maybe both, were growing bolder and bolder, the timeline moving faster and faster. The conversation with Miller kept playing in her head. *I know my way around the violent types*. Jess prayed she did.

She turned to the door and Burnett. The grave face he wore had fear pumping again. 'What is it you're not telling me?' Lily's husband and son had gone to Nashville this morning. Surely they were safe.

'He gave your sister a message for you.'

The thoughts racing in her head slowed as she braced for the worst.

'He said, *Manning up just for you, Jess.*'

Chapter Thirteen

Lorna Road, Hoover, 1.58 P.M.

Dr Strickland's office had been cleared. There were no wounded on the scene. Upon first glance, not one thing appeared out of place. A simple spill in an exam room where an instrument tray had been overturned. The mess could have been made by a clumsy technician or a patient. It happened all the time.

But that wasn't how it happened this morning. The monster taunting Jess had been here and gone.

She stood at the rear entrance of the clinic and retraced the steps the witnesses stated were taken by the intruder. He'd entered the small clinic through the rear. The door was steel with an automatic lock. Whenever the door closed it could only be opened by a key or from the inside. The door was always locked,

Strickland had insisted. But one of the techs had admitted that she propped a small, common rubber stop at the threshold to prevent the door from closing and locking her out while she had a much needed hit of nicotine.

Trouble was, she'd forgotten to remove the small rubber stop when she rushed back in to attend to her waiting patient. She'd been in a hurry since one cigarette had become two while she fought with her boyfriend via her cell. She'd been distracted. She'd made a mistake.

The man, identified as looking exactly like the sandy-blond-haired devil in the photo on Jess's cell that was, in fact, Spears, had waltzed into the clinic without the least bit of fanfare.

It was Spears but not really. How was that for getting nowhere fast?

Jess moved along the corridor from the back door toward the front where another door separated the clinic from the lobby.

He had smiled and said good morning in that charismatic voice of his to the two techs, including the smoker, employed by the orthodontist. He then walked right into the exam room where Alice's braces were being removed and stuck a weapon in Agent Miller's face.

In the exam room, he closed the door, ordered Alice, Lily, Dr Strickland and his assistant down on the floor. After threatening their lives if they moved, he and the agent had exited the room, strolled out the back door – which no one considered odd – and vanished into thin air.

The techs went about their business with their patients, as did the two women working the front desk. When Dr Strickland had gathered his wits he used the cell phone in his pocket to call the police.

Meanwhile, Spears or his twin or whoever, drove away with a federal agent as a hostage. Because Jess had pissed him off with her comment and forced him to feel the need to prove himself.

She had fucked up.

Jess closed her eyes. Whatever he did to Miller would be on her. He could have taken Lily or Alice. This whole damned mess was on her. Maybe Gant was right and she had no business on this case. Next time it could be her sister or her niece . . . or Dan.

Jess shoved the painful thoughts away and focused on the scene and what she knew. She couldn't help anyone unless she did her job.

Lieutenant Prescott and another detective had arrived and were conducting interviews with the doctor and his employees. Agent Manning was doing the same. Wentworth was monitoring the goings-on. Mostly he was watching her, but Jess no longer cared. Two BPD officers were canvassing the neighboring suites and parking lot for anyone who might have seen the man or his vehicle.

There were no exterior security cameras to have captured anyone's entrance or exit. The man, who no one except Jess wanted to call Spears, and the agent had simply vanished.

Burnett and Gant were interviewing Lily and Alice in Strickland's private office. Lily and her daughter had been sequestered there, away from Jess, after much hugging and copious tears.

Jess walked back out the rear door and surveyed the alley. Wide enough for two cars headed in opposite directions to pass each other as long as no one had illegally parked in the alley that was posted for deliveries only. Signs to that effect were displayed on the wall every twenty or so feet the length of the one-story building that housed seven suites.

Trash receptacles sat next to each rear entrance.

Even if Jess had ticked him off, why would Spears or anyone else make such a bold move? There were now no less than ten witnesses who could identify him, six of them at this scene.

If this was Spears, was he planning an escape to some exotic island he'd bought with the fortune he'd made when he wasn't playing killer? Some country where he could spend the next five years torturing and murdering women until someone got too close the way Jess had. Then he'd just move again. Another country. Another realm of prey at his disposal.

He would never stop.

What was he trying to prove? Why had he allowed Belinda Howard to live? Was that an accident or a calculated strategy? What the hell was his point? He'd gone from no witnesses and no evidence to flaunting his mug all over town and leaving evidence of his suddenly sloppy work for anyone to find.

The messages, including the one left at her house in Virginia, left no question as to his ultimate goal. Why not just come and get her? That strategy would certainly save a lot of time and energy. Anyone with the guts to abduct a federal agent in broad daylight wasn't afraid of going straight for his target.

Three victims in thirty hours. Four counting her neighbor in Virginia who was murdered. No one man could accomplish so much, considering the geography involved.

Jess pushed her hair behind her ears. Braced her hands on her hips. Then crossed her arms. There was no question in her mind now. There had to be two, working together. Spears and an accomplice. There simply was no other rational explanation. Particularly considering they had no prints that matched those of Spears unless a match was found here today.

Hinges squeaked, alerting Jess to the door opening. The dental tech who smoked stalked out, paused long enough to light a cigarette then walked across the pavement to the painted cinderblock wall that divided the back of this property from the next. The woman took a couple of long puffs then started to sob.

Jess considered assuring her that the man they encountered this morning would have gotten in one way or another, then she decided against it. If the experience prevented her from making that mistake again, let her carry the guilt for a while. Security was no trivial matter these days.

The door opened again. Burnett motioned her inside.

'Did you learn anything else?' she asked, hoping for something, anything.

He shook his head. 'As soon as Lily's husband and son arrive, they're out of here. They're not even going back to the house for their things.'

Relief stole Jess's equilibrium for a moment. 'Good.' At least she wouldn't have to worry about whoever the hell this was getting to her family now.

Burnett ushered her toward Strickland's office. 'They want to see you.'

That awful trembling started in her limbs again as she moved past the exam rooms. Prescott flashed her a smile from the other end of the corridor where she was still interviewing the receptionist and insurance clerk. The other detective whose name Jess couldn't remember was getting a statement from the second tech. Gant loitered at the door to Strickland's office. He said nothing to Jess as he stepped aside. From the expression on his face, he was as horrified as she was.

Two evidence techs were milling about. It all suddenly seemed surreal. Whether it was plain old exhaustion or stress, Jess felt ready to crumple to the floor. This evil had gotten that close to her sister . . . to her niece. Lori was still out there and now Agent Miller was missing.

As soon as Jess entered the office, Lily pulled her into a group hug with Alice. The tears started anew.

Jess should never have come back here. Just look at what she had done.

Lily drew back, swiped at her eyes with the heels of

her hands. 'You have to go with us, Jess. You can't stay here.'

Before Jess could say anything, Alice tugged at her arm. 'Please, Aunt Jess. You have to listen to Mom.' She shook her head and burst into tears again.

Burnett moved up beside Jess. 'They're right, Jess. This is way out of control.'

Was he out of his mind? She stared at him, wanted to shake the hell out of him. How could he put her in this position? He knew she couldn't go . . . not until this was done.

Grabbing her courage with both hands, she set all those logic-stealing emotions aside and did what she had to do. 'I need to speak to my family alone.'

The statement pricked his pride. She saw it in his eyes. But that was too bad. His undermining carried a barb of its own.

Burnett acquiesced, closing the door behind him. She imagined he was right outside the door listening. Good. Then she wouldn't have to say it twice.

'Let's sit, okay?'

Lily nodded. She dropped into the nearest chair and ushered her daughter into the one next to her. Jess dragged the doctor's chair from behind his cluttered desk and joined them.

'This man,' she got out without swearing, 'who took Agent Miller falls into the category of *most* evil. He has no conscience.' She wanted them to understand she couldn't just walk away from this case. There was too much at stake. Trying to explain the possibility that there were two involved, who bore the same face, would only confuse Lily and Alice and add to their fears. Better to keep it simple. 'He knows right from wrong but he doesn't care. Taking another person's life is inconsequential to him.'

'Is he the worst kind of criminal you've ever tried to stop, Aunt Jess?'

Jess had to think about that one a moment. 'No. He's not the worst.' She had no intention of going into those details with her niece. 'But he's one of the most elusive.'

'Why does he want to hurt the people around you?' Lily asked.

There was no easy way to answer that one. 'I'm not sure. I can only assume he has some sort of fixation on getting back at me for the final case I worked with the Bureau. I'm trying hard to figure that part out.' She let go a deep breath. 'But the truth is, I might never know. If I can stop him, that's all that matters.'

'Why does it have to be you?' Alice wanted to know. Her lips trembled. 'Can't someone else do it? Chief

Burnett said he was going to get him.'

Bless her heart. The braces were only partially removed. Jess wondered if she would ever be able to sit in that chair again for long enough for her orthodontist and his assistant to finish the job.

And damn Burnett for making this harder than it needed to be.

'That's the tricky part.' If Jess explained the gory details that would only scare them more. If she didn't . . . well that wasn't an option. 'If he's intent on getting to me, he might not stop until he makes that happen.'

Tears streamed down Lily's cheeks as Jess spoke. She wished she could reassure her sister but there were no reassurances in this.

'Unless I find him and stop him, he may keep haunting me. If I follow you guys to Pensacola. He might follow me there. I can't take that risk.'

A light rap on the door drew their attention as it opened. Burnett stuck his head in. 'Blake and Blake Junior are here.'

Jess stood. 'I want you guys to get on the road right away. No changing your mind about going back home to pick up your things. It's just not safe.'

Lily pushed out of her chair. 'Alice, you go wait

with your brother and father. I need to talk to Jess a minute.'

Alice gave Jess a hug before hurrying out to the safety of her father's arms. Lily closed the door and turned to her baby sister, as she loved to refer to Jess at moments like this. Jess braced for the older-sister-knows-better talk. Instead, Lily hugged her tight.

They both cried a little more then laughed at each other as they brushed the tears away. Their make-up was a mess.

'I understand that you have to do this,' Lily said finally. She nodded. 'I didn't want to at first, but now I do. I'll be praying for you.'

Jess squeezed her sister's hand, grateful for the support. 'Thanks, Lil.'

Lily hesitated at the door before joining her family. 'You be careful, Jess.'

She nodded. 'I will.'

Lily held her gaze a moment longer. 'When you find this monster, you make sure he can't ever hurt you or anyone else again, you hear me?'

Jess managed a shaky smile. 'That's the plan.'

Another group hug waited in the corridor as Jess said her goodbyes. Two officers were escorting them to Pensacola. Part of Jess wished she could go. Just walk away from the whole situation. But she owed it to Lori to stay and try her hardest. And to Agent Miller.

'You okay?' Burnett asked softly.

Jess shrugged. 'Yeah.' She didn't look at him. She couldn't. Having him hug her or something with Prescott and the others around would only make bad matters worse. Her reputation was in sad enough shape without adding something new to the rumor mill. And if she were completely blunt with herself, maybe she didn't deserve any better. She was single-handedly making as big a mess here as she had last month in Richmond.

'Chief Burnett,' Prescott called from the lobby. 'Agent Gant was called away. He asked that you and Deputy Chief Harris meet him at the Bureau office downtown as soon as possible.'

She glanced at Jess as if that, too, was her fault. Jess supposed it was.

'Give me an update when you finish up here,' Burnett instructed the detective.

'Yes, sir.'

Outside, Jess raised her hand to block the sun from her eyes. She didn't have the wherewithal to dig for her sunglasses.

Two uniforms were keeping the media exiled to a

neighboring parking lot. Even from that distance, questions were shouted at her and Burnett. He ignored them. Jess did the same. She'd already made enough of a mess with her last eloquent statement.

She climbed into the passenger seat of Burnett's SUV and buckled up. The world spun a little so she leaned back and closed her eyes. Spears and/or his accomplice had her cell number. Burnett's, too. Why didn't he contact one of them directly?

Why keep taking other people if it was Jess he wanted?

He said he was waiting for her and yet he failed to show her the way. Was she missing the clues to the damned map here?

'Jess, you really need to think about going to Pensacola with Lily.'

She did not want to have that conversation again. 'He'll just follow me there.' Her sister and her family wouldn't be safe with Jess anywhere near them.

Why didn't Burnett get that?

The fear started clawing at her from somewhere deep inside. Jess fought hard to slow it but that wasn't happening. The idea that this monster had gotten close enough to touch her family shattered some part of her that she desperately needed to be strong.

Burnett kept giving her reasons why she should do the right thing and disappear until this was done. Somewhere, anywhere, he insisted.

She couldn't listen. Her stomach roiled and the overwhelming sensation of needing to vomit slammed her.

'I have to get out.' She sat up straighter. Looked up ahead for a place to pull over. 'I have to get out now, Burnett.' Otherwise the passenger side of his fancy Mercedes was about to be decorated with puke.

'Give me a minute.' He eased over into the right hand lane.

Jess held her hand over her mouth, closed her eyes and fought the dizzying, sickening sensation. Her heart pounded as her chest seemed to close in on itself. She could not let this case get to her like this. She had to stay focused. Objective.

Burnett turned into the parking lot of a strip mall not unlike the one they had just left. As soon as the car stopped, she bailed out.

Deep breaths. She drew in slow, deep breaths. Her belly ached, but the urge to vomit eased. Her heart wouldn't stop pounding. Her chest constricted tighter and tighter. A panic attack. She'd had a couple when she was younger.

Walk it off.

She walked back and forth between Burnett's SUV and the far end of the building. The parking lot was practically deserted. Four of the six shops were for lease and in various stages of disrepair. Reminded her of her life. Falling apart. She was struggling to find her footing again and things just kept tumbling downhill.

The sensations started to fade. She breathed a little easier now. Back and forth. Walk off that adrenalin.

Burnett stayed back. Let her do what she needed to do.

When her respiration and heart rate were normal again, she walked back to where he waited by his SUV. 'Sorry.' She shook her head. 'I haven't had that happen in a long time.'

'This has been a tough few weeks for you.'

She nodded. Didn't trust her voice.

'The good news is your sister and her family will be safe and away from all this insanity.'

'But not Lori . . . or Agent Miller.' Both were her fault.

'We will find them, Jess.'

Another jerky nod. God, she was going to cry. She hated crying.

'And we will get whoever is responsible for this,

whether it's Spears or his accomplice or both. He won't get away this time.'

'I know.' Her voice wobbled.

Burnett stared at her for a moment with those blue eyes that had always seen way too much. She needed to be stronger than this. Showing him this kind of weakness was no way to start off a working relationship.

'Come here.'

He pulled her into his arms and held her close. She wanted to resist. She really did. But she couldn't. She needed to feel his strength. To inhale his familiar scent. To have those reassuring arms around her.

Surrendering, she wrapped her arms around his waist, closed her eyes and just sank into the warmth and strength he offered. He held her that way for a long time. Neither spoke. It wasn't necessary. Just the feel of his arms around her was enough. When her pulse started to flutter for reasons she recognized all too well and understood were absolutely unrelated to this case she knew it was time to step back.

'Thank you.' She gave him a real smile, weak though it might be. 'I needed that.'

He touched her cheek, just the softest, fleeting touch and she melted a little more.

'Let's go see what Gant has to say.'

'I can't wait.'

1000 18th Street, 3.15 P.M.

Gant had fast-tracked their sign-in process so she and Burnett wouldn't have to wait. The receptionist in the main lobby led them to a conference room where Gant, Wentworth and Manning waited.

When they were seated and offered refreshments, Wentworth kicked off the briefing or whatever the hell it was.

'I'd like you to consider these photos taken at your home after the break-in.' Agent Wentworth pushed the file down the table to Jess.

She opened it and stared at the first of several photos. The message, written in blood like the one at the Howard crime scene, disrupted the rhythm of her heart. *Why did you leave me?* She pushed that one aside. The next two showed pictures of Spears literally covering one wall in her office. A close-up of one particular picture showed there were actually two, one of her cropped to match with one of Spears as if they were together.

She passed the folder back across the conference

table. 'Whoever killed my neighbor and broke into my house put those pictures on the wall.'

'Did you have all these photos of Spears in your home?'

'What? No! I've never seen those photos before.' Did Wentworth really think she was that screwed up? 'I have the few photos of the scenes of his most recent victims, his official ID photo from when he was brought in for questioning and the one on my cell but all of that is with me. There were no photos related to him or the Player investigation in my house.' She held up her hands to halt any further debate. 'Whoever did this brought the photos with him.'

'Surely you can understand why we felt compelled to look into the situation.'

'Surely.' She shrugged, feigned a smile at Wentworth. 'Doesn't the Bureau always make it a habit to believe the accusations of sociopaths?'

Wentworth ignored her jab. 'You remain convinced that this is Spears? That he is here in Birmingham stalking you?'

Was this a trick question? Why were they wasting time having this conversation? And why was Gant just sitting there staring at her?

'Whether Spears is here or not, his accomplice or

protégé is. There's no other explanation.' Jess leaned back in her chair and crossed her arms over her chest. 'I don't know why we're arguing the point. We need to be out there trying to find him. Honestly, your concern for the safety of my family and for your missing agent is absolutely underwhelming.'

'That,' Gant came alive and jabbed a finger in her direction, 'is uncalled for. We are concerned about your family's safety and for God's sake you know we're sick about Agent Miller. We have assets in the field just as you do. We want Miller found quickly and alive just as you do your detective.'

Jess threw up her hands again. '*This* is uncalled for. We're sitting around here having these ridiculous and redundant conversations when Spears or someone who looks like him, maybe both, is out there with two victims whose lives are at stake.'

'You really do believe it's him, don't you?' her ex-boss said, his tone resigned now.

'Jesus Christ, Gant, I honestly don't know. But if it's not him, it's someone he's associated with.'

'Eric Spears was cleared of suspicion,' he reminded her as if she could have forgotten. 'Why would he jeopardize his freedom like this?'

He was asking her this? She wasn't going to bother

regaling him with her theories. Instead, she laughed, the sound dry, brittle. 'I can't fathom his ultimate motive just yet. But he's not jeopardizing a whole lot. The man is rich. If his fancy lawyers can't head off trouble, he can take his assets and go to Thailand or wherever. One less member of the big One-Percent Club in our capitalist society.' She took a breath. 'The fact is, no one in this room can say for sure whether this is Spears or not.'

'I think you're going to be interested in watching this feed we just received from Quantico.' Gant picked up the remote on the table and fired up the monitor on the wall.

Jess watched while a local Richmond news anchor hurriedly moved through a minute or two of breaking news.

Suddenly Spears' face appeared on the screen.

Jess felt herself leaning across the table to get a better view. He was being ushered along by two agents Jess recognized, Taylor and Bedford.

'Is this footage from before?' she asked despite the fact that the newscast had today's date in the scroll at the bottom of the screen.

Gant put down the remote. 'It's from today. And, as you can see, it was taken in Richmond shortly before noon. Spears claims his attorney contacted him about the mess going on down here and suggested he make an appearance. That's the reason I can say with complete certainty that the unsub who took Agent Miller is not Spears. However much he resembles Spears, it is assuredly not him.'

Jess looked from him to the screen and back.

'Unless you found documentation he was out of the country as his assistant claimed, where has he been?' Jess charged. 'He could have murdered my neighbor and broken into my house to plant the evidence Wentworth wants to hold against me. And he could have left that message. He may be working in concert with an accomplice here.'

'We can't dismiss that possibility, that's true,' Gant agreed. 'But our most pressing concern at the moment is the unsub who abducted Detective Wells and Agent Miller. And whoever that unsub is, it is not Eric Spears.'

Jess stared at the screen now frozen on Spears' face. Her heart rocked against her sternum as the reality settled deep into her bones.

'When he turned himself in, his prints confirmed he's the real McCoy, Jess,' Gant added, his voice as grim as the expression he wore.

How had her instincts led her so far astray?

'Maybe now we can focus on the real case we have in front of us,' he went on to suggest. 'But, to close this quickly, we're going to need your help, Jess.'

She swung her attention to him fast enough to suffer whiplash.

'You're the only connection we have to this son of a bitch. We need to use that to reel him in.'

Chapter Fourteen

Lori pretended to be asleep.

Spears shuffled across the concrete. His steps sounded unusually heavy. But it was dark so she couldn't see a damned thing.

He'd been gone for what felt like hours.

The injection he'd given her before he left had knocked her out almost immediately. Since she'd come around it felt like a long time before he returned. The heat was getting to her. She needed water. And her body ached. Her face hurt but she had no energy to waste suffering the pain so she ignored it.

Something plunked, like bags of potatoes hitting the floor.

She jerked at the sound.

Don't move.

The more time she had before he realized she was awake the better.

She'd used his absence to search around the dark space for as far as her chain would allow for anything new he might have brought in and forgotten about.

Thankfully she hadn't stumbled over the other woman's body. But he'd said she was still alive. Lori had no idea what he had done with her. She wasn't within Lori's reach and she had called out to her several times with no response.

She tried to remember what she'd read about his victims. Was there a common element about where the bodies were discovered?

Where would they find *her* body?

A shiver stole over Lori's skin.

She'd thought it was over when he put his hand over her face. She'd tried to break free of his hold but all she had done was use up the oxygen in her lungs even faster. When she'd roused after that she had been startled that she was still alive, lying here on her stomach, her cheek pressed to this filthy floor.

Alive was good. Gave her a little more time to figure a way out.

He'd paced the warehouse talking to himself again before he'd injected her.

Even had she not known what she did about his past crimes, she knew for sure by watching and listening to him that he was bat shit crazy.

How the hell did a guy that nuts continue committing the perfect murders, leaving behind no trace of evidence?

Didn't seem reasonable.

If Jess were here she would know what to make of his erratic behavior.

And Harper. Tears welled in Lori's eyes as that last time they'd made love filtered through her fragmented thoughts. He'd shown her the difference between making love and having sex. She wondered if he was taking care of her mother and her sister. They would need him. Lori felt confident that he wouldn't let them down.

She licked at her sore lip. Though she didn't have a mirror, she was pretty sure she had a black eye to go with the busted lip. More of those shuffling noises drew her attention to the side of the warehouse closest to the crates stacked along the wall.

She couldn't be sure how long he'd been gone since he'd sedated her. With no windows, she'd pretty much lost any concept of the time. He'd forced her to drink cans of Ensure. At first she hadn't wanted to cooperate but then she'd realized that the nutrient drink would keep her from growing too weak to fight.

What was he doing? How did he see to do anything in the dark? And why hadn't he killed her yet? Not that she wanted to die . . . but she knew his MO.

A low moan filled the darkness.

Lori's heart started to hammer. She held her breath. Listened.

More of the soft moaning.

She wanted to say something. To get up and find out what was happening. But then he would know she was awake and the element of surprise would be lost.

What was that sound? The woman? Was she still here after all?

Another sound grated against her senses.

Grinding?

No . . . sawing.

It went on and on and on.

The moaning grew louder. Spears was muttering to himself again.

Lori tried to make sense of his words. Something hit the floor next to her. She jumped. Reminded herself to stay still. She didn't dare reach out to touch whatever had hit the floor.

That flop of something soft hitting the concrete

echoed again. The moaning grew louder, more urgent and that other sound . . . the sawing or grinding filled the darkness, intensifying and somehow growing more rhythmic.

She put her hands over her ears and tried to block the noises. Her mind kept putting pictures with the sounds and she didn't want to see.

The tang of blood weighted the humid air.

God, make it stop!

'Stupid bitch.'

Lori jerked at the words but he wasn't near her . . . he was still on the other side of the room. He was moving around.

Light filled the space, the old fluorescent tubes flickering with the sudden surge of electricity.

She blinked to focus.

A scream echoed around her.

Lori sucked in a breath. Her brain ranted at her not to scream again.

Had she been the one screaming?

She wasn't sure.

Her attention was fastened on the woman lying on the floor by the crates.

She was naked like before. Duct tape sealed her mouth . . . blood was everywhere. Her body convulsed and jerked like a fish tossed onto the bank. Her dark hair stuck this way and that where it had come loose from the pins she'd used to bundle it against the back of her head. Her feet . . . lay on the floor . . . oh God . . . they were no longer attached to her legs. The woman shuddered and quivered . . . her hands were missing, too.

No . . . Lori shook her head. This had to be a bad dream.

Unable to take her eyes off the woman's juddering body . . . Lori felt the warmth of urine spread beneath her pelvis. Bile burned her throat.

Not the woman from before. This was a different woman . . . another victim.

Oh God . . . *no*.

Spears walked over to the woman, kicked a foot across the concrete. 'You shouldn't have tried to run away. You made me angry and look what happened. This is your fault.'

His hands were bloody . . . something hung from his right one.

A hacksaw?

No!

He turned to Lori.

She froze.

She hadn't said that out loud, had she? Blood was splattered over his shirt and the front of his jeans. Bright red drops slid down his lean jaw as he glared at Lori.

'You see what she made me do?' He shook his head then held up the saw. 'Bone saw. I borrowed it.' He stared at the bloody saw. 'He won't mind.'

He tossed the saw aside and walked closer to the woman. She flopped around as if she were trying to get away. Blood gushed with each movement . . . or maybe it was the beating of her heart.

Agony swelled inside Lori. Tears spilled from her eyes. *Please, someone, help us.* Someone had to come soon or it would be too late.

Unless Lori sucked it up and did more than just lie here. Rage flooded her trembling body. She flattened her hands on the concrete and braced to propel herself upward.

Spears turned to her.

Lori froze.

He swaggered over to where she lay and crouched down. 'Do you know what you call a fed with no hands and no feet?'

Lori held very still. She kept her gaze away from his. *Sick mother fucker.*

'Look at me when I'm speaking to you, detective!'

Lori shifted her attention to him. The urge to tear off his head stormed inside her.

'Do you know what you call a fed with no hands and no feet?'

'No.' Her body shook with the effort of lying still.

He smiled. 'Done.' He glanced at the woman. 'See, she's hardly moving now. Barely breathing. No one can save her now.' He laughed. 'Even if a skilled surgeon had his hands on her right this second, the blood loss and shock would be too much.'

Lori positioned her feet first, toes down, heels up. While he stared, mesmerized by the dying woman, she eased her hands into place flat on the floor beneath her shoulders.

He turned to her. 'I think this might finally get Jess's attention.' He leaned a little closer. 'I could have taken her sister or that sweet little niece of hers, but I didn't. I knew that would make her too emotional. I don't want that kind of emotion getting in the way.' He laughed. 'Just the fear. Let her stew over what I could have done. Who's the man now?' He laughed again. 'I love it.'

He glanced back at the woman. 'Looks like she's down for the count.'

Lori sprang at him.

The chain rattled.

She knocked him over.

He tried to get a grip on her neck. She grabbed him by the hair and banged his head against the floor. He manacled her arms.

She rolled away from him, scooted away on her belly. Ignored the blood. Weapon! She needed a weapon. The saw was in her peripheral vision, she reached out for it.

He was climbing on top of her.

Reach! Lori! Get it!

Her fingers wrapped around the bloody handle.

He flipped her over.

She swung the saw, blade side out, aiming for his neck. He caught her by the forearm, stopping the blow.

'Women never learn,' he mocked. 'Stupid bitches.'

He ripped the saw out of her hand and threw it across the room.

She clawed at his face with her free hand. He banged her upper body against the concrete over and over. Then he let go.

Before Lori could shake off the spinning in her head, he was off her and walking away.

She rolled weakly onto her stomach and tried to push up on all fours.

Her hands slipped and she went down.

Blood was everywhere. Her stomach heaved, sending more bitter bile into her throat. She strained upward, her arms shaking as she got onto all fours.

'Where do you think you're going?'

Before she could react, he stuck something to her back.

Fire rushed through her body.

Taser.

She collapsed to the floor, her body jerking from the jolt of electricity.

He leaned down and glared at her. 'I know what you need, Lori Doodle. I almost forgot this part. You're gonna love it.'

He walked away.

Lori tried to move. Couldn't. She couldn't scream . . . not that it mattered. No one would hear her.

Seconds or minutes passed, she wasn't sure which. The jerking and quivering slowed but still her limbs would not obey her brain's commands.

He was coming back.

She tried to turn her head . . . couldn't yet.

A squeaking sound accompanied his steps. Something rolled up next to her head. She moved her eyes as far to the right as possible to see.

A big bucket on wheels.

Mop bucket. Industrial size.

He grabbed her by the hair and jerked her up to her knees. Her arms wouldn't work . . . wouldn't fight him.

'Take a deep breath, Lori Doodle.'

Terror flooded her heart.

Face first, he shoved her head into the bucket of water.

Chapter Fifteen

Dunbrooke Drive, 10.00 P.M.

Dan scrubbed the towel over his body, soaking up the water on his skin.

The hot shower had felt damned good against his tense muscles. But nothing he did relieved the helpless feeling that they were getting nowhere on this investigation.

Detective Wells had been missing since 7.30 Monday morning. Two more women had gone missing in the thirty-eight hours since. This bastard was moving at warp speed. Though Belinda Howard had survived the encounter and was improving, there had been no word about Wells. No threats, nothing. The same for Agent Miller.

Jess was pretending to be strong but Dan sensed she

was falling apart inside. Eric Spears had turned himself in before noon today, about the same time Agent Miller had gone missing. Abducted by a man who looked like Spears and who appeared to be manipulating the same sort of game used by the Player, who Jess remained convinced was, in fact, Spears – but the Bureau remained equally convinced he was not. The only good to come of this day was the confirmation that Lily and her family had made it safely to Pensacola.

Dan rubbed his hair until it was dry enough, then he dragged on a tee-shirt and jeans. Unless there was a Christmas gift around here some place he'd forgotten, he didn't own a pair of pajamas and walking around the house in his boxers with Jess here was out of the question. More for his peace of mind than for any awkwardness she might feel.

Knowing her, she would make a face and toss some snarky comment at him. She was far too distracted by this puzzling and emotionally wrenching case to care what he walked around in, he suspected.

Dan picked up his clothes and damp towel and headed for the mudroom. Jess had taken a shower already and changed into jeans and a tee. He liked that more comfortable side of her though he doubted she let anyone see her like that often. Nearly an hour after her own shower, she was right where he'd left her. At the dining room table poring over her case file on the Player. Comparing notes with what little they had in this one, just like she'd done last night. And rubbing at that damned ring, turning it round and round.

After he'd tossed the laundry into the hamper he grabbed two beers from the fridge and joined her. Pepsi wouldn't do the trick tonight and he didn't have any wine chilled.

He sat a beer in front of her. 'It might help you relax.'

She glanced up, seeming surprised that he had entered the room. 'Do I look like I want to relax? I'm missing something here and I have to find it.'

A smile tugged at the corners of his mouth. He couldn't resist. She actually looked soft and tousled and way too vulnerable. She'd pinned her hair haphazardly atop her head. Her glasses were a little smudged and there was a tiny speck of chocolate on that lush bottom lip of hers. She carried a stash of M&Ms and chocolate mints in her bag.

He supposed it was true. Women turned to chocolate far more often than alcohol when stressed.

Her expression darkened. 'Why are you smiling? There is absolutely nothing to smile about.'

'Lily and her family made it to Pensacola safely.

Belinda Howard is greatly improved. Both are under police protection. We haven't won this war but we haven't lost either.' Damn. He needed this moment of optimism. He needed to believe Wells and Miller would be found alive. 'Isn't that something to smile about?'

Jess laid her pencil down. 'Detective Wells has been missing for nearly forty hours. The chances she will be found alive considering the kind of twisted member of the species who took her, are about zero – particularly since I don't know who the hell he is. He's apparently pissed at me for giving him that shout-out and we have no idea how that will play into his next move. We have no leads . . . we can do nothing but react to whatever he does next. There is nothing to smile about.'

'I think he's growing more careless with every hour that passes and somehow his actions have caused the real Eric Spears to surface,' Dan proposed. 'That's what I think.'

She shook her head, disgusted. 'He's taunting me. He could have taken Alice or Lily as easily as he did Agent Miller. He wants me to sweat. He hasn't made an attempt to get to me but I believe that's the finale he's building up to. He believes if he makes me desperate enough I'll comply. Who else but Spears would have it in for me like that? If it's not him, what's the motive?'

'If he does come after you,' Dan warned, 'it'll be the last thing he does.'

She faked a smile. 'That's sweet of you, Burnett, and I do appreciate your concern. But if he makes a move against me, you won't have to protect me. I'll protect myself.'

'Let's just hope we don't have to find out who does what.'

She propped her elbows on the table and rested her head in her hands. 'Honestly, I'm ready for him to make a direct move. The longer this drags out, the more likely someone will end up dead. Belinda Howard was lucky. Lori and Agent Miller may not be so fortunate. There just doesn't seem to be any rhyme or reason to his methods. No logic or pattern other than the fact that two of his three victims are law enforcement and all three are somehow, however vaguely, connected to me.'

The pain on her face told him just how deeply she meant those words. She would trade herself right now if Wells and Miller were released. That Gant wanted to capitalize on that infuriated him.

The search teams continued to come up empty-handed. Harper was personally following up on each location that was or had been used to house motorized vehicles of any kind or vehicle parts considering the trace evidence he'd found on Howard's feet.

And still they had nothing.

The Bureau had nothing except the fact that the Eric Spears they had held as a person of interest in the Player investigation in Virginia last month had turned himself in to the local authorities in Richmond. Four hours later those same authorities had no choice but to release him.

Gant had put Spears under surveillance for his own protection. At least that was what he'd told Spears. If Dan had his guess, he'd also told the guy that the surveillance might be best until the suspicions related to Jess were cleared up. The idea burned but, in reality, he understood Gant had a protocol to follow. Once in a while a damned good cop went off the deep end and committed far worse atrocities than tacking up photos on a wall.

As long as the Bureau kept an eye on Spears, Dan didn't care what they told him.

Jess shuffled her photos and reports back into the dog-eared folder she'd been wagging around for God knows how long. She'd made a lot of notes on her pad.

Everyone else had moved into the twenty-first century with their note taking, using their smart phones or electronic tablets, but not Jess. She still carried her trusty pencil and paper in that big old bag of hers.

'What are you smiling about now?'

Dan figured she was far more annoyed with his intrusion than with the fact he was determined to find some bright spot in this mess. 'You've made a lot of notes. Care to share?' He took a swig from his beer.

Visibly skeptical of his motive, she picked up her pad and reviewed the notes. 'Like we talked about last night, there are only two ways that our unsub can bear such a striking resemblance to Spears.' Her brow puckered with frustration as she studied more of her notes. 'One would be a blood relative. But we turned Spears' background upside down. He has no living family. If he had a sibling, twin or otherwise, that sibling's birth was never documented in connection with his family.'

He was fairly certain she wasn't waiting for a response from him. More likely she was analyzing.

'But let's reach . . . assume there was a sealed adoption or something, it's possible a brother could look so similar. Like Lily and me. But why didn't we find something?'

Babies were born even today who ended up being sold or given away with no legal documentation so that was certainly possible. 'What about option two?' Dan queried as he propped against the table.

'Option two is the one I find more complicated and requiring a broader stretch of the imagination. Our copycat may be or have been an apprentice for the real Spears. Last month as we closed in on Spears, the anonymous source who baited me with the potential discovery of evidence is a perfect candidate. During his apprenticeship he may have altered his appearance with hair color, colored contacts and even plastic surgery to become like Spears. These steps may or may not have been at Spears' bidding. Whatever the reason, anyone who would go that far would be a very unwell individual.'

'I think that's what we're dealing with.' Dan couldn't reconcile what he knew about motive with what had taken place today. 'This Spears copycat burst into a clinic full of people and kidnapped a federal agent at gunpoint. That kind of move wouldn't be so difficult to label if it was about the usual – money or revenge – but, as far as we know, it isn't about either of those. It's about a fixation on you. Getting your attention or setting the stage for a bigger strike related to you.'

Jess chewed on her lower lip and considered his conclusion. 'An individual who would go to such extreme measures would have to worship the real Spears. He wants to be him or to bask in his favor. Or maybe he wants his life. His reverence may have turned to envy and Spears may have shut him out, igniting this frenzy.'

'Where does that put you in the scenario?'

Her shoulders heaved then sagged. 'I don't know. Logically I would assume that I became a target of one or both after the events in Richmond. The real Spears, the one I interviewed in that investigation, may have made statements that prompted his apprentice to seek me out as a way to gain his mentor's favor. Then again, if our unsub's motive is envy, he may simply be doing this because he realized how intrigued Spears was with me and he wants to prove something.'

She seemed to consider the idea for a moment before sharing her next thought. 'Whatever the motive, I'm not the only one feeling desperate. This guy is feeling the pressure, too. That could explain his haphazard work.'

The way she stated the facts as she saw them scared the hell out of him. 'You make this sound so matter of fact.' He didn't mean to allow anger to slip into his voice. He wasn't angry with her, just the potential he heard in her voice for putting herself more at risk. 'It isn't, Jess. This is your life and the lives of at least two other people we're talking about. Both of these men are clearly insane. They may see this as a game, but it's not.'

She threw down her pencil. 'If I can't set my emotions aside for the part of this case that impacts me personally, how do you expect me to do so when looking at Lori's situation or Miller's? Don't make this different just because it's me. The facts and theories have to be explored with at least some level of objectivity. Jesus.' She snatched up her pencil and focused on her notes, a warning that she was through debating the issue.

'I need another beer.'

Leaving the unopened one he'd offered her on the table, he pushed away from the table. If he didn't walk away he would only say too much. This time last night she wasn't speaking to him. He didn't want to go there again. They'd spent the better part of the past twenty years doing that.

When he closed the fridge door Jess was standing there staring at him, hands on hips and glasses pushed up into her hair. The image of her, barefoot and glaring at him, was so familiar it took his breath. All those years together . . . fighting like wildcats and making love as if there were no tomorrow.

'We need to talk about how you see me in the field.'

As much as he might assuredly need another cold one for this, he would be smart to keep a clear head. He set the beer on the counter. 'Okay. Talk.'

Sitting down wouldn't make it any easier.

'You asked me to take the position of deputy chief over a unit that will investigate major crimes, maybe even cases like this one, and yet you persist in treating me like a helpless civilian,' she charged. 'Worse, like a helpless woman.'

Okay, maybe he did. 'I'm trying, Jess,' he admitted. 'It's just a different role for me where you're concerned.' He held up his hands when she would have lit into him again. 'My brain knows that you are as capable as I am when it comes to the job. Maybe more capable. But here,' he flattened his palm on his chest, 'I just haven't been able to get that yet.'

The truth was out. So shoot him. He still had feelings for her, strong feelings. Anything that would hang on this long had to be real.

She looked stunned or horrified or maybe both.

'You wanted the truth, right? Or did you want me to tell you something that feels less awkward?' He couldn't ignore this any longer and tiptoeing around the idea wasn't working for him.

'They're all watching us, Burnett. Every sergeant and lieutenant and damned deputy chief in Birmingham PD is watching and waiting to see if you gave me this job to keep me here for personal reasons.'

He couldn't tell if she was worried, hurt or angry. But he was angry.

'I wanted you to stay.' He held up his hands in surrender. 'I wanted it and still do more than I've wanted anything in a long time. *But*, I offered you the position because you're more than qualified and we need you. End of story.' He held up his hands in surrender. 'Wait, you probably can't accept my word on that since you don't trust me anymore.'

She crossed her arms over her chest, signaling she was ready for battle. 'You want to talk about trust? Here's a perfect example. You want me to stay more than you've wanted anything since when exactly? Since you married Annette Denton? Or,' she shrugged "I can't remember the names of your other two wives. Or maybe since the last time that reporter brought take-out to your door and you wanted her.'

'You expect me to feel guilty because I tried to move on with my life and failed three times or because I have needs? What does that have to do with trust?'

'No! I want you to feel guilty because you walked out on us twenty years ago and now you have the audacity to pretend you are so here for me. *That* was about trust and you broke mine.'

He looked away, tried to slow the emotions churning inside him before meeting her expectant gaze. 'Are we never going to get past the past?' *Bring it down a decibel.* Shouting was not the adult thing to do and they were both adults now. 'I thought we talked about this already. Last week, remember? How many times are we going to do this? We can't just go from here?' Christ, she was like a dog with a bone.

'As soon as you drag yourself out of denial,' she charged, 'we can move on. What do you say, *Dan*, are you up to the challenge?'

'What denial?' he snapped. 'I told you why I came back home after college. We had different visions of how we wanted to spend our lives. I just didn't realize it in the beginning. You wanted free of family entanglements. You wanted to live half a country away. I didn't!'

She nodded. 'Oh yeah. I almost forgot that part. You needed to be close to your parents. Bullshit!'

Take a breath. He stared at his feet, anywhere but at her while he grappled for control yet again. 'Look, this isn't accomplishing anything.' Dan ran a hand over his face. 'We should take a break.'

'Why? So you can find a distraction from the truth?'

Fury expanded in his chest. 'I told you the truth.'

'Admit it, you have commitment issues. We were planning our wedding, what kind of house we'd buy for Christ's sakes, and you bailed. You came running back home. Made your career and subsequently bailed out of three marriages! That's a pattern, Dan! You cannot do the forever thing. You just can't. And I'm not going to live in this whole storybook fantasy you've created about us. There is no us! There hasn't been an us since you walked out and left me to build my future alone.'

Her words hit their mark. He couldn't respond to that . . . he wasn't sure which hurt the most, the idea that he had wounded her that badly or that she refused to forgive him.

She snatched off her glasses, tossed them on the counter and rubbed at her temples. 'I'm in crisis right now, Burnett. I blew that case in Richmond. Four months before that my divorce papers came in the mail – for a marriage that was as wrong and screwed up as any one of yours. And now the ghost of that goddamned case has followed me here. I'm scared to death every decision I make is the wrong one.' She turned her hands up in frustration. 'Lives are depending on me to be smart and strong and perceptive. And I don't even know who *I* am anymore!'

He took her face in his hands. She tried to pull away but he held on. He needed her to look him in the eye.

'You're right.' He had some trouble of his own holding her gaze then. 'About all of it. I couldn't do it. You were so strong and independent and ambitious and I was afraid.'

'That's crazy.' Her lips trembled. 'Afraid of what?'

His gut clenched, but he wasn't stopping there.

'Afraid of you, Jess. Afraid you would always outshine me. That I would never be good enough or strong enough. I was just plain scared. I was twenty-two and stupid. So I came home and I grew up. I tried to pretend that we were just kids back then and had different visions. I worked hard at moving on. Yeah, okay, my marriages did end because I had commitment issues. I had commitment issues *to you*. My marriages died swift and certain deaths because no one could live up to my memories of you, Jess. No one.'

For a long time they just stood there . . . looking into each other's eyes with the weight of twenty years slowly lifting – as least for him. He'd said it. The truth he hadn't wanted to admit even to himself. She'd helped him understand and he desperately and selfishly wanted her to understand, too.

'Well,' her lips trembled into a smile, 'that was certainly a mouthful.'

He nodded. Relief rushing through him. 'I'm sorry, Jess. I made a mistake and I've regretted it ever since.'

By now they would have had that house they'd dreamed of . . . kids . . . and he screwed it all up.

She reached for him, caressed his jaw. 'You are and always have been a good, strong man. We were young.' She shrugged. 'Women do mature faster than men and you—'

He hushed her with his lips. She tasted hot and sweet, like chocolate. She tensed at first but didn't resist. Her arms went around his neck and he took that as a sign. His hands went to her bottom, and he pulled her against him. She made a soft sound that confirmed he'd gotten it right. He picked her up, settled her on the counter, and then moved between her legs without breaking the fiery connection of their mouths.

When catching a breath became necessary, he drew back, reveled in the look of her just kissed, all flushed and breathless. He showered more kisses on her cheeks, her nose, along the line of her delicate jaw and down the slender length of her neck.

Her fingers roved over his back, along his sides and up and over his chest, as if she needed to learn him again.

'Jess,' he murmured against her ear, 'I want—'

Her phone made that sound that signaled she had received a new text message.

She stiffened. 'I should check that.' As much as he wanted to say she could check it later, that wasn't an option. He set her onto her feet and she hurried to the dining room. He moved a bit more slowly in an effort to get his body back under control.

Jess made a small sound. She turned to face him and the fear in her eyes had him rushing to her side. He took the phone from her and read the message.

Riverchase Drive A Fed EX delivery just for you.

Chapter Sixteen

Riverchase Drive, Wednesday, July 21st, 12.01 A.M.

The scene was one straight out of a grotesque horror film.

Agent Nora Miller's nude body was draped over a FedEx self-service drop box. Her hands and feet had been severed from her body.

Jess prayed she had been sedated during the execution of that shocking mutilation. If the killer had been the Player she would have been wide awake during each excruciating moment, with only enough Ketamine to heighten the experience. But this might not be the Player. Jess had no choice but to consider that cold, hard fact. That Belinda Howard had very little memory of the wounds inflicted on her body gave Jess hope that Miller had perhaps been spared some amount of the agony.

Agony that Jess had goaded this monster into employing. She had pushed his buttons and this was the result. He had been enraged . . . determined to make a point. The ache that twisted through her tugged at her ability to remain upright. Dear God, look what she had caused. Jess squeezed her eyes shut. She'd made a mistake. A terrible, terrible mistake.

Remorse jolted her. She sucked in a ragged breath.

That's right, Jess. You did this. Are you going to stand here and feel sorry for yourself or are you going to do something about it?

Lips trembling with the effort to restrain a scream of frustration, she forced her eyes open. Deep breath. She cleared her mind and did what she knew best. Studying the body's positioning in hopes of determining if there were any other messages left by the killer was difficult in this environment. Moving the body before the evidence techs had arrived and done their work wasn't an option.

Jess replayed the one conversation she'd had with the agent. Miller had insisted she had the situation under control, that she had the necessary experience.

No one could have been prepared for *this*.

'I'm sorry,' Jess murmured. Then she turned away. Inside Jess the tiniest thread of hope held on that maybe Lori was still alive and that he was saving her for some sick, twisted reason.

She scanned the street, wondered if the monster was out there somewhere watching. Birmingham PD had blocked Riverchase at a sufficient distance in either direction to keep the media and curiosity seekers at bay. Agent Manning, since he knew Miller's family, was making that painful visit. The crime scene unit was en route. It was the middle of the night so there were no potential witnesses to canvass. The brick wall and tree line blocked the view of the crime scene from the nearest neighboring office building. There were several businesses along this stretch of Riverchase Drive, but none that operated at night.

The unsub had little to worry about in terms of being seen, not that the presence of witnesses had stopped him so far. All he'd had to do here was drive up, position the body and drive away. If not for the text, Miller's body would not have been discovered before morning. The sooner the necessary evidence collection and photos were taken, the sooner the mangled body could be taken away. When the techs arrived Jess would see that a trace sheet was draped over Miller's body.

The anguish tried again to consume her. Jess gritted her teeth, shoved it back. She had to be stronger than this. She could not let this sociopath win.

Jess looked away. But there was no peace to be found. Gant and Burnett were headed her way. She steeled herself for the accusations she would see in their eyes. Her actions had prompted this horror.

Stop, Jess. Just stop. It's done.

As her boss and her former boss neared, her beleaguered attention focused on the contrast between the two men. Gant looked as haggard as she felt in his travel-weary suit. Burnett, on the other hand, though equally exhausted, looked strong and determined in his jeans and BPD tee-shirt. Jess almost smiled as she remembered the nineteen-year-old version of him.

What in the world had happened to them? Why hadn't they done more to work things out all those years ago? Young, foolish. Now look at them. Work – these kinds of nightmares – was their lives. Neither of them knew how to have a normal relationship. How had they gotten to this place?

Gant abruptly stopped and turned back to shout at one of his colleagues, 'Get a trace sheet over here and cover her up, for God's sake.' He muttered a few choice expletives as he took the final steps to reach

Jess. Wentworth, she noticed, was conspicuously missing.

This was the side of Gant she knew best. The familiarity had emotion stinging her eyes. She had worked with him for a lot of years. Under normal circumstances, he was fiercely loyal. Under all circumstances he was damned good at his job.

The Spears case had destroyed their working relationship. Jess was nearly certain that Spears himself was the one to set her up, with the investigation and with the bizarre evidence found at her home. The only questions were for what purpose and what connection did that move have to do with this – if any?

More importantly, what did she have to do to stop it?

'The crime scene unit is almost here,' Burnett said to her.

Jess nodded. Didn't meet his gaze. If she'd listened to him and kept her mouth shut, maybe this wouldn't have happened.

'Chief Burnett told me about the solid profile you'd developed on a possible apprentice.'

She cleared her head and her throat of emotions. 'It may be the same unsub who led me on a wild goose chase last month in Richmond. If I'm correct, that would confirm your conclusion that this is the work of a copycat.'

Might as well give credit where credit was due. She had been wrong about a lot. Mainly because she had desperately wanted to believe this was Spears. Burnett should have listened to her when she suggested he delay announcing the job offer. If this didn't make him regret his decision . . . she didn't know what would.

'I think we may be on the right track,' Gant agreed.

Jess squared her shoulders and said the rest of what needed to be said, 'I antagonized the unsub with that comment to the reporter. This,' she gestured to the poor woman behind her, 'is the result. Whatever aspects of this case I was right about, doesn't justify my irrational behavior.' She deserved the OPR investigation. She'd operated on emotion rather than her training.

Burnett shook his head and started to speak, but Gant jumped ahead of him, 'You're wrong, Harris.' His gaze rested on the body of his fallen colleague for a few moments. 'This is my responsibility. I was so convinced that you had,' he shrugged, 'I don't know, had a breakdown of some sort. To that end, I latched onto Spears' allegation.' He shook his head. 'It was easier to let you take the fall than to see how badly we'd all screwed up. Bottom line, I failed to warn all involved in this investigation of the possible true danger. Agent Miller was not properly prepared and that, Deputy Chief Harris, is on me.'

Gant fell silent as Miller's body was covered. Down the street the officers holding back any traffic that might be out at this hour, allowed the crime scene folks and the coroner through.

'There's been another development,' Burnett said, breaking the silence.

Jess's heart stumbled. 'What new development?'

'Just before you called,' Gant said as if he dreaded passing along even worse news, 'I had a call from Agent Bedford.' Gant heaved a big breath. 'Agent Taylor is dead.'

'What happened?' Jess and Taylor had gone to the academy together. Could this night suck any worse?

'He had surveillance detail on Spears,' Gant explained. 'Once again, he was not adequately prepared for the true danger. We were so damned busy tiptoeing around the legal ramifications of accusing Spears again . . .' He shook his head, visibly overcome.

Her own regret wouldn't allow any feelings of triumph for Jess. 'Spears killed him?'

'I can't see any other explanation. Bedford says there was no sign of a struggle. Taylor was in his car. The unsub walked right up to his window, reached in and cut his throat. And Spears has disappeared.'

'This happened when?' A terrifying scenario started to form.

'Taylor's body was found less than an hour ago.' Gant's expression was grim with defeat. 'Spears' private jet departed Finagin Airfield at midnight.'

Could the two, Spears and his apprentice, have plotted a double homicide, one here and one in Virginia, as some sort of lead in to the finale? To distract and confuse?

'It appears,' Gant admitted, 'you were right about Spears, too. At least in part. We may never find any evidence to prove he murdered Taylor, but I know it was him. It had to be.'

Jess felt some amount of relief at the confirmation that she wasn't completely irrational, but it failed to assuage the immense regret she felt for the senseless murder of a colleague and friend. 'I believe Spears is either in control of what's going on down here or attempting to gain control. He would never have put himself at risk by killing a federal agent assigned to his own surveillance unless he felt the step was unavoidable.'

Before Gant could comment, Jess tacked on, 'He

didn't have to. We had nothing on him. He was in the clear. As intelligent and careful as he usually is, something had to have seriously pissed him off and he's feeling some measure of desperation.'

Was Spears upset that his protégé was down here screwing up his reputation or was it because the sloppy student had made such a mess and still hadn't gotten Jess where Spears wanted her?

'I am inclined to agree with you.' Gant shook his head in disgust.

Burnett reached for his cell, checked the screen and said, 'Excuse me,' before stepping away

'I'd like to continue assessing the scene,' she said to Gant. She glanced at Burnett's retreating back and wondered what that look on his face had been about. Not more bad news, she hoped.

Worry roiled in her stomach. *Please don't let it be about Lori.*

'Take as much time as you need,' Gant said, drawing her attention back to him. He gave his head a weary shake. 'I have calls to make.'

When Gant was gone, Burnett reappeared. 'Harper thinks he may have a good lead on three locations based on the trace evidence from Howard's feet. As soon as you're finished here, I thought we'd check those out personally with him.' He glanced at the white sheet covering the victim that was now mottled with varying shades of pink and crimson. 'We have to stop this.'

That was the best idea she'd heard all night. 'I need ten minutes and then I'll be ready.'

'There's a snag.'

He was wearing that look again. 'The call you received?'

'That was Annette. There's a problem with Andrea.' Burnett rubbed at his forehead. 'I need to go over there. I won't be long.' The worry in his voice and in his posture warned that this was no small matter. 'When Harper gets here, he can bring you up to speed on his discovery.'

'I understand.' She gave him a nod. 'Do what you have to do.'

He turned and started to go, then hesitated. 'Stay right here, Jess, until Harper arrives. He should be here any second.' He dropped his hands to his sides. 'I should stay until he gets here.'

There he went again. What was she going to do with him? 'What does it take—?' She stopped. Harper was striding toward them. 'Go. He's here.'

When Burnett caught sight of Sergeant Harper, his relief was palpable. 'Okay. Good. We'll rendezvous at the first site. I should have this situation squared away by the time you're done here.'

Jess watched him hurry to meet Harper. She didn't need a bionic ear to know how the conversation would go. *Don't let Jess out of your sight. She's vulnerable. A target . . . unable to protect herself. And make sure she doesn't talk to any reporters.*

Damn. Damn. Damn. What did she have to do to get the man over the whole protector thing? She did not need him playing that role in their personal lives and she certainly didn't need it in their professional relationship.

The techs had started setting up and Jess waited for their lights to go up before she began another walk through. The drop box was located in the parking area between a four-story corporate office building and a post office. The owner of the office building as well as the post master had already been contacted to determine if there was any outside security surveillance. It would be a few hours before they had access to any recorded data if it existed.

Harper joined her. He took a long look at the bloody trace sheet before turning to Jess. 'I heard it's bad.'

'Not a death you'd wish on your worst enemy.' He would know the details already. 'Burnett said you had some promising locations to check out.'

'Yes, ma'am. I was en route to the first location but Chief Burnett suggested we should go together. I have a team prepared to meet us there.'

'Go, now,' she urged. 'I'll be a few more minutes here and I'll catch up with you.'

'Sorry, ma'am. My orders are—'

She held up a hand to stop him. 'Fine. Let's get this done.'

Jess walked the perimeter of the parking lot, Harper right behind her. She didn't see any exterior cameras on the office building. The unsub had likely considered exposure before choosing the location. Though he'd shown his face repeatedly, he hadn't allowed a glimpse of the vehicle he used. That prevented the possibility of tracking him that way.

BPD would run a trace on the cell number he'd used to send the text to Jess. Probably another prepaid and sent from right here in Birmingham. Turning off the phone and removing the battery would prevent the ability to track the pings from here after he'd dumped the body. Could be that he disposed of the phone after this one use. Damned thing could be lying around here somewhere. Since the number was different, he had likely done that with the phone he'd used to contact her about dropping Howard at Lori's apartment.

Jess couldn't bear to consider that Lori might be dead already. But why would he reserve delivering her body if she were already dead? The notion that he might be holding Lori for when he had Jess where he wanted her gave her hope. But, if that were the case, it was only so he could torture Lori to hurt Jess. The idea gave her little comfort.

There was no comfort in any of this.

She walked in a wide circle around the drop box, moving closer to the placement of the body with each sweep. As usual, nothing had been left behind except the body. This time he hadn't bothered even a half-assed attempt at cleaning the victim's body. The likelihood of trace evidence was far greater this time than any other. It was a crying shame that Miller had to die to give them the potential for useful evidence.

Once the coroner and his assistant had moved the body to a gurney, Jess considered the condition. No bruising that she could see but there were a lot of blood smears and traces of what she believed might be that grimy substance they had found on Howard's feet. There was some discoloration on the wrists and lowest portion of the calves where he may have held down each limb while he sawed off the hands and feet. The idea of how long it would have taken to accomplish this savagery made Jess sick to her stomach.

Rage threatened to steal her control. She took a step back from the body and the anger. Not even outrage was a good thing when assessing this kind of killer's next move.

She turned to Harper. 'I'm done here, sergeant.'

'I'll call the unit en route and have them meet us at the first location.'

As they headed for Harper's car she wondered at the decision to hit the places one at a time versus simultaneously. She had a feeling that Harper wanted to oversee each one personally to ensure – if the unsub and Lori were there – no one made a mistake.

While Harper drove, Jess reviewed the details from each scene in the case. The three abductions were vastly different. When the unsub had taken Lori he had lured her to the scene and then departed, leaving none of the dirty details he'd left behind after luring Belinda Howard to the Liberty Park Lane property. The first victim remained unaccounted for while the last two had been tortured, in Miller's case murdered, and then dumped.

Why had the degree of his torture deviated so from Howard to Miller? Why leave Howard clinging to life with, compared to the Player's victims, scarcely more than superficial wounds? Clearly, Howard could have died from blood loss, but in comparison with Miller's horrendous and fatal wounds, the injuries were barely a scratch. The abrupt change not only signified an unsub whose technique was far from polished but also that there was an emotional element driving the killer. What he had done to Miller reeked of anger and determination to prove a point.

He'd manned up.

The thought constricted her throat, made a decent breath impossible. Possibly it was a combination of Jess's smart ass message and the fact that Howard had survived, forcing him to try harder to accomplish his goal of impressing the killer he obviously idolized. And showing Jess who was boss in the process.

No matter the motives and emotions involved, every step led back to Eric Spears. Jess had been a key member of the team investigating the Player case and his connection to it. The anonymous contacts began after her interview with Spears.

What if Spears wasn't the Player? But was somehow connected to the games he played? Exactly how many killers were behind this elusive Player?

One? Two? A whole team?

North 31st Street, 3.55 A.M.

The former car wash on Parkway East had been a bust. Though part of the building had been used for detailing cars, the entire property was clean save a few layers of dust. There was no indication anyone had been inside the building in years. The unmarred layer of dust confirmed that conclusion.

An old gas station with mechanic's bay the other side of town certainly had the grease and oil spills on the concrete, but again, no indication of occupancy in many years.

Jess waited with Harper at his SUV as the search team checked the perimeter of the final location on his latest priority list. The building sat in the middle of a large and long neglected parking lot. A high metal fence contained the area. There was a considerable distance on all sides from surrounding buildings. Most of the windows had been boarded up. According to the realtor who had the property listed there was a large storage warehouse located in the rear portion of the building that had no windows and only one walk-through door from the rest of the building as well as an overhead door leading to the outside.

With its thick brick walls, definitely the perfect place for torturing victims.

She and Harper, sporting vests and communication links, remained on the street until they were cleared to enter the property. Standard Operating Procedure. She doubted that would have prevented Harper from being right in the middle of moving in if Burnett hadn't ordered him to keep Jess out of danger. Forcing both her and Harper to stay back until the search team was sure there was no threat.

Once this case was closed, she intended to see that the we-must-protect-poor-Jess mentality changed.

Where the hell was Burnett? She understood his need to check on the girl who had up until a year ago been his stepdaughter. She really did. But why wasn't he here yet? Was it a life-or-death situation? The bigger question was why hadn't he told Jess what was going on?

When she'd first arrived back in Birmingham last Wednesday – had it only been a week? – she had immediately sensed the connection between Burnett and one of the missing young women. Andrea Denton had been his stepdaughter. Thankfully she and the other four girls had escaped uninjured for the most part from a tragically twisted couple. But after what they had been through, much counseling would be needed. Particularly Andrea. Jess wouldn't be surprised if issues hadn't already come up.

The girl was close to Dan. The family would certainly call upon him. But why was it taking so long in light of what was going on with this case at this very moment?

Jesus, she was repeating herself to *herself*.

Bad sign.

And, if she were completely honest, she might even be a little jealous. A killer appeared to be taken with her and all Burnett could talk about was protecting her then suddenly – in the middle of a homicide scene – he has to go see about his ex-stepdaughter whose mother just happens to be drop-dead gorgeous?

Jess booted out the green monster. She had no right to be jealous of anything about Burnett.

'We can move in now, ma'am.'

Jess hauled her wayward attention back to Harper. 'Excellent.'

She hitched her bag higher on her shoulder, followed Harper through the gate and across the parking lot. She checked her cell. Still nothing from Burnett. They didn't need him for this, but the idea that he hadn't shown in more than two hours under the circumstances felt wrong.

A *Jesus Christ* buzzed across the communications link.

'Sergeant Harper, you need to get in here . . . now!' echoed next.

Jess broke into a run. She had a hell of a time keeping up with Harper but she managed.

'South side. Overhead door entry,' rattled in her ear next.

The lights were blazing and the three members of the search team stood just inside the doorway.

There was blood all over the place. A couple of chairs, one overturned. And a length of chain attached to a steel post near the center of the room. Lots of wooden crates with Grimes stamped on the sides.

Harper turned to her and she nodded, dread coagulating in her stomach. 'This is it.'

She dragged shoe covers and gloves for her and Harper from her bag as he ordered a crime scene unit. They were going to need more than a couple of techs.

Moving carefully so as to disturb as little as possible, she and Harper progressed through the warehouse. Near what appeared to be a mop bucket filled with water, a hand . . . and then a foot lay on the floor.

'Call Agent Gant,' Jess murmured, 'tell him to get over here. We've found the primary scene.' This was where Agent Nora Miller had been heinously tortured and mutilated before taking her last breath.

Jess surveyed the bloody floor, then the bucket of water. Lori was terrified of drowning.

Jess prayed she was still alive.

Chapter Seventeen

5.01 A.M.

Evidence techs were crawling all over the warehouse. Jess had ensured the feet and hands had been carefully collected and tagged for Gant. She tried Burnett's cell phone again. She'd called him at least six or seven times in the past hour. Straight to voicemail. Where the hell was he?

To her immense relief, no other body parts had been discovered in the warehouse other than Miller's. A scrap of a yellow blouse had been found. The collar and upper part of the back of the blouse. Harper confirmed that it was Lori's size. Lending more credence to the possibility that she had used her own blouse to attempt first aid for Belinda Howard.

The unsub had obviously gotten nervous about the

mess he'd made and departed the premises.

Agent Gant hadn't arrived yet, but Manning was here. Jess felt reasonably confident that the agent had never worked a scene quite like this one. To say he was green around the gills would be an enormous understatement.

She needed to find Burnett. He *needed* to know about this.

Had something happened to Andrea? Surely he would have let Jess know if the situation – whatever the situation was – had deteriorated. Were he and the Denton family at the hospital?

Jess made yet another attempt at reaching him. When that failed, too, she made a decision. No matter that it was only shortly after five in the morning she saw no other recourse. All she needed was the number for the Denton family home. If there was an ongoing issue, surely one of the two was able to answer their phone. She went in search of Harper. He'd taken a breather outside away from the smell of blood and death. He was immensely disappointed that they hadn't found Lori. And at the same time relieved that no readily discernible evidence of her murder had been discovered either.

'You hanging in there, sergeant?'

Harper looked up as she approached. He nodded. 'Yes, ma'am.' Then he shook his head. 'I just keep thinking that she was probably the one chained.' He exhaled a ragged breath. 'It's very difficult.'

Jess placed her hand on his arm. 'I'm sorry, Chet. I know this is extra hard on you. I also know that Lori would want us to do all within our power to stop this from happening to anyone else.'

Another shaky breath hissed past his lips. 'She would.'

'Have you kept in contact with her family?' It seemed incredible to Jess that it had been only two days since Lori disappeared. Felt like months.

'I spoke to her mother twice yesterday. Terri, her sister, calls me several times a day. What they'll see on the news today will break their hearts.'

When they had left the scene on Riverchase the media was still being kept at bay. But Gant or Black would have made some sort of statement by now.

'Have you heard from Burnett?'

'Not yet.' He glanced at Jess. 'I'm beginning to get worried. It's not like him to just drop off the radar like this.'

'I've tried his cell over and over.'

'I've called three times in the last half hour myself.'

'Do you still have a number for the Dentons in your cell?' Until Saturday their daughter had been missing and both Jess and Harper had worked the case. Jess hadn't had the occasion to call the family but maybe Harper had.

'I believe I have a contact number I can try.'

'See if you can get one of them and find out what's going on. I'll take a last look around.'

'Yes, ma'am.'

Jess couldn't shake the mounting dread that something had happened with Burnett. They would have heard by now if he had been in an accident and she still couldn't believe he wouldn't call if something had happened to Andrea.

'Ma'am.'

Jess turned back to Harper.

'Why don't I take that last look around with you?' He walked toward her as he spoke. 'I can check with the Dentons as we go.'

'Sure, sergeant.'

Burnett had told him to keep an eye on her and other than that moment he stepped outside to get a breath, he'd followed the order to the letter – even with more than a dozen members of law enforcement all around her.

Jess walked the warehouse again, ignoring the techs and uniforms. Deputy Chief Black was overseeing the collection of evidence personally, along with the redhead, Prescott.

Agent Manning was deep in a cell phone conversation, with Gant probably.

In a twelve-hour span the unsub had abducted a federal agent in broad daylight from a public place, brought her here, tortured her, murdered her, dumped her body and then evacuated with a hostage in tow.

Where would he go? How could he have possibly had time to make all these plans and contingencies?

'Ma'am.'

Jess tuned back in to the present.

'There is no answer at either of the numbers I have listed for the Dentons. But I'm not sure if what I have is home or work or cell numbers. Lori – Detective Wells or Chief Burnett usually communicated with them.'

Apprehension coiled tighter around her ribs. 'Sergeant, I think we need to make a drive by. Manning and Black are here,' Jess pointed out. 'There's no need for us to hang around.'

'I'll let Deputy Chief Black know we're leaving.'

Tremendous willpower was required to keep Jess

waiting for Harper to cross the warehouse, give Deputy Chief Black a heads-up and to walk back to where she waited.

Move it, Harper!

'Ready, ma'am?'

'Past ready, sergeant.'

By the time they reached Harper's SUV way across the parking lot and on the street Jess fully comprehended that Harper absolutely knew how to hurry and that she had to start running again. She was seriously out of shape.

With no traffic to speak of, the drive to Montclair Road took less than twenty minutes. Harper said nothing. She said nothing. Each second seemed to echo in the silence, a taunting reminder that her cell phone had not rung.

Burnett was not going to call.

Best case scenario, there was new trouble. Worst . . . he was *in* trouble.

Harper slowed as he reached the Denton residence. The downstairs lights seeped through the slits in the blinds covering the front windows. Burnett's Mercedes was not in the driveway. Where the hell was he?

'Ma'am,' Harper said, shattering the silence as he parked at the curb in front of the Denton home, 'I'm thinking we should just go to the front door and see if anyone's up.'

Jess moistened her lips. 'I think you're right, sergeant.'

'If it turns out the chief was called away for some personal reason, like an emergency with his parents, we'll just be a little embarrassed showing up here like this looking for him.'

For once Jess would be thrilled to learn dear old Katherine had needed her son. She wished it would be as simple as that, but the potential for that possibility had come and gone in her estimation. Something was wrong or she would have heard from Burnett by now. 'I've been embarrassed before.'

Harper offered her a faint smile. 'Won't kill us.'

'Definitely not.'

Harper pulled into the drive and shut off the engine. Her hand shaking, Jess reached into her bag to make sure her weapon was handy. With her other hand she tugged at the Kevlar vest she still wore. She hadn't thought to take it off. Just as well.

Keeping an eye out for trouble, Jess joined Harper at the front of his SUV. They walked to the front door together. Her pulse rate revved faster and faster. She refused to allow any of those worst case scenarios related to Burnett to totally form in her head.

He was too smart to let this son of a bitch get to him. But Lori had been smart, too . . . and Agent Miller.

If Burnett had been ambushed, why hadn't she gotten a message of some sort?

Harper pounded on the door. The sound made Jess jump even though she knew it was coming. Brandon Denton opened the door. His expression went from worried to fearful in a heartbeat.

'Jesus Christ, what's happened?'

'I'm Deputy Chief Harris and this is—'

'I know who you are, where's Andrea?'

The bottom dropped out of Jess's stomach. Before she could find her voice, Harper asked, 'Sir, we were not aware that your daughter wasn't home. We came here looking for Chief Burnett. He left to meet with you nearly three hours ago.'

Annette Denton pushed past her husband and stood trembling in the doorway. 'Andrea didn't come home last night. She said she needed some time away,' her lips quivered, 'from us. She sounded so distraught I called Dan. Brandon was out driving around looking for her car.'

Jess managed a nod. 'Did Chief Burnett come here after you spoke?'

Annette shook her head. 'It wasn't half an hour after I called him that he called me back and said he'd gotten Andrea on her cell.' Pain lined her face. 'She wouldn't answer our calls. She had gone to Dan's house. He was on his way to meet her there. They were going to talk. He promised me everything would be fine. That was more than two hours ago.'

Fear thudded in Jess's brain, the thump-thump-thump keeping time with the beating of her heart. 'You haven't heard from either since?' she deduced.

Annette shook her head, tears streaming down her cheeks. 'He said we should wait here and be patient. He would call.'

'I got tired of waiting so I drove to his house,' Denton interjected. 'I just got back. His SUV is there but Andrea's car is not. There was no answer at the door. He's not answering his phone. Andrea isn't either. I was just telling Annette that we needed to call nine-one-one or something. What the hell is going on?'

Jess and Harper exchanged a look.

'Sir, we will find out what's happened,' Harper assured him.

Somewhere in the house a phone rang. Denton rushed to answer it. Annette went after him. Jess wasn't waiting for an invitation. She walked into the house with Harper trailing her.

In the massive great room Denton grabbed the back of the nearest chair in an apparent move to remain vertical, tears slid down his cheeks. 'It's okay, baby. Just tell me where you are.'

Annette clung to her husband and through her sobs demanded, 'Is she okay?'

The girl's father frowned. 'Wait . . . honey, slow down. Who are you talking about? Is Dan with you?'

Goosebumps rose on Jess's flesh. She needed to talk to the girl, but the parents were so emotionally overwhelmed that outside of jerking the phone out of the man's hand, she wasn't sure she could make that happen.

'Baby, listen to me,' Denton urged. 'I'm giving the phone to your mother. We're heading to you right now. Stay right where you are.'

He handed the cell phone to his wife and turned to Jess. 'I couldn't understand everything she said. But we have to go to her.'

'We'll escort you, Mr Denton,' Jess offered, struggling to sound calm. 'Can you tell us where she is and what she said about Chief Burnett so we can make the necessary calls en route?'

'She was angry. She went to Dan's house to talk but he wasn't home. She has a key so she opened the garage and hid her car so we wouldn't know where she was. She was angry with us,' he repeated. He stopped. Seemed lost for a moment. 'I have to get over there.'

'Sergeant Harper, get a unit over to Chief Burnett's residence now.' Jess fixed her firmest gaze back on Denton. 'Sir, did Burnett show up eventually?'

'Yes,' Denton said, visibly confused and shaken. 'She thinks he did. But someone else was already there when she first arrived. He was in the house when Andrea went inside and . . . he drugged her with some sort of injection.' Denton made a keening sound. 'When she woke up just now, the man was gone and Dan's SUV is in the drive but he isn't anywhere in the house . . . she's hysterical. I have to go to her.'

'Come with us,' Jess urged, fighting for calm herself. 'We'll take you there.' These people were in no condition to drive anywhere. 'Sergeant, get the paramedics to Burnett's house in case Andrea needs any medical attention.'

Jess led the Dentons to Harper's SUV.

She sat in the passenger seat as Harper drove as fast as he dared through the quiet neighborhood. Burnett's house was only a few minutes away. But that was a few too many. Wouldn't matter anyway . . . he wouldn't be there.

Jess bit her lips together. Tears crawled down her cheeks just the same.

As they approached Burnett's house that wasn't a home but it was the place where he lived . . . where he'd kissed her last night . . . where he'd admitted his fears about their relationship after all these years . . . that tiny thread of hope she'd been clinging to in order to get through this nightmare snapped.

Jess entered the number she needed to call. When he answered, she cleared her throat of the emotion and said, 'Agent Gant, he's taken another victim.'

Gant said some things but Jess didn't get any of it until he repeated the demand for a name and location.

'Dunbrooke Drive in Mountain Brook,' she said, her lips trembling, 'Police Chief Daniel Burnett.'

Chapter Eighteen

Dunbrooke Drive, 9.01 A.M.

Jess stood in the middle of the kitchen. She stared at the place next to the fridge where Dan had lifted her onto the counter and kissed her so longingly just a few hours ago. The case file still lay on the dining room table. Everything was exactly as they had left it around midnight.

Except Dan wasn't here . . .

Evidence techs and cops were all over the house. Deputy Chief Black and Sheriff Griggs were working with Sergeant Harper, orchestrating the activities. The Dentons had gone to the hospital with their daughter.

Andrea had awakened on the sofa to find herself alone and Dan's SUV in the driveway. The paramedics had found no indication of any physical assault to her.

The man she had identified as the one in the photo on Jess's phone, had already been at the house when she arrived. He'd followed Andrea inside. Based on Dan's call to Annette saying that he had spoken to Andrea, Dan had arrived here perhaps thirty or so minutes after Andrea.

The girl had come here thinking she could talk to Dan about how her parents were driving her crazy about every word she said and every move she made. After her abduction not two weeks ago and several days as a hostage, Jess could understand their concerns. Andrea had scarcely been home four days. Emotionally exhausted, she'd come to the one person she had known would understand. She hadn't expected to find Dan gone. As the chief of police he rarely got called out to a scene in the middle of the night. But this was different. Evil had intruded into his life, following on Jess's heels.

She shouldn't have come back to Birmingham. She was long past the terror. What she felt now was something along the lines of numb. And defeated.

'Ma'am.'

Jess turned to Harper. 'Yes, sergeant.'

'We're heading downtown now. Are you ready to go?'

Jess looked around, lost for what to do. 'Yes.' She managed a nod. 'I'm ready.'

'Deputy Chief Black has called a conference with all the other division chiefs, Sheriff Griggs and Agent Gant. Afterward there'll be a press conference.'

'All right.'

Jess moved through the house, unable to meet the gazes of all who stopped and stared. She knew what they were thinking.

This was her doing. She had to make it right.

Outside, the sun had already turned the interior of Harper's SUV into an oven. Jess settled into the passenger seat, her bag in her lap. The air rushing from the vents was stifling. She didn't care.

Harper drove for several minutes before he spoke. 'What's your assessment of the situation, ma'am?'

He wanted to know if she believed either one, Lori or Dan, would survive. She wanted to turn to him and demand to know how he expected her to have a damned clue. None of this fit the Player's pattern – Spears' pattern. None of her theories seemed to hold together as each new development evolved.

Jess closed her eyes and fought a wave of emotion. Harper had kept his cool extremely well through this whole travesty. He'd called Lily en route to Dan's house and ensured they were safe. He'd called the chief of police in Pensacola and given him an update so that another layer of protection could be added to Lily's family. He'd ordered another unit on surveillance duty at the Wells' home and at the hospital where Belinda Howard was recovering.

Jess had done nothing but wallow in the nothingness.

He waited for her answer so she gave him all she had. 'My assessment is that we can turn this city upside down and we won't find him until he wants us to find him.'

It was simple really. She should have narrowed in on the goal hours ago. To some degree she had, only she'd flittered all around it rather than honed in on the exact definition of what he wanted. Too many unclear signals from the unsub. His communications with her were sporadic. His MO all over the map.

But now she understood. He could have taken her sister or her niece but he hadn't. Jess had assumed he'd taken Lori because she was his type and because of the camaraderie he'd noted between them. He'd even sent that text last Saturday – or had it been Friday – saying he liked her friend. But that hadn't been the reason he'd taken Lori.

The realtor fit the new scenario coming together,

piece by slow piece. That one had thrown Jess off at first. Seemed reasonable to assume he was targeting people he deemed close to her. Like perhaps seeing the realtor give her that hug at Lily's house.

But Miller didn't fit that scenario. Taking Dan now rather than Lily or Alice before they were moved out of his immediate reach didn't fit either.

Except that this wasn't about Jess Harris the woman, the sister, the aunt or friend. This insane game revolved around Jess the agent . . . the deputy chief.

'Are we supposed to just give up?'

Harper was mentally and physically exhausted and emotionally devastated. He needed hope and she couldn't give it to him. He braked for a traffic light. She felt his gaze on her but she couldn't meet his eyes. What he wanted was something she couldn't give him. What she had to offer as the only solution he wouldn't want to hear.

Harper would only get in her way and if she was correct in her conclusions, he was already a target. Gant and the others with whom she had worked on the Player case were safe because they had turned on her. Discredited her in the media, which evidently tripped the bastard's trigger. That was what he'd wanted . . . why he'd set her up. He'd wanted to ruin her as punishment for getting too close and, no doubt, as a new way to achieve pleasure. Her move to Birmingham had rained on his terrorize-Jess parade. But how could he have anticipated that Dan would offer her a position here? Even she hadn't seen that coming.

Jess had taken something from Spears. Whether it was his playing field or something else, she wasn't sure. There wasn't enough information available to her yet to determine if he had sent this lookalike accomplice to Birmingham to keep an eye on her or if that was part of the reason he'd cut his losses by killing Special Agent Taylor and vanishing.

Was the lookalike working for him or against him? Whatever the reason, Spears had at least one more move on his agenda. If she was right, she could move first and usurp his finale . . . but if she was wrong, both Lori and Dan might end up paying the price.

A horn blew behind them, forcing Harper to start moving again.

'I need to speak to Deputy Chief Black before the briefing.'

There was no way to know which man, Spears or his protégé, had intercepted Dan. There was no way to estimate the timeline one or both were working on. Or if they were working together . . . if they had always been. And absolutely no way to validate her conclusion one way or the other.

'With all due respect, ma'am,' Harper protested, 'you didn't answer my question.' Harper waited for a break in the traffic to make the left turn into the downtown parking garage. And he waited for her answer.

'I need you to trust me, sergeant. Giving up is not on my agenda.'

Seemingly satisfied, he made the turn and parked in his assigned slot.

He reached for the door handle. Jess touched his arm and he hesitated. 'Do you trust me, Chet?' She was the one needing an answer now. Jess felt herself holding her breath. She had one last preemptive strategy and if it didn't work . . . she couldn't go there.

Harper held her gaze for a long moment. 'Yes, ma'am.'

The numbness eased a bit with a spark of hope as her plan formulated at an unprecedented speed. 'Then I need you to give me your word that no matter what happens in the next few hours you will not question my words or my actions. You will go along with whatever I say and do. If you trust me, you'll know that whatever happens, it's the only way. Can you do that?'

His hesitation was longer this time. He gave Jess a nod. 'I can do that.'

She managed a smile. 'All right then. Let's do what has to be done.'

The walk to the entrance of BPD headquarters reminded Jess that she was not dressed for a briefing and certainly not for a press conference. The jeans and tee-shirt and sneakers she'd been wearing last night looked far from professional but she wasn't out to impress anyone this morning.

Funny, she realized, mostly because her brain needed a distraction, no one else seemed to have that problem. Harper, Gant, Deputy Chief Black had all traipsed around that murder scene in their suits and their polished leather shoes. She and Dan had shown up in their jeans and tees.

And then Dan was gone.

Her lips trembled as she smiled.

Don't worry, Dan. I'm going to save *you* this time.

Her cell rang out with that old-fashioned jangle. She paused in the BPD lobby and fished out her phone. Took forever. Damn, she needed to get organized. 'Harris.'

'We got a print match from the Miller crime scene.'

Her breath trapped in her chest. *Gant*. 'Spears?'

'Not Spears, but we may now have the identity of his accomplice.'

She had no idea how they could possibly have made a connection this quickly but she was ready for any kind of break.

'Matthew Reed, Caucasian, twenty-eight. Encino, California.'

'Why didn't we get that with Howard's business card?' The man hadn't been wearing gloves according to the two witnesses at the florist.

'You wouldn't have since he's not in any national databases. But he is in the SpearNet database.'

'This Matthew is employed by Eric Spears' company?' Adrenalin fired, igniting the urge to act. Spears had provided the Bureau with access to his company's files as well as all personal files. He had been so damned sure of himself.

'Was for three years. His file went inactive two years ago.'

Fury twisted in her belly. 'I guess so. Matthew couldn't exactly go to work wearing his boss's face.'

'Exactly. Let Chief Black know I'm en route. I've been waiting for confirmation. This,' Gant said, anticipation in his voice, 'was worth waiting for.'

Jess dropped her phone back into her bag. Yes, this

was worth waiting for. A smile tugged at her lips. *I'm gonna get you, Spears*. He'd made his own little clone for his evil purposes. Just went to show what a man with too much money and a warped mind could do.

Deputy Chief Black waited at the elevator. Jess hurried to catch the car that arrived.

'Good morning, Chief Harris, sergeant,' he offered.

Along with the professional suit, he wore that same tired and troubled expression as everyone involved with this investigation sported.

'Morning, chief. I need a few moments of your time,' Jess told him, 'in private before you start the conference.'

The older man's eyebrows reared up. 'Most everyone has arrived already. Is it necessary to make them wait?'

'It's essential.'

'Very well. We can talk in Chief Burnett's office.'

'Thank you. Oh, and Agent Gant is running behind but he has an important development to share.' Jess could feel Harper's gaze burning into her again but she couldn't make eye contact this time. Not and maintain the necessary composure until this was done.

'I hope this development will point us in the right direction.'

Jess didn't elaborate on Gant's news. No need to

steal his glory. She had her own breaking news to announce this morning.

The elevator doors opened and she exited and headed straight for the chief's door. Black was right behind her.

'Deputy Chief Harris,' Harper called after her.

Dammit. 'I'll be right there,' she said to Black.

He glanced at his watch before moving on, a silent reminder that they had a conference room full of people waiting.

When he'd continued into Burnett's office, Harper asked, 'Ma'am, you didn't say why you're meeting privately with Deputy Chief Black.'

Harper was worried but he was also suspicious. 'Remember, sergeant. You said you trust me. Don't back out on me now.'

'I do, ma'am, but I know Chief Burnett would be very upset if I allowed anything to happen to you.'

Damn these hard-headed southern men.

'You made a promise and I'm counting on you not to let me down. Now go down to the conference room and let the others know that Black will be there in just a minute. And brace yourself, Agent Gant has good news.'

Harper hesitated, then walked away.

As long as he kept his word until she was out of this building, she would be good to go.

In the chief of police's waiting room, a teary-eyed Tara offered her a weak smile but didn't say good morning. Jess nodded, couldn't quite summon even a fake smile. Everyone here was worried about their chief. They all loved Daniel Burnett. Jess's throat threatened to close. She forced back the emotions and went to Dan's office.

Deputy Chief Black stood in the middle of the room waiting for her. 'What's this about, Harris?'

Jess plunked her bag on the small conference table. 'I have to give you this before you start your meeting.' She dug for her pad and pencil as she spoke.

'Have you learned something new?'

His patience was scarcely holding under the circumstances. Jess understood. Hers had already cracked. She quickly wrote the necessary words on the page, signed her name, tore off the sheet and gave it to him. While he read the note, she tucked her pad and pencil away and shouldered her bag.

'What's the meaning of this?' He stared at her as if she'd lost her mind.

She probably had. 'I'm not required to give you an explanation.' Jess turned for the door.

'This is unacceptable, Chief Harris.'

She hesitated at the door but didn't look back.

'Whatever this is about,' Black resumed, 'you will need to take it up with Chief Burnett. I will not accept your resignation.'

Jess walked out the door. She didn't bother with the elevator. Waiting for someone to notice her leaving would just create a scene she did not need or want. By the time she was outside on the sidewalk, her heart was pounding and her nerves were frazzled. She looked around at the busy morning traffic.

Damn.

Her car was at Dan's.

No problem. A taxi would work. As long as it got her out of here fast. There was just one other thing she needed to do first and for that she needed Gina Coleman.

Chapter Nineteen

10.28 A.M.

'She's still alive.'

'I can see that.'

Matthew watched his mentor as he spoke. The way his lips moved mesmerized him. But it was the sound of his voice that truly, truly inspired him. Deep, soothing.

He would do anything for Eric. Anything at all.

But Eric was disappointed. Angry even. His voice, of course, did not reflect either of those emotions, but Matthew knew. He recognized that his work was not up to the expected standards.

'Have you been feeding her?'

'Of course. Ensure. When she would have it.' Which was only twice since he'd taken her. No need for Eric to learn that part.

'What methods have you used for self-gratification?'

Matthew shook his head. 'None. I saved her for you and Jess.' It was a lie . . . he hoped Eric wouldn't notice the subtle change in the timbre of his voice.

'Really? Then why the bruising?' He indicated her cheek and the swollen lip.

Fear trickled inside Matthew. 'She's rather a stupid little twat. No appreciation or respect for rules. So I taught her a lesson.' He lifted one shoulder in a nonchalant shrug. 'She's terrified of drowning.' He laughed, relishing the memory of her screams and pleas. He'd gotten rock hard playing that game with her. 'I gave her a few dunks for starters. Then I tried the water-boarding made famous by our esteemed military. It's quite interesting to watch the subject's reaction. Especially one as phobic as this one.'

The water-boarding had caused him to ejaculate twice but he wouldn't share that with Eric either. Discipline was vital to his mentor. Matthew had shown little discipline the past few days.

But he would do better.

'You injected her every day?'

'It was the only way to keep her under control.'

Her body was completely relaxed now. He'd gotten rid of her slacks and undergarments. Such nice breasts.

Slim, narrow waist with nicely flared hips. He found it interesting that she had not removed her silky tuft of pubic hair. So many young women bared those thick lips, leaving nothing to the imagination.

'I think she might have cracked just a little with the water-boarding.' He smiled, ignored the pain that pierced his damaged lip. The bitch had come at him like a wildcat, more than once. 'Exquisite, isn't she?'

Eric surveyed Lori Wells' nude body stretched out on the old wooden table. 'Quite. Just like Eve in the Garden of Eden.' He sighed. 'Her beauty brings out the worst in man and for that she must be punished.'

'Indeed.' Matthew had known he would approve.

When Eric lifted his gaze back to him, Matthew saw disapproval rather than the approval he had anticipated. A rush of apprehension tightened his body.

'You've made quite a mess, my friend.'

'Yes.' He bowed his head in humility. 'In my eagerness to carry out your wishes, I may have overstepped.'

'Harris' career with the Bureau was destroyed,' Eric noted. 'All went exactly as planned. The message I left at her home added the perfect touch.'

Of course, Eric's work was always flawless. Still, hope thrust aside the apprehension. Her career at the Bureau had been destroyed and that was *Matthew's* work. 'Pretty little bird flew against the wind. Got her wings broken.'

'But the damage was only temporary.'

'I watched her as you asked and she redeemed herself by finding those missing girls.' Matthew shook his head. Jess Harris was far too clever. 'I knew Burnett would want to keep her, both at work and in his bed. Obviously her talents extend beyond her investigative skills.'

Matthew glared at the man silenced and bound to one of the two steel support columns in the room. Burnett had ruined everything. If he hadn't called Jess . . . she would still be in Virginia facing the demise of her career, floundering amid doubt and self-disgust. Right where Eric had wanted her.

'So you failed.' Eric inclined his head and studied Matthew. 'Your marginal success could not be sustained.'

'That would seem to be the case.' *Marginal?* There was nothing marginal about his work in Virginia, but he knew better than to argue with Eric. 'The damage was not sufficient to ruin her. But she has suffered another blow. That luscious reporter, Coleman, announced this morning that she had inside information that Jess Harris resigned under pressure from the department. My strategy is working still.'

'Is that what you believe?'

Matthew went rigid with renewed uncertainty at the mocking tone Eric used. 'Is there reason to believe otherwise?'

'Whether she has resigned or not is no longer relevant. I was forced to terminate the federal agent assigned to my surveillance,' Eric admonished, 'so I could come here straightaway. My patience for your chaotic and rudimentary tactics is at an end. You were to watch her after her arrival in Birmingham, nothing more. Instead, you have set in motion Armageddon for us both.'

Matthew swallowed the tiny whisper of pride he had allowed. 'I'm prepared to properly finish the work. My lacking performance is inexcusable, but you are well aware that I'm far more talented than this. I have proven my worth numerous times. I *will* salvage this situation while you escape to safety.'

'But then you would only break more rules. Your lackluster performance allowed one to live. Did you give the other a fighting chance at survival before ending her useless existence?'

'There was no time.' Sweat dampened Matthew's body. He had come here prepared, with the necessary tools and a plan. He had done everything to draw attention to himself. To protect Eric. Matthew knew nothing of this city. He could not have his prey running about in those final hours before her death. The risk had been far too great.

'You showed your face – our face – time and again, did you not?'

He was angry. 'I . . .' Matthew steadied his voice. 'I was forced to take desperate measures.'

'Measures for which *I* will pay the consequences.'

Matthew dared to meet his gaze. 'That was not my intent. My goal was to increase *her* desperation in the interest of complete obedience to your wishes. Still, as you say, this is my failure. I will make the proper adjustments.'

'The only desperation you have increased is your own. Your actions were neither fully calculated nor well planned. You acted on impulse and that is a grave error under any circumstances.'

'Allow me to rectify my errors,' Matthew urged.

'You have left me no alternative but to start over elsewhere. There is no turning back. I've already made arrangements.'

'What about Jess?' Matthew wasn't supposed to, but he wanted to touch her. She intrigued him more than any of the others. To feel the terror pulsing in her blood would transcend all other experiences. Outrage at the thought of missing that opportunity dared to kindle deep in his belly.

'I will attend to the rest personally.'

Envy jarred him. After all Matthew had done? *He* would finish the rest?

'And Burnett?' Matthew had never punished a male before . . . his cock stirred at the challenge . . . at the remembered rush of the esteemed chief of police's fist pounding into his flesh.

'Are you listening, Matthew?' Eric's eyes mirrored the irritation in his voice. 'I have answered that question already.'

'Of course.' Then it was finished. He offered his teacher a smile. There was nothing more to be said.

'There are rules, Matthew,' Eric reiterated. 'Each rule has a purpose. The discipline required to master and maintain those rules has been my protection for more than a decade. You have destroyed that in a matter of days.'

Matthew nodded succinctly in acknowledgement of that pronouncement. Then he met his beloved mentor's eyes. 'My fate is of no consequence. Save yourself and allow me to do what must be done to finish this.'

Eric laughed at his sincere plea. 'Perhaps my

investment in you need not be a total loss.' He glanced around the room. 'For every game there must be a final, impressive move. Allowing that finale to be trumped would be a travesty.'

Anticipation swept through Matthew. 'A complete travesty,' he agreed.

'Time is short,' Eric warned, 'you will need supplies for a thorough preparation.'

Matthew smiled. 'I won't fail you this time.'

'No,' Eric confirmed. 'You will not.'

Chapter Twenty

Dan squeezed his eyes shut. Tried to clear his vision. It was like seeing double. The lookalike *and* Spears.

As he watched, the two left the room. If not for the difference in the way they were dressed and the battered face one sported, it would be impossible to tell them apart. The guy who'd brought him here wore a tailored suit that suggested a man of means. The other one, Matthew, was dressed in jeans and a blood-splattered white shirt. But then, the wooziness in Dan's head hampered his senses. At the moment he wasn't sure of anything except that he had to get loose.

He worked harder at stretching the duct tape wrapped around his wrists. He had to stop these sick fucks before they hurt Wells and figured out a way to get to Jess. He hadn't gotten the entire conversation but he fully grasped that there was a plan.

Estimating the length of time he'd been unconscious was impossible. There were no windows to determine if it was daylight yet. The man in the suit, who he suspected was Spears, had waited at Dan's house for his and Jess's return. Only Andrea had shown up instead. Spears had seized the opportunity and been lying in wait for Dan.

He'd been seriously pissed off when Dan had arrived alone. He'd demanded to know where Jess was as he disarmed Dan, then forced him into the trunk of the rented car he'd parked in the garage alongside Andrea's and Jess's. Dan should have killed him. But he'd been unprepared. There had been no reason to draw his weapon before entering the house and once he'd found Andrea unconscious on the sofa with a gun to her head, it had been too late.

He prayed Andrea was safe.

Spears had gotten behind the wheel and backed out of the garage immediately after closing the trunk on Dan. He hadn't stopped for anything until they arrived here, giving Dan hope that Andrea had been left on the sofa safely sleeping off the drug Spears typically used on his victims. By now, maybe Annette or her husband had called 911. But, considering Dan had assured her everything was fine, he couldn't hazard a guess as to how long she would wait before calling for help when she couldn't reach him or Andrea.

And Jess. How many times would she have called before demanding that Harper take her to Annette's?

At least Dan knew where Spears and his accomplice were at the moment.

The one called Matthew, the younger version, had been tasked with getting Dan out of the trunk. Readied for the opportunity when the trunk opened, Dan had beaten the hell out of the piece of shit before Spears Tasered him.

Dan had a busted lip for his trouble but the other guy had a black eye and at least one tooth missing.

Gut twisting with renewed fury, Dan worked his wrists harder still, stretching the tape with all his might. His damaged knuckles protested but he ignored the nuisance. Wells was stretched out on a long wood table. Like Dan, the tape secured her and covered her mouth. Steel instruments, knives and scalpels, lay in a neat line next to her. She hadn't made a sound since he arrived but she was alive.

Thank God.

Dan figured she had given Matthew some trouble, too, since his face had looked a little the worse for wear even before Dan lit into him. He tried not to look at

Wells. Her clothes had been stripped off, leaving her naked and vulnerable. Seeing her that way pained Dan. After what had been done to Miller and Howard, it was a miracle Wells was still breathing.

Spears had taken Dan's cell and left it in his garage, ensuring it couldn't be used to trace them to wherever the hell they were. Dan's one hope was to get loose and kill one, or preferably both, with his bare hands or with one of those shiny tools.

He surveyed the room which appeared to be separated from what he believed was a larger space, likely a defunct factory. He hadn't gotten much of a look around outside. A brief glance of an extensive parking lot gone to seed. He hadn't seen the street or highway or anything else.

The room that served as his and Wells' prison was fair sized with pipes snaking overhead. Two steel posts, one of which he'd been strapped to after being Tasered, supported the wide expanse. A commercial-sized sink to the left and two tubs or vats, like large round washing machines, to the right. Beyond the door Spears and his lookalike had exited Dan could see rows of some kind of machines. There were several industrial parks in the Birmingham area; this could be in any one of the older areas.

If he could get his hands loose, he could free his feet and then he would be the one doing the hunting.

Spears, suit guy, entered the room.

Dan stilled.

He paused at the table and surveyed Wells. When Spears reached for one of the torture instruments Dan started to struggle. He grunted, tried to speak, made as much noise as possible.

Spears turned to him. 'So, you are paying attention.' He smiled. 'All the better.' He turned the gleaming knife beneath the light and admired it. 'Not to worry: I'm saving both you and Detective Wells for Jess. I wouldn't want her to miss any of the fun.'

Dan railed at the son of a bitch but the words were muffled by the tape over his mouth and rendered impotent by his bound hands. He jerked his arms, tried to twist his hands.

'Yes,' Spears said as if Dan had asked a question. 'Jess is coming.'

Dan wanted to kill him now. All he had to do was get loose, dammit!

'No.' Spears shook his head, his attention still on Wells. 'I'm not concerned at all that she might lead the police here. You see,' he turned to Dan then, 'she won't risk what I might do to one or both of you.'

Spears resumed his scrutiny of Wells. 'Jess would be devastated if either of you were damaged beyond recovery.' A smile spread across his evil face. 'That hardly precludes a little fun and games.'

Dan's right hand came free. He stilled, kept his free hand behind him as if he were still fully restrained.

While Spears traced the blade along Wells' ribcage, Dan worked on his feet, trying different moves, twisting, tugging to loosen the tape. Bending down to tear the tape loose from his ankles was not an option. If Spears left the room again, maybe then.

'Her skin is perfect.' Spears sighed. 'I would love to open her and see inside but that would be a waste since she sleeps. What's the point without the beauty of the pain? The hot, stinging temptation of the first slice into her skin. None are as potent as the first. The mind tricks the body into suppressing the sweet agony beyond a certain point. Such a pity.' He placed the knife back on the table. 'Obviously, a flaw of nature.'

Dan dared a bolder move, tugging one leg away from the other as far as the tape would allow and pushing to stretch beyond that limit. It was only a few inches but if he could stretch it enough, he might get one foot free. That was all he needed.

'Ah, you're awake.'

Dan froze.

Wells started to struggle against her bindings.

Don't move! Dan tried to shout but the words were nothing more than muffled grunts. Wells tried to lift her head but she collapsed against the table. He couldn't be sure if she saw him or not. Her body shuddered and rocked.

Spears stood back and laughed at her struggle.

When she fell still, her labored breathing filling the room, Spears stepped forward once more. 'Would you like to be my playmate, Detective Lori Wells?'

Like Dan's, her rants were rendered indistinguishable by the tape.

Spears removed the tape from her mouth. She screamed in his face.

'Yes! Let it all out. I want you to scream until it hurts.'

Wells' screams settled into soul-shattering sobs.

After enjoying her agony for a time, Spears ripped off another piece of tape from the roll on the table and attempted to re-cover her mouth. Wells tried to evade him but he eventually succeeded. Dan used the distraction to work at his bindings.

Then Spears rolled the table, its metal wheels squeaking across the concrete floor, until it stood in front of Dan. 'You want to watch? It's quite a miraculous thing to see. The blood blooms like the bud of a flower, swelling until it opens into wide beautiful petals.' He picked up the knife he'd been toying with. 'This instrument holds the power. Shall we watch her flower bloom?'

Dan struggled against his bindings, ranted at the monster for the good it did.

Spears' attention lingered on Lori for a time before he shoved the table aside and stepped closer to Dan. He ripped the tape from Dan's mouth, smiled at the automatic grimace the move garnered.

'Let's see how long it takes *you* to scream, Chief Burnett.'

Dan flinched when Spears sliced open his BPD tee-shirt.

Spears raised his eyebrows in surprise. 'Very nice, chief.' He traced a line down the center of Dan's chest with the tip of the blade. 'Well-muscled. Not a centimeter of flab. Jess must love that.' He made a sound of approval. 'And not the first scar. In all these years you've never been shot?' He hitched his head toward Wells. 'Even the good detective has taken a bullet in the line of duty. She has the scar to prove it.'

Dan said nothing. Met his menacing eyes with murder in his own.

'Of course, there may be scars earned in the line of

duty somewhere on that admirably toned body. Shall we see?'

'Cut me loose,' Dan suggested, 'and I'll show you what I can do in the line of duty.'

'Such big talk. Perhaps,' Spears leaned closer, the tip of the blade now poised on end against Dan's chest directly above his heart, 'you're not the man you want everyone to believe you are. Possibly that's why you've had three failed marriages.'

Dan clenched his jaw. Allowed the scumbag to enjoy the moment.

Spears smiled. 'Are you a closet homosexual, Chief of Police Daniel Burnett?'

Dan didn't move. Refused to breathe to avoid sucking in the stench of his rotten soul.

'No? Perhaps then, you're just a plain old *pussy*.'

Dan looked him straight in the eye. 'Fuck you.'

'That's not a bad starting place, chief. I could,' he pierced Dan's flesh, the bloom of warm blood seeming to captivate him, 'show you how a real man gives it to his *bitch*.'

'Let's see who the real *pussy* is,' Dan growled. 'Cut me loose.'

Spears laughed. 'Why don't we find out my way, chief?'

The tip of the knife ripped down his abdomen.

Dan flinched and bit back a gasp.

Spears stood back a step and watched the blood slide down Dan's skin. The wound wasn't deep enough to do anything but sting like hell and bleed.

Wells flailed and tried screaming.

Dan blanked out the sounds. She wrestled harder against her bindings. He prayed that whatever happened to him, she and Jess would be okay.

Spears turned to stare at Wells.

'Is that all you've got, Spears?' Dan demanded.

Spears whipped his attention back to Dan, a mixture of fury and anticipation in his eyes. He slashed out with the blade, slicing a horizontal path across Dan's chest. Then another.

Dan steeled himself against the pain. More warm blood oozed down to soak into the waistband of his jeans.

When Spears glared at him, obviously pissed at the lack of audible and visible reaction, Dan laughed. 'I'm still waiting to feel you and it ain't happening, you piece of shit.'

Spears dared to put his face right in Dan's. 'Trust me, you will feel me.'

'Feel this.' Dan swung his right arm around and

crushed him in a choke hold. He deflected Spears' attempt to plunge the knife into his chest.

Spears twisted, stumbled back. They toppled to the floor.

Dan held Spears' right arm and the knife at bay while shoving the heel of his free hand under the bastard's chin, snapping his head back. Feet still encumbered with the fucking tape, but he was on top . . . had the upper hand for the moment.

Spears fumbled in his pocket. Dan tried to get a hold on his left arm. Spears head-butted him. Tried to knee him in the groin. Dan twisted his hips to avoid the blow. He needed his feet free! Dammit!

A sting in his side splintered Dan's focus.

Spears heat-butted him again. Tried to break Dan's hold on his right hand . . . the hand with the knife.

Suddenly Dan was on his back. How had that happened? The room was moving. He grabbed Spears by the throat with both hands but he couldn't get a good grasp. His arms and hands wouldn't cooperate.

Spears shrugged him off, smiled down at him. 'Here's a little something you will absolutely feel.'

The blade buried in Dan's gut.

The burn and pain roared through him, consumed him.

Spears laughed, got up and walked away.

Dan told himself to go after him but he couldn't move.

Wells' muffled screams followed him into the darkness.

Chapter Twenty-One

BPD, 12.51 P.M.

Chet waited for his turn to speak privately with Deputy Chief Black. Finally Sheriff Griggs and Agent Gant exited Burnett's office. Black motioned for Chet to enter.

'You've been waiting since the press conference ended to speak to me.' Black gestured for Chet to have a seat at the small conference table.

Chet settled in a chair and bit the bullet. He'd taken certain steps without authorization but he felt compelled to do what he had to in order to protect Jess and to find Lori and the chief. 'Sir, I've been concerned since Deputy Chief Harris walked out of your office this morning.'

'I found her abrupt decision unsettling myself.'

Black braced his hands on the table and shook his head. 'Frankly, I was so concerned that I ordered a unit to follow her but I was too late. She was gone by the time I had someone on the street.'

'I felt compelled to do the same, sir. Chief Burnett's final order to me was to ensure that I did not allow Deputy Chief Harris out of my sight. Since I was in the conference room when she left, I was unaware until, as you say, she had vanished.'

'Do you have reason to believe that she would attempt to intercept the perpetrators in this case, sergeant?'

Chet nodded. 'Absolutely, sir. Before she asked for that private meeting with you, she urged me to trust her. Whatever she said or did, that I was to trust her.'

Black frowned. 'So she had some sort of plan in mind.'

'Yes, sir, and I do certainly trust her, but I believed from the moment you announced her resignation in the briefing that her safety might be at risk.'

'What did you do about that concern, sergeant?'

'Since she has received several texts from Spears and possibly his accomplice, Reed, we've tapped into her cell phone record several times to attempt a handle on the location of the sender of those texts. It was a simple matter to resume that tracking.'

'Only without her permission, a direct order or warrant this time.'

'Yes, sir. I felt imminent danger applied to her situation.'

'And what did you ascertain as to her activities?'

'That she left the downtown area probably in a taxi and went to Chief Burnett's house. After that she became mobile once more. Her car was in the chief's garage, so I assume she's using that vehicle.'

Chet hated this feeling of going behind Jess's back, but he couldn't take the risk. 'She drove north on 31 until she exited onto Messer Airport Road. After that she turned onto 39th Street going north. Moments ago she arrived at what appears to be her destination.'

'I'm familiar with the area. Is this a factory or a warehouse?'

'It's an old fabric mill that hasn't been used in years. Located in the light industrial development area.'

'Deputy Chief Harris is armed?'

'Yes, sir, she carries a Glock .40 cal. I'm not aware of any other weapons she may have in her possession.'

'Sergeant Harper, we have one murder victim, one victim who is still recovering, a missing detective who may very well be dead and now our chief of police has disappeared. Before I pull all our resources and converge on this location you believe Deputy Chief Harris has somehow determined is the place to go to prevent more of the same, are you certain that we can rely on whatever prompted Harris to go to this location?'

'Yes, sir, I'm positive. I was tempted to go after her alone, but I'm also aware that back-up is essential. We don't want this killer to get away again.'

Spears had escaped Jess and the Bureau once already. He and his accomplice had been eluding BPD for three days now. It was time this bastard went down.

Before anyone else died.

Chet refused to believe that it was too late for Lori. She was out there waiting for back-up. He did not want her to have to wait any longer. He trusted Jess's instincts. She was on to something, had gotten another message from Spears or maybe even a call. But she had gone to that location for a good reason.

Every minute they wasted added more risk to the safety of all three.

'In that case, we'll assemble a tactical team and get out there with everything we've got.'

Chet stood. 'Thank you, sir.' He hesitated . . . waiting was not what he'd had in mind.

As if he'd telegraphed the urgency he felt, Black

added, 'Select two of the best we have and go ahead of the team, sergeant. But,' he qualified, 'as you already pointed out, we don't want any hasty moves. Proceed with caution and keep me informed. We'll be right behind you.'

'What about Agent Gant, sir?'

Black considered that for a moment. 'I'll contact Agent Gant once we're in position.' He shook his head. 'No need to draw the Bureau into a search for our own. For all we know, Harris could be out there meeting an old friend.'

Chet smiled. 'Understood, sir.'

He moved quickly from the office and fished out his cell. He knew just the two detectives he needed on his advance team.

Forty-five, fifty minutes tops was the best ETA he could hope for.

He prayed Lori and the others could hang on that long.

Chapter Twenty-Two

12.59 P.M.

Jess flattened against the wall near the front entrance of the old Ballet Fabrics building. No vehicles in the lot. She'd left her Audi out front, visible from the street. For the good it would do, the area was fairly congested with warehouses and factories. As soon as she confirmed that someone was actually here she intended to text Harper her location.

She wasn't stupid enough to jump in without back-up but if Spears was here she needed him to believe she had come alone. A head start before law enforcement surrounded the place was crucial. Harper was suspicious and knowing him he wouldn't wait for her signal. He would know what to do.

No wasting time, Jess.

Weapon palmed, she reached with her free hand for the door. Locked. Nothing visible beyond the heavily tinted glass door. She eased along the length of the building's front façade. Holding her breath and with a three count, she pivoted and checked the west side.

There was a side door near the rear corner. No windows so far. Checking behind her as she went, she hurried to the next door. Steel. Locked.

Damn.

She should text Spears and ask how the hell she was supposed to get in. He would know she had arrived. He would be watching. Or have his associate watching. There had been no documented proof he worked with anyone, not until now. But she had known the last time this sociopath messed with her head there was no way he had managed certain feats without assistance. The near simultaneous murders of two federal agents in two different states left no doubt in her mind.

If Spears and Reed were here, the odds would be two against one, but all she had to do was keep them distracted until back-up arrived.

After giving Deputy Chief Black her resignation, she'd taken a taxi to Dan's house to get her Audi. En route she'd called Gina Coleman. Once at Dan's, she'd had to hurry. As soon as Harper was out of that briefing and realized she was off the BPD radar he would be trying to track her movements. Though she had a full magazine in her Glock, she'd spared a few minutes to search Dan's place for any usable back-up weapons. His gun safe had been locked and the key was probably on the ring in his pocket along with his house key. She had entered the house with the key he kept in one of the exterior electrical outlets that was actually a secret hidey hole. She had the code for the security system so that hadn't slowed her down. But the search effort was wasted. No pepper spray or usable, easily concealed weapons.

Emotion had almost gotten the better of her as she lingered in his bedroom. A small box of photos had been stowed in the top drawer of his dresser. Dozens of snapshots of the two of them at parties and just hanging out during high school and college. She'd sat down on the bed and sifted through the memories. The pain and worry pressing against her heart had given way to regret and fear. She had similar photos at her house in Virginia – if Spears hadn't destroyed them. She and Dan had spent every possible second together. God, they had been so in love.

And so blind to the pitfalls the future held.

Jess had fully believed at the time that she and Dan

would be together forever. Just like he'd written in their senior yearbook. But fate had proven that not all dreams and plans could withstand reality.

And here they were . . . proving that theory while still clinging to what if.

Before she left his bedroom, she had hugged his pillow and inhaled his scent. Then she'd prayed. *Please, please, let him be alive.*

Hours later, with her driving around town wasting three-dollar-a-gallon gas to prevent the possibility of being found by BPD, Spears had finally responded to her via text. He'd given her a general direction in which to head but the final turn-by-turn instructions hadn't come until she had almost passed the necessary exit.

All she had to do now was go in there and rescue Lori and Dan.

She recognized that was what Spears wanted anyway. During the interview three weeks ago in Richmond, he'd reached across the table and touched her. Just a quick caress of his fingers across the top of her hand. She'd had no idea then that the bastard was marking her. This whole sick game was about getting to her and he held the bait he knew would reel her in, Lori and Dan.

Dan was the unknown variable in this equation that

most worried her. As far back as documented history went on the Player and the murders attributed to him, there had never been a single male victim. She couldn't accurately gauge how Spears would handle the situation. And the wannabe Spears, there was no casting him into a particular mold. He was scattered and careless – a man with a solitary goal who would stop at nothing to accomplish it, no matter how messy things got.

If the end game was to lure Jess in and torture her . . . maybe for that purpose these sadistic bastards had kept both Dan and Lori alive.

Jess steeled herself and then rounded the next corner.

Two vehicles were parked in the rear lot, one sedan, one SUV. Both had rental decals. Jess's pulse accelerated with a wallop of adrenalin. Oh, yes. *Visitors.* She dragged her cell from her back pocket and entered her location into the text box addressed to Harper. She hit Send and shoved the phone back into her pocket.

Three entrances in the rear. A walk-through door. An overhead door allowing vehicles to enter from the parking lot and another, smaller overhead door on the loading dock at the east end.

Steadying herself, she kept an eye on the two vehicles and moved toward the walk-through door. Steel, like the last, hopefully not locked. With another one-eighty scan around her, she reached for the knob. Her fingers tightened around it and twisted. The latch mechanism released. The door opened with a groan of neglected hinges.

Leading with her weapon, her heart pounding, she eased past the door. It slammed shut behind her.

'Well, hello, Jess. Glad you could make it.'

Her aim zeroed in on the voice.

She froze.

Spears stood dead ahead. Ten yards away maybe.

He had Dan. Wait, Jesus Christ. A yellow nylon rope hung from a large overhead pipe, the other end coiled around Dan's neck. The air trapped in her lungs. Spears' arms were wrapped around Dan's bound legs, holding him up to prevent . . . *oh dear God* . . . him hanging from his neck.

'Don't you move, Spears.' She steadied her aim on him, her arms shaking. There was no ladder. A sink against the left wall; two vat-like tubs to her right. An old wood table in the center of the room. Knives and scalpels were spread across its top. Blood darkened the blade of one.

Defeat taunted her. She needed back-up now. Only they would be too far away. Her fault.

If Spears let go . . . Dan's body would drop and he would be hanged. Broken neck, maybe. Asphyxiated in five minutes or less for sure. He looked in bad shape already. Lot of blood. His arms were restrained behind him. Was he unconscious?

She had to do something.

She couldn't shoot Spears. He'd let go for sure then. Could she shoot the rope? Doubtful. She was good but not that good.

Where was Lori?

Focus. Spears' hands were in sight. No weapon. She had to do something. She took a step toward him. 'You make one move, Spears, and—'

'Bad idea, Jess,' he warned. She stalled. 'As much as I'd love some up-close one-on-one time with you, you come any closer and I'm walking away.' He shrugged. 'I'd have to let go of your friend first, of course.'

Fear grabbed her heart and fisted. 'Cut him down! Now!'

Spears laughed. 'Which is it, Jess? Cut him down or don't move?' Arms still supporting Dan, he waved his hands. 'You see a knife?'

His ultimatum jarred her. This wasn't right . . . the voice was wrong. Was this Spears or the other guy? 'You try to walk away, you make a mistake, you're dead,' she warned. 'I'm coming over there to get him down.'

'I'm afraid you can't do that.' He let go with one arm. She gasped. He reached as high as he could. 'It's quite a reach.' Spears grinned. His face was scratched and battered, one eye swollen. His white shirt was as spattered and smeared with crimson as the trace sheet that had lain over Miller's body.

'I fear that's going to be a problem for *you*.' He slapped Dan on the belly. Dan's body jerked, he groaned, the tape over his mouth muffling the sound. 'And an even bigger problem for him.' He smeared the blood he'd gotten on his hand on the leg of Dan's jeans.

Where had all that blood on Spears' shirt come from? Dan? Or Lori? She resisted the urge to look around. Where was Lori? What was that sound? Water running? A quaking she couldn't control started deep inside her. *Lori isn't afraid of a thing in this world except water.*

Jess steadied her lethal bead on her target. 'Where is Detective Wells?'

'Let's cut to the chase, Jess. We have a dilemma.' Spears or whoever the hell he was braced his right hand on his hip.

'Keep your hands away from your body,' she

ordered. That sound . . . water running. She could still hear it. Where the hell was it coming from? Not the sink. The lids on the vats were closed.

'The clock is ticking, Jess,' he singsonged.

Her attention flew back to him. Dan groaned, managed to lift his head. He looked at Jess and the ache that swelled inside her nearly overwhelmed her. She had to help him!

She readied her grip on the Glock. 'I'll ask you once more, where is Detective Wells?'

Spears flashed another of those million-dollar smiles. 'We've had this problem all along, Jess. You just won't pay attention.' Rage darkened his face. 'Now listen!'

Jess flinched. *Keep it together.*

'Listen carefully,' he said, as calmly as if the outburst hadn't occurred. 'We don't have much time.'

'All right. I'm listening.' Think, Jess. *What's his next move?* He has a precise plan. *What's yours?*

'You see, Jess, I'm going to walk out of here. And you—'

Her hands shook. *Dammit!*

He smiled.

Fury lit in her veins. She wanted to shoot this son of a bitch so badly. If she did, could she help Dan? Get him down? How would she hold him up and find a ladder at the same time? *Shit!*

And where was Lori? She glanced around the room again, her gaze landing lastly on the bloody knife on the table. *Please don't let her be dead.*

'You have a choice,' Spears continued in that voice that was wrong.

And then she knew what to do.

'I'm sorry,' she interrupted his monologue, 'I wasn't paying attention.'

Fury twisted his battered face. 'You,' he roared, 'can waste valuable time trying to stop me or you can save the chief.' He patted Dan's legs. '*Or*,' he inclined his head for emphasis, 'you can save your friend Detective Wells.'

Completely focused now, frame after frame of the hours she'd spent interviewing Spears flashed in her brain . . . watching his every expression and mannerism . . . listening to the nuances of his voice.

The calm she desperately needed settled over her. 'I guess you have it all figured out, *Reed*.'

He wasn't outwardly surprised that she recognized the differences, but he was disappointed. The cocky expression and posture waned.

'That's right,' she taunted, giving him a taste of his

own medicine, 'I know who you *aren't*. Did your friend leave you here to do his dirty work? Seems like you got the short end of the stick. A smart guy like you should've seen this coming.'

Water splashed on the floor. Jess glanced to her right before she could stop the automatic reaction. Water gushed from beneath the lid and over the rim of one of the vats.

'And that's my cue.'

Her attention snapped back to Reed.

'One last question,' he said, 'do you have any idea how long Detective Wells can hold her breath?'

Oh God! Lori was in the vat! The urge to run to her slammed into Jess.

Reed licked his lips as if he could taste Jess's fear. 'I do, and I'd say you have maybe two minutes max.'

The fear, the sound of the water splashing . . . all of it faded. There was only the weapon in Jess's hand and the target in her sight.

'Then I guess you'd better run,' she advised.

Reed stepped away from Dan.

Jess fired.

The shot exploded in the room, shattering the trance that had blocked all else.

Reed crumpled to the floor.

Jess rushed against the wood table. Knives and scalpels rattled and flew across the floor as the table rolled the few yards necessary.

Dan's sneakers dragged across the table, he stumbled, got his feet under him and steadied himself. He tried to speak, his words muffled.

She got it. He was okay.

Shoving her weapon into her waistband, Jess ran for the vat. She slipped. Hit the floor hard. She scrambled up. Grabbed the lid and shoved it out of the way. It banged against the wall.

Lori's green eyes stared up at Jess through the water. A burst of terror tried to paralyze her. *Just get her out!*

Her body was duct taped in an awkward position, arms around her knees, knees against her chest. The tape was wrapped around her mummy style, scarcely any skin showing. Her body was wedged down in the vat and her head was leaned back in an attempt to get her nose above the water line.

Jess reached in with both arms to get a solid hold on her. She pulled.

Lori's face broke the surface.

She gasped.

Jess couldn't pull her up high enough to get her over the rim . . . couldn't hold on to her well enough to keep her face up those few necessary inches.

Lori slipped back under the water. Water sloshed over the side.

Jess shoved at the vat to turn it over. Too heavy. Wouldn't budge. She couldn't climb in. Not enough room. She'd be on top of Lori. Couldn't reach inside and shoot a hole through the wall . . . too confined and risky. Her searching fingers found the switch. Turned off the water. Couldn't find a drain. She needed a damned bucket to bail out the water . . . something.

Forget it. She reached in and dug her fingers into the rows of tape around Lori's body and pulled. She pulled with all the strength she could summon. Lori's face broke the surface again.

Another gasp . . . cough.

If Jess could get her over the rim this time . . . she gritted her teeth and tried harder.

Tape snapped. Lori went under again.

'Dammit!'

This wasn't working! What now? She reached into the water, got a good hold on Lori again and pulled her up as far as she could.

Lori didn't gasp for air this time. Fear lanced Jess's heart. She shoved Lori down, hard. Water sloshed over the rim. Jess pulled her up again. Shoved her down. More water sloshed out of the vat.

This time the water level had dropped enough so Lori's head didn't go fully under the water. She tilted her head back, dragged in some more air and started to cough.

Thank God.

She coughed and coughed, water spurted from her nose. 'Thank . . . you,' she muttered between gasps.

Relief made Jess's knees weak as she grabbed a knife from the floor and freed Lori's hands and arms. 'I'll be right back.'

Reed hadn't moved. The bullet she'd put in his skull had done its job.

Jess hurried to the table and climbed up onto it. She grabbed one of the scalpels and reached up to saw through the rope just above Dan's neck. It was too tight around him to risk trying to slip the scalpel between the rope and his throat. When the rope snapped in two Dan collapsed to his knees.

'I've got you,' she assured him as she removed the tape from his mouth. She needed to get him flat down on the table and still. There was a lot of blood and she couldn't be sure what kind of neck or spine injury he might have sustained. She dragged out her cell, hit 911.

With the cell tucked between her chin and shoulder, she removed the duct tape from Dan's wrists and ankles and helped him to lie down.

'You okay?' There was so much blood. She checked his wounds. Lots of shallow injuries. One nasty looking stab wound. The bleeding had slowed so she flattened her palm over the wound and applied pressure.

'I'm . . .' he licked his lips, 'I'm okay.'

Why the hell wasn't Harper here yet? 'You okay over there, Lori?' The screen on her cell still said Calling. Hurry! Damned thick walls were slowing down reception.

'I'm okay,' Lori called out, still sounding breathless. 'I just need . . . out of here.' Her voice got a little high pitched on the last.

The 911 dispatcher came on the line. Jess identified herself and provided the location.

The back door burst open.

Harper and two others rushed in.

Jess dropped the phone. 'We're clear,' she said to Harper. 'Reed's down. Burnett's lost a lot of blood and he may have a neck injury.'

'ALS is right behind us,' Harper assured her.

'Harper!' Lori cried. 'I need your jacket! Get me out of here!'

Lori sounded strong, like herself. Jess managed her first deep breath since walking into this nightmare. 'Take care of Lori,' she said to Harper. 'I've got Dan.'

Harper was already headed that way. The other two detectives were securing the scene.

Jess felt ready to collapse but there was a way to go yet.

Dan looked so pale. 'You hang in there,' she warned. 'I'll be mad as hell if you ruin my big rescue.'

His lips quirked the tiniest bit.

He was lethargic. Had trouble focusing his eyes. *The Ketamine.*

Keeping the pressure on the wound, Jess leaned down close and caressed his face. Fear tightened her throat at the possibility that Reed may have given Dan too much on purpose as a back-up strategy. 'Hey, did he drug you?'

Dan blinked, stared at her as if he couldn't actually see her. 'Yeah.'

That would explain the lethargy. Still, he'd lost a lot of blood, too. And she was worried sick about his neck and spine.

Paramedics hustled into the room. Jess explained about the possible Ketamine and neck injury, then she got out of the way. She swiped at the tears spilling down her cheeks with the backs of her hands. The sight of Dan's blood on her hands had her body quaking.

Lori's sobs filtered through Jess's worries. She turned to go to her, but Harper was already holding her tightly. She was wearing his jacket.

Lori would be okay.

They all would.

Jess walked over to where Reed lay. She crouched down and examined his face more closely. She found the telltale scars in his hairline and behind his ears. Studied his bloody hands and fingers. Though she'd only been face-to-face with Spears for that one lengthy interview, she remembered every detail. The long, slender fingers. Not these blunt-tipped, thicker ones.

This was definitely not Spears. Just another run-of-the-mill sociopath who'd fallen under the influence of a far more devious and intelligent sociopath.

Spears could be anywhere. Already scoping out his new hunting grounds.

'Jess!'

She pushed to her feet and hurried back to Dan's side.

'Take it easy, chief,' one of the paramedics urged. 'We're prepping you for the ride to the hospital.'

'Jess!'

She reached for his flailing arm. 'I'm here. It's okay, Dan.'

His fingers fisted in her tee and he pulled her close. She searched his face, got sick all over again at the pain etched there. The paramedic had applied a neck brace in deference to the possible neck injury.

'I'm going with you to the hospital, Dan, don't worry.' The Ketamine, if that was what he'd been given, sometimes caused hallucinations and amplified fears.

'Spears,' he murmured.

Jess shook her head, caressed his jaw gently to comfort him. 'It wasn't Spears. It was Reed and he's dead. Spears is—'

'He was here.'

Jess went cold. The sound of a gurney rolling up behind her signaled that she needed to get out of the way. 'In Birmingham? Or *here*?'

'Here,' Dan muttered, his gaze fixed on hers now. 'Spears was *here*.'

Chapter Twenty-Three

UAB Hospital, 5.30 P.M.

Chet waited outside Lori's room. He needed a moment to compose himself before going back inside.

Her mother and sister were gathered around her. They had arrived at the ER half an hour after Chet and Lori. The reunion had filled his heart with relief and happiness. Lori was alive and safe.

Until he'd gotten her out of that vat and the rest of that damned tape off her, he'd wanted to scream with the agony tearing at his soul. He kept imagining what sort of injuries her folded-up position and the tape might be hiding. So many bruises. The possibilities of what that son of a bitch had done to her kept twisting in his head.

Other than one cracked rib, too many bruises to

count and being dehydrated, Lori was fine.

If he spent the rest of his life on his knees in prayer, he would never be able to thank God enough. Once they'd taken Lori away for x-rays and refused to allow him to accompany her, he'd made another decision. Beginning this Sunday, if his ex-wife was agreeable, he wanted to start taking Chester to church – the same one where his parents had taken him to as a kid.

Maybe one day Lori would go with them.

That was probably too much to hope for.

He'd checked on Chief Burnett. He, too, was holding up well considering what he'd been through. He wasn't happy that Spears had gotten away, but the Bureau was on top of that. Spears wasn't BPD's problem anymore.

'Chet.'

He snapped to attention and smiled for Mrs Wells. 'Yes, ma'am?'

Lori's mother and her sister Terri slipped out into the quiet corridor. Mrs Wells gave him another hug. As she drew back she blinked at fresh tears. 'We're going to the cafeteria for a few minutes.' She smiled. 'I think she wants some time alone with you.'

Chet's heart skipped a beat. 'I'll keep her company while you're gone.'

'You want us to bring you some coffee or something?' Terri asked.

Chet shook his head. 'I don't need anything. Thank you.'

He lingered in the corridor a moment after they were gone. Not because he wasn't looking forward to a few minutes alone with Lori but because he didn't trust himself not to break down emotionally.

It was a risk he'd simply have to take.

The room was quiet. The TV muted. Some silly sitcom on the screen. The lights were low but not so low that he couldn't pause a moment just to look at her. Her long dark hair spread across the pillow made him yearn to feel it sliding across his skin or slipping through his fingers. And though her face and throat were badly bruised, one eye swollen, she was more beautiful than any woman he had ever seen.

Her eyes opened and she smiled, then winced. She patted the mattress. 'Come sit with me.'

He crossed the room, barely hanging on to his composure, and settled carefully on the edge of the bed. 'Did they give you anything for the pain?'

'Yeah. I'm feeling pretty good right now.'

The silence settled between them. It wasn't particularly uncomfortable, just there, sort of in the way. But he wasn't sure what to say to break it. What he wanted to say was probably the wrong thing.

'While I was in the warehouse,' she said, saving him from the awkwardness, 'I worried about my mother and my sister and whether or not they'd be okay if . . . if I didn't make it.'

A fierce surge of emotion pounded him. 'I knew you'd make it.' That was all he trusted himself to say.

'I thought about you, too.'

She looked up at him and his chest constricted with emotion. He wanted to take her in his arms and promise her anything if she would only give him a chance to be the man in her life. If that made him weak, he didn't care.

'What did you think about me?' His voice cracked.

'I thought that maybe I made a mistake.'

Hope nudged him. He smiled. 'You rarely make mistakes, detective. You've told me so many times.'

She laughed. Put her hand to her mouth. 'Ouch!'

'Sorry.'

She waved him off. 'To hell with this beating around the bush. I kept thinking that I should have given you a chance.' Tears glittered in her eyes. 'I was terrified that I might not be able to make that right.'

As much as he wanted to hear those words, she was

vulnerable and emotional right now. Not to mention on pain meds. He took her hand in his and gave it a little squeeze. 'Tell you what, we'll take it slow and if you still feel this way in a month or so we'll move it to the next level.'

'Sounds good to me, sergeant.'

They talked and laughed and Chet was almost afraid to close his eyes even to blink for fear that he would open them and find that this was only a dream.

But it was real. What they felt for each other was real.

The only mystery was who would cave and admit it first.

His money was on Lori.

Which was a no-brainer since he'd already caved.

Chapter Twenty-Four

8.31 P.M.

Jess paced the room. She couldn't sit still if her life depended on it. They'd taken Dan down for an MRI just to be sure they hadn't missed anything with all the other tests. She'd showered and changed into a pair of scrubs kindly provided by one of the ER nurses. A call to her sister had confirmed they were all still safe and enjoying their getaway. The kids were having so much fun they had decided to stay in Pensacola through the weekend.

The man responsible for Lori's and Howard's abductions and Agent Miller's murder was dead. As best they could determine, Matthew Reed was responsible for all the events that took place here. Except for Dan's stabbing. If they matched the blood on the knife to Dan's and discovered Spears' prints matched any lifted from that knife's handle, they would finally have evidence connecting him to a crime. Attempted murder, maybe. It was far less than he deserved but it was better than nothing.

The good news, Jess had to bear in mind, was that Dan's injuries were not nearly as bad as they could have been. The blade had missed anything vital. The CT scan had ruled out any fractures to the spine or any other permanent damage, unless something was discovered in the MRI. He would be sore as hell for a while, but everything would heal. The doctor insisted he stay overnight just in case any swelling or other unexpected complications occurred. They were keeping Lori overnight, too. Jess and Chet had played musical rooms a couple hours ago. He'd spent a few minutes with Dan and she'd visited with Lori.

Whenever Jess closed her eyes she saw him dangling in the air for those few seconds before she'd gotten the table under him.

She shook off the haunting memories. He was fine now. They were all fine.

Except that Eric Spears had gotten away.

Fury lit inside her at the idea that he was out there somewhere instead of in hell where he belonged.

Gant had called while she and Dan were headed to the ER. Spears' Cessna had taken off from Montgomery Regional Airfield at two that afternoon. The Bureau had every airport in the country on alert. The flight plan filed had listed the destination as Richmond and a single passenger, Eric Spears. Four hours later and there had been no communication with the pilot and no report of a crash or a landing.

But the plane had to come down sometime.

Jess stalled at the window and leaned against the frame. She stared out at the dark sky. A week ago she had come back here with her tail tucked between her legs and her entire career crashing down around her. Now, after three tortured hostages and one heinous murder, the Bureau finally had the necessary evidence to clear her with OPR. She wanted to be angry that it had taken all that. But the truth was, Spears wasn't the typical criminal. Smart with endless financial resources at his disposal and a total malignant narcissist. He had been doing this a long time. Far longer, Jess estimated, than anyone knew. He executed each step carefully and could have numerous associates like Matthew Reed ready to die, if necessary, to protect him.

Yet, Spears hadn't been quite as brilliant as he'd thought. Otherwise he wouldn't have taken the risk and showed up here, even if only to give his protégé a pep talk. Recalling the way he'd watched her and that one touch during their interview last month made her shudder with disgust. There was nothing she could do about his twisted obsession. He was gone and if he was half as smart as she believed he was, he wouldn't be back.

He was the Bureau's problem now. He had extensive international contacts. He literally could be anywhere. Considered the prime suspect in the murder of Agent Taylor and the attempted murder of Dan, Spears would be a fool to return to the States.

She refused to be a prisoner to what-if. If the Bureau didn't get him and she doubted they would, she wasn't looking over her shoulder the rest of her life. Her cell vibrating against the laminate top of the table next to the bed dragged her from her troubled thoughts.

She shuffled over and glanced at the screen. Gant. 'Harris.'

'Spears wasn't on the plane.'

Despite being braced for this news, Jess's gut wrenched. 'The pilot have any idea how or where he went?'

'His instructions were to file a flight plan for Richmond at two. Once in the air he was to divert to a private airfield in Texas. We had agents waiting at the pilot's home. Apparently he forgot to tell his wife that no one was supposed to know where he landed. He claims he has no idea how Spears planned to leave the Birmingham area.'

Fear trickled inside her. 'He wouldn't still be here.' She glanced at the door. She should have gone with Dan for the MRI but the tech had insisted she would only have to sit in the lobby.

'That's the next part I regret having to pass along.'

Jess wilted onto the bed. 'Get it over with.'

'We had the commercial airlines on alert. But you know how it is, sometimes there's a failure in the system.'

'Where's he headed?' Jess rubbed her eyes with her thumb and forefinger. Spears, of course, would travel under an alias. Unfortunately the facial-recognition software didn't always work as hoped when attempting to catch a fleeing criminal.

'We haven't pinned down how he got from Birmingham to New York, but he left JFK just before seven this evening headed to Bangkok. We can try to intercept him in Shanghai but you know how that will turn out.'

'Yeah.' She tucked her still damp hair behind her

ear. 'Well, let's hope it works better if he tries to come back.'

'We'll do all we can, Jess.'

Her next thought was almost amusing. 'I guess his assistant was right about Bangkok. She was just a few days off on his travel plans.' Knowing Spears he'd told his assistant to say that just so they would look back on it now and wonder.

'Creepy bastard.'

She nodded. 'Yeah. Thanks for the newsflash.'

Gant asked about Dan. He was glad to hear that he would be released from the hospital tomorrow. They spoke a moment more but basically there was nothing else to say. Spears was gone.

Jess checked the time on her phone. Dan should be back by now. A soft rap on the door launched her to her feet. 'It's about time.'

A cart burdened with a large Peace Lily squeaked into the room. The person pushing the cart was impossible to see beyond the massive plant. Jess snagged her Glock from the bedside table.

'Sorry this took so long.' A young man wearing scrubs stepped from behind the plant. His jaw dropped and his eyes rounded.

Jess took a breath, lowered her weapon. 'Sorry.'

The guy stood there in a kind of shock. Not that she blamed him. It wasn't everyday a hospital volunteer came face-to-face with the business end of a gun just for delivering a plant. She glanced at his crotch to make sure he hadn't peed his pants.

'What's this?' She placed her weapon on the bedside table.

'It came a couple hours ago but none of the girls could pick it up to get it on the cart.' His eyes were still big as saucers but he kept his bladder under control.

'Thanks.'

He nodded, the move jerky.

Before he could get away she figured she'd better explain or she'd be getting a visit from hospital security. 'This is the chief of police's room. I'm one of his deputy chiefs. Jess Harris.' She offered her hand.

He stared at her hand a full ten seconds before he accepted the gesture.

'You can verify that at the nurses' desk.'

Another jerky nod. 'Where do you want this thing?'

He was right. It was huge. 'Let's just leave it on the cart for now. I'll be sure you get your cart back.'

'Whatever you say.' He glanced at the weapon on the table.

'Do you know which florist made the delivery?'

His head wagged side-to-side. 'It was here when I showed up for my shift.'

'Thanks for bringing it up.'

When he was gone, she plucked the card from the plant. Dan's name was scrawled on the front. The card inside was a preprinted one. *Get well soon.* Could be from anyone.

Jess stared at the plant. She hated Peace Lilies. Maybe because that was the one thing she remembered about her parents' funeral. A big, glossy plant just like this one. She shook it off. Dan was the chief of police. He had a lot of friends. His parents had a lot of friends. Lucky for her, they'd dropped by while Jess was visiting Lori. A run-in with Queen Katherine was not the way to end a day like today, especially with Jess looking like hell.

Her cell vibrated again. She jumped. Almost dropped the damned thing. She took a breath and touched the screen to view the message.

Private Number.

The silence in the room suddenly closed in on her. The sound of her heart beating pounded in her ears.

Until next time.

Her heart bumped harder and harder against her sternum. This didn't mean *he* had sent the plant. Just a coincidence. He couldn't know she hated those damned things. Besides, the card was addressed to Dan.

The door opened again. Dan sat in the wheelchair looking impatient. Jess tossed her phone onto the table next to her Glock. She scrubbed her sweaty palms over her hips.

'Looks like you survived the fun.' She pushed a smile into place.

The cute young tech with the huge boobs beamed a smile at her. 'I think he's tired.'

Jess imagined the word she was looking for was grumpy. Men didn't make good patients even when attended to by sweet young things. Jess offered her hand and he scowled at her. Instead of accepting the help, he pushed up from the chair and shuffled to the bed.

The tech and Jess got a glimpse of his cute ass when he climbed into the bed. Damned hospital gowns.

The tech giggled and started maneuvering the wheelchair out of the room. 'Goodnight, chief!'

'G'night,' Dan grumbled. 'I did not need a wheelchair for that,' he complained to Jess.

'Hospital policy,' she assured him. 'Besides, I'm sure the pretty tech still thought you were a big, handsome tough guy whether you were walking or rolling.'

'Right.' He glared at her, then the plant. 'Did somebody die?'

Jess flinched. Wished she had rolled it out into the corridor. 'It's for you.'

He rearranged the pillow under his head. 'Great. Who's it from?'

'Dunno. Maybe the department or the mayor sent it.'

He reached for her hand. 'Sit with me.'

She took his hand and settled on the edge of the bed. It was hard not to stare at all the bruises and bandages. She'd only get all emotional again if she did. He could have died today. Dammit. She swallowed back the swell of anxiety and other stuff she didn't want to analyze right now.

'Did you hear from Gant?'

'Yeah. They're reasonably sure Spears is on his way to Bangkok.'

'He got away? Dammit.'

'That's pretty much what I said.'

His fingers entwined with hers. 'What're you gonna do about that?'

He was worried she'd leave. 'That's the Bureau's problem. I'm going to be the best deputy chief in BPD.'

'You sure about that?'

She nodded. 'If he wants me, he'll find me. Doesn't matter where I run.'

He reached up, touched her cheek and smiled. 'I guess you showed me today.'

A frown lined her brow. She rubbed it away. 'Showed you what?'

'You saved my life, Jess. Lori's, too.'

'I did my job.' She made a scoffing sound. 'How would it have looked to the department if I'd gotten their chief killed my first week?'

He toyed with her hair. 'Not many people, no matter how well-trained, could have reacted with such swift decisiveness in that situation. You did good, Jess.'

Tears leaked from the corners of her eyes. 'Damn you, Burnett. Now look what you've done.' She swiped at her eyes.

She stood, dragged the lounge chair closer to the bed and plopped into it. 'Now go to sleep. You need your rest.'

He searched her eyes. 'You won't sneak out while I'm asleep? I've got a feeling those pain meds they gave me are going to work really well.'

'I'll be right here,' she promised. 'All night.'

They watched each other until his eyes grew too heavy and he drifted off to sleep. Then Jess watched him. She had never seen him look vulnerable. It terrified her. Tomorrow he would be better, stronger.

And Spears would be a world away.

Chapter Twenty-Five

Saturday, July 24th, Howard Johnson's Inn, 9.00 A.M.

Good thing Jess had bought hangers, too. The hotel only provided six.

She'd tucked her suitcase over to one side and made a nice neat row of shoes on the rest of the floor space in the closet. After a trip to the one-hour cleaners yesterday, that had actually taken three hours, the suits and one dress she'd brought with her when she left Virginia twelve days ago hung in another nice, neat row.

Tomorrow she would have to go shopping for more work clothes and other things she would need.

Jess closed the sliding door and stared at her reflection. Vaguely she wondered if management would be upset if she removed the mirrored doors. She supposed at some point she would come to appreciate them. Mostly they reminded her that she was getting old. Needed to workout.

'Tomorrow,' she promised her reflection.

Her cosmetics were assembled in order of necessity on the bathroom counter. Luckily, it was good-sized with plenty of working room.

She padded to the desk. The handy-dandy shredder she'd picked up had done better than she'd expected. Shredded the photos as well as the papers. Made a mess on the carpet when it overflowed. She should clean that up but she didn't want to touch anything related to Spears again.

It had been more than forty-eight hours since she'd gotten that text.

Whatever he was doing or planning, she couldn't live her life wondering if he was coming for her. She had to move on.

She stared at the tiny pieces of the Player's case scattered on the floor around the shredder. Maybe she'd just let the maid get it.

Jess smiled. She had a maid. The woman didn't speak a word of English but she smiled a lot. And Jess didn't have to make the bed or scrub the toilet.

She could get used to that.

Lori had helped her find this place. She'd gone to Dan's with her, helped her gather her stuff and bring it here. Not that Jess had much stuff. Mostly she'd needed Lori for support. Jess had worried that she would give in if Dan tried to talk her into staying.

She laughed. Lori had been held hostage for two and a half days and she was helping Jess. She and Lori made quite a team.

Jess dropped onto the end of the bed. Dan was disappointed she wouldn't stay with him or Lori until she found a permanent place. But she needed some space. Last night she'd awakened in a panic. Had to walk it off around the pool. She'd dreamed that Spears had showed up at her door with one of those damned Peace Lilies.

A rap on her door yanked her from the disturbing replay of the dream.

She pushed to her feet and went to the window. Gant. What was he doing here? He was supposed to be on his way back to Quantico.

Jess opened the door. 'Morning, Gant.'

'Morning, Harris.'

She nodded. 'You headed to the airport?' If so, he'd taken the long way around town.

'Wentworth left yesterday. I stayed for Agent

Miller's memorial service. But it's time for me to be on my way.'

Jess nodded. 'Have a safe trip.'

Gant looked around, hands tucked in his trouser pockets. 'I want to apologize to you, Harris. I was wrong to let anyone think you were the reason the Spears case went south. I was wrong and I'm man enough to admit when I'm wrong. What happened here . . . shouldn't have.'

'Nothing we can do about that now.' Okay, say the rest. 'But, in retrospect, I understand you did what you had to do.'

He nodded. 'I'll keep you briefed on any updates we get on Spears.'

'I appreciate that.'

He looked her in the eye then. 'I also wanted you to know that your job is waiting if you ever decide to return to the Bureau.'

Funny, but the offer was in no way appealing. 'Thank you but I'll be staying here. My family is here.' Lily and her husband and kids would be home tomorrow. 'This is where I need to be.'

Gant nodded. 'I can understand that. Birmingham PD is lucky to have you.' He stuck out his hand. 'If you ever need anything, just call.'

Jess took his hand and gave it a shake. 'Thank you. I'll remember that.'

Gant walked away. She watched, grateful that they could be friends again. That was another funny thing. All these years Gant had been the closest thing to a friend she had, but actually they were just work friends. Not personal friends. Jess couldn't remember when she'd last had a friend like that. Lori was her friend now, on and off the job.

And there was Gina Coleman. She'd helped Jess out considerably with that leak about her resignation. She and Gina could be friends.

Jess considered how gorgeous the woman was and her thing for Dan.

Maybe not.

Jess closed the door and picked up her bag. She had a lot to do today. Check out some apartments, maybe drop by her new office. She'd contacted a realtor yesterday about selling her house in Virginia. She'd mailed the keys and, for a fee, the realtor would have her things packed and put in storage. The furnishings could go with the house. And of course there was the repainting that had to be done in the living room.

The possibility that Spears had touched any of her stuff was reason enough to never want to see it again.

The personal belongings she would need to go through at some point.

Just not now.

Eventually she would find a place here. Something small and private. Away from the noise and traffic of downtown . . . away from Dunbrooke Street and Dan.

Her sister was annoyed that Jess wouldn't move in with her but one good thing had come of this whole ordeal. Lily's husband had decided that moving to Nashville was out of the question. That would put them an additional three hours away from the colleges the kids would be attending and this nightmare had made Blake realize that his family meant more to him than a salary increase.

Maybe two, Jess supposed. She had decided that life was too short to give everything to her career.

From now on, she was taking some time for herself.

The job was no longer going to control her destiny.

She stared at her left hand and the band she still wore. She rubbed it around and around for the last time. Hesitation slowed her, but she slid it off and tossed it into the drawer of the bedside table. She closed the drawer and effectively closed that chapter of her life.

She drew a deep breath. Felt a sense of freedom.

From her past. From her regrets. From a lot of things.

Maybe she'd just go shopping today. Why not? She had at least one credit card that wasn't maxed out.

Just as she reached the door another knock sounded.

She checked out the window. Dan. Her pulse tripped as she opened the door. Her knees went a little weak with the way he stared at her. For a man who'd been stabbed and sliced a couple days ago he looked damned good.

'What brings you to the low-rent district on Saturday morning?'

'I came by to take you to breakfast.' Those blue eyes swept over her, returning to meet hers with something fierce in their depths. Hunger. And not for eggs and pancakes.

The sound of his voice flowed over her senses, made her warm and shivery inside. God, he looked good. Beneath the short-sleeved tan crew neck that muscled chest was marred and bandaged, but that knowledge did nothing to diminish how strong he looked. The jeans were worn soft and well-fitted to his body. The memory of the way he'd kissed her that night in his kitchen made her a little giddy with her own fierce hunger that had nothing to do with breakfast either.

But he was her boss now. She lifted a shoulder, let it

fall. 'I was going shopping. I need stuff.'

He grinned and leaned against the door frame. 'You'd need less stuff if you'd continue staying with me.'

The desire that glittered in his eyes was almost her undoing. 'I can't stay with you, chief. Not if I ever hope to gain the respect of the other deputy chiefs, not to mention the detectives in my unit. And we won't even go into all the legal crap.'

He reached out, toyed with a wisp of her hair. 'Is this the way it's going to be? I know what I felt the other night. . . I know what you wanted.'

'We can't always have what we want, Burnett.' She had to get the situation under control. Her body was humming with need . . . she wanted him. Damn, she wanted him. Ten years . . . they hadn't been together in ten long years.

He straightened, took a step inside.

Her breath caught. She backed up a step.

'Our private business is just that, private.' He took another step. This time he closed the door behind him.

Jess stood her ground. 'Is that what this is? Business?'

He wrapped his fingers around the strap resting on her shoulder and lifted her bag away, dropped it to the floor.

'I think you know the answer to that.' His hands molded to her face and he leaned down to kiss her.

She encircled his wrists and pulled free. 'If we're going to do this . . . there have to be rules.'

He dropped his hands to his sides. 'All right. Tell me your rules.'

'First and foremost, just because we have sex doesn't mean you own me.'

He rolled his eyes. 'This is not the same as when we were kids, Jess. I think I've matured a little since then. Hopefully we both have.'

She folded her arms over her chest. 'Are you listening or are we finished already?'

He held up his hands. 'Okay. Okay. Rules.'

'You will not do that whole protector thing. I am a deputy chief in your department, you will treat me with the same respect and confidence you do Black or any of the others.'

'You wouldn't have the job if I didn't respect you and have confidence in your ability, Jess.'

'Do you hover over Deputy Chief Black and try to protect him?'

Dan said nothing.

'Do you agree to that rule or not?'

'Agreed.'

'Third, this . . . thing between us . . . it's about sex.' She forced the words past the lump in her throat. 'This does not constitute a relationship. Agreed?'

'Wow.' He folded his arms over his chest. 'I think I've lost interest now.' He glared at her. 'Why is it you have to make everything so damned complicated? Can't we just let things take their natural course?'

Lost interest? Like hell. Her fingers threaded into his hair and she kissed him with all the repressed anger and passion, need and desperation that had been mounting inside her for days. She showed him with her mouth that she could get him plenty interested in about five seconds. She wanted him right now. No more ignoring her personal needs.

She kicked off her sandals. He toed off his sneakers. Slowly they peeled off each other's clothes. It was terrifying and exciting at the same time. Would he still find her body sexy now that she was over forty?

No matter that his chest and abdomen were covered with bandages, he still looked amazing. She glided her palms down those muscular arms . . . walked all the way around him admiring the lean power of his body.

He molded his hands to her breasts, traced her ribcage down to her waist and then pulled her close. 'How can you be more beautiful now,' he murmured against her ear, 'than you were at seventeen the first time we made love?'

Emotion burned her eyes. 'You need your eyes checked, Burnett.'

He cradled her face in his hands and looked deeply into her eyes. 'The only thing I need checked is my head for letting you get away the first time.'

She pressed her finger to his lips. 'Shh. Remember rule number three.'

He lifted her into his arms and carried her to the bed.

Her body curled around his and he settled fully between her thighs. There was no need for all that foreplay required back when they were crazy teenagers. Their bodies meshed skin to skin, heartbeat to heartbeat, he filled her completely . . . and that was the perfect starting place.

Felt like home . . . where she had always belonged.

At least until Monday morning when she became Deputy Chief Jess Harris again and he became her boss.

But they had nearly forty-eight hours before that happened. *Unless* some freak took a hostage or there was a heinous murder . . .

Dan tangled his fingers with hers and braced their arms on the pillow above her head. He nuzzled her neck with his lips, trailed kisses along her skin, and then he whispered such sweet words that she forgot all about psychos and killers and everything else beyond this moment.

'I've missed you, Jess.'

She smiled. 'Missed you, too.'

Power

Debra Webb

EVIL WILL FOLLOW YOU

When a celebrated ballet instructor is found dead, the court rules that it was a tragic accident. But new Deputy Police Chief, Jess Harris, isn't convinced, and she can't rest easy until she's discovered the truth, however horrifying it may be.

WHEREVER YOU GO

Jess has not long been appointed to her new role and she was hoping to leave the troubles of her haunted past behind. But with the possibility of a killer on the loose, she has no choice but to risk everything.

CAN YOU FIND A WAY TO HIDE?

As she delves deeper into the seedy underworld of Birmingham's gangs and their powerful allies, Jess finds herself targeted. With so much at stake, does she already know too much?

Acclaim for Debra Webb:

'Compelling main characters and chilling villains elevate Debra Webb's *Faces of Evil* series into the realm of high-intensity thrillers that readers won't be able to resist' *New York Times* bestselling author C. J. Lyons

978 0 7553 9690 0

headline